FULL CIRCLE

JULIE HOLLAND

hearts and minds art

MALLORY CAMPBELL WAS A LOTTERY WINNER. In real life. Like ice-cream on a summer day, hope and excitement had flowed into the cracks in her heart when she had learnt of her win. She had trusted the future, and had dared to dream that this could be the stunning turning point in her life, in her marriage. It could offer her a tiny foothold on a life that was heading dangerously in a direction she didn't dare contemplate.

With the thrill of expectation tingling through her veins, she had decided to take the first step and book a trip for two to Venice – imagine John's surprise when she held aloft the first-class tickets.

But that was all dirty water under the bridge now; literally the Rialto Bridge. And the water was foul and polluted like a discarded, frayed lotto ticket stuck to bubble gum under her tennis shoe.

Now, a little hard stone of regret remained lodged in her stomach. Here she was, a mature woman of means with a meaningless life. *Not true Mallory Campbell.* She mentally pulled herself up and voiced her latest affirmation: 'You're a very fortunate, independent woman, on your way to a beautiful country town, you have the freedom to do whatever takes your fancy.'

And yet here she was, heading back to Appletree Hill, to her childhood haunt, to attempt to rebuild fractured family ties. No marriage, no Venice, just an ailing father and a hillside of memories. She tried not to dwell on the series of events that had led to this path, but there was something about a solo road trip and kilometres of smooth bitumen that prodded her mind to wander ...

Chapter One

NEARLY SIXTEEN MONTHS EARLIER:

Mallory sagged into the pink plastic chair. She had never ventured to the food hall at the local plaza before. She preferred the latte and lemon slice at the quiet little café on level one. *Whatever that place is called* – her mind was so fuddled she couldn't even remember, despite enjoying a coffee there every Friday for the last couple of years. Was it Puddles? Puberty? No that couldn't be right. It didn't matter.

The food hall offered noise and anonymity which were what she needed, not a sweet smile from her usual waitress or gentle background music. To her right was a Clearance Sale at Discount King, its balloons and energetic jugglers encroaching on the eating space; to her left was the children's playground where a boy called Bryson was being yelled at to come and finish his fries. Her own tray bulged with a Muffin Madness large double shot coffee and a pineapple non-GF muffin.

Mallory poked her wooden stirrer into a splodge of sticky soft drink left on the table by the previous diner. She glanced around her, nervous that people would wonder why a woman her age, sitting alone in the family area, was gazing blankly into space. Maybe they presume I'm watching grandchildren shimmying down the mini slide. There were no grandchildren in Mallory's life, and no one paid her any attention. Perhaps being invisible was worse.

The blue light on her phone flashed. She snatched it up, hopeful the missed message would be from John saying he was sorry, he had been mistaken. He wouldn't be staying late at the office after all. Mallory flicked her finger through the muffin's yellow icing and let it sour her tongue as the message chirped: 'Hey Mallory. It's Zarni. Just ringing to say happy anniversary. Hope your special dinner tonight is, um, romantic. Anyway, have a fun night.'

Mallory quickly rang her friend back, ready to put on a devil-may-care tone. She had become accustomed to doing that.

'Hi, Zarni. No, you're not interrupting anything.' She paused, unable to keep up any pretence with her best friend. 'Actually, John seems to have forgotten our anniversary.'

'No way. Maybe he's planning some kind of surprise?'

'No, apparently he's snowed under at work and might have to head to the office.' Unbidden, a hitch in her voice gave away her true feelings.

'But what about Vivien? Didn't she tell Warren to handle whatever came up? Good Lord, Mallory he's John's business partner and she's your sister.' A pause and a deep sigh came from Zarni. 'How could John forget when I know you would have left quite a few post-it notes around the place.'

It was an obvious attempt to lighten the mood, but Zarni's joke fell flat.

Mallory's husband was challenged by life's celebratory dates. How intentional that was, Mallory was unsure. Year after year for over a decade, she had marked their anniversary and her birthday on the Daily Aspirations calendar on the kitchen wall. Then as the day approached, she would leave gentle reminders; a new restaurant pamphlet or something sparkly circled in a jewellery catalogue. But this was the first time her prompts had failed. His announcement that morning proved he had paid little attention or had better places to be.

'Okay, well if you're sure there's no surprise, how about we go catch a movie together? Gold Class,' Zarni offered.

Mallory pushed the muffin aside. 'Thanks, but I'll go home. Maybe you're right and he has something wonderful planned.' With a deep sigh, she hung up.

She abandoned the food hall and meandered through the lunchtime crowd and up the escalator, her fingers tapping on the rail. Where had she read there were more germs on that long rubber strip than on most bathroom floors? She quickly searched for her mini sanitiser as she stepped off the escalator, reflecting on the strange habits the world had adopted since Covid. She paused outside a luggage store and rubbed her hands together vigorously.

'It's our new range, complete with TSA lock,' a female voice trilled beside her. 'Unbreakable polycarbonate with custom aluminium bumper corners. But incredibly light in case there isn't a hunky fellow to lift it for you.'

Mallory hadn't realised she was even looking at the range of super sleek luggage. Nothing seems to be registering with me today, she thought. 'Away with the fairies' my mother would have said. Back in the day when Mallory had always yearned to be on a plane exploring the world, her luggage had been the latest design of heavy tapestry-look finishes. Now, like heavy Mary Poppin rejects, they were relegated to gather dust in her attic.

'Does it come in blue?' she blurted.

'Yes, in check-in and carry-on sizes. French navy or cornflower?'

'Cornflower in both. And I'll also have one of those shoulder bags with straps that can't be cut through. Maybe black.'

'And where are you travelling to?' the assistant asked as she snipped off tags and wrapped receipts around fully retractable handles.

'I have no idea,' Mallory said, shaking her head.

Why on earth had she bought cases? She wasn't going anywhere, not unless she won the lottery. With the current ticket she hadn't checked yet. The coffee detour had thrown her right out, and for a moment she considered skipping purchasing a ticket for the next draw. But she just couldn't; her Tatts check-and-spend had become a serious Friday ritual. If the ticket was a winner, she would allocate that meagre amount to another ticket and so it went on. Week after week, year after year. With every new ticket, a tingle would spread quickly through her body as though a fairy had sprinkled lucky dust across her shoulders. She would smile smugly, with vibes of 'I've got a good feeling about this ticket'.

Back at home, the Campbell fridge was littered with Dream Home and Cancer Council raffle tickets and Tattersalls printouts; all regularly rotated as the date when Mallory's win was supposed to appear came and went unsuccessfully. Non-winning tickets lay scrunched and abandoned at the bottom of her handbag. She tried to be pleased for the winners who, somewhere, were getting drunk on their enviable luck.

'I don't know why you bother hiking down to the shops when you can just get a ticket online,' John had told her more than once. She'd ignore him as he'd laugh at all the hopeful pieces of paper that sat on the fridge, curling under Magic Happens magnets.

Also, he didn't fancy the newsagent knowing if he had won his millions. 'You're too trusting. Who knows what would happen, Mallory. He could suddenly appear on our doorstep with some sob story, asking us to pay for his mother's hip replacement or something,' John had explained, nodding seriously but ignoring her frown.

'Well, you can have your Pokies, John and I'll enjoy my little flutter,' she'd often reply. Small prizes had materialised over the years; she had even scratched away $100 on a Santa Square one Christmas. All enough to keep her in the game.

Her chosen point of purchase, never varying in case it altered her position in life's queue of winners, was the Lucky Cat Newsagency. She liked Jin, the owner, who would always greet her so warmly. Her potential winning ticket consistently had her own special numbers, chosen years ago.

With the suitcases safely stowed in her car, Mallory retraced her steps to the newsagency.

Normally, her routine would be to slide her ticket under the self-scanner herself, but she wanted to check out the new edition of Travellers' Highlife magazine, and its feature on northern Italy. She had been enamoured with Europe ever since her twenties when a ConTiki tour had bussed her through the It's Tuesday We Must be in Rome Tour. She passed the ticket to Jin to check when he had a moment. Her nose was buried deep in an article about where best to see George Clooney around Lake Como when she felt Jin and his wife Helen sidle next to her. Mallory reached for the offered ticket, but Jin refused to release it.

'You've won a prize,' he whispered.

Helen nodded. 'A big prize.'

'How big?' Mallory asked. 'I'll just put it toward next week's draw please.'

'Our machine said a very big prize. Division 1,' Jin responded, holding up his pointer finger. 'Come look.' They ushered her across to the Lotto screen where Mallory saw the unbelievable announcement that she indeed had won Division 1. $20,000,000.

Mallory's hand flew to her mouth. 'Fuck,' she whispered. She turned to the newsagents. 'Really?'

The wide grins on both Jin and Helen's kind faces said it all. 'Oh, my God!' Mallory gathered the couple to her chest, stifling happy sobs that threatened to explode.

Jin held the ticket high, perhaps worried it would be torn in the embrace. Mallory took a step back, her shaking hands cupping around her blushing face. Quickly she glanced around the shop, thankful to see it was empty. Jin passed her the ticket with a little bow and instructions to contact the lottery's Head Office as soon as she could.

IT ALL SEEMED SO IMPROBABLE. Mallory dashed back to her car, started the engine then just sat there, her clammy hands clutching the steering wheel. Little puffs of nervous breath escaped her pursed lips, but her thoughts refused to calm. She closed her eyes, unwilling to have a heart attack before she knew what $20 million looked like. Was it all stacked somewhere deep in a vault, safe from any possible heist?

Once, twice, three times she checked that the ticket still sat deep inside a zipped pocket of her handbag. Surely it couldn't be true, but had she unknowingly had an inkling? After all, she had bought suitcases! Italy was suddenly a whole lot closer.

She turned on the ignition. Her win was almost tangible, like a warm gift box or happy red balloon that only she could hold, safe against her for the moment. It was her own little secret in a world where nothing was truly just hers. Once everyone knew, then everything would change. She would be tugged in a hundred directions by family and those she didn't even know; and she didn't want to be prodded, let alone tugged, by anyone anymore. With a nod of her head, she decided not to share news of her good luck with anyone except John, not even her sister Vivien just yet.

Her thoughts tumbled over each other as she drove carefully home. She had seen on the news how other little suburban businesses had celebrated. DIVISION 1 SELLER!! would be blazoned across the window and walls, bunting and balloons spreading from one corner of the store to the other. Jin, Helen and employees would all be wearing rosette badges that read Winner! Yes, everything would have an exclamation mark and Mallory would be expected to give interviews to the local press. The signs would outlast the shop's Chinese New Year banners, but she was happy for them and their, no doubt, increase in ticket sales that would follow. Mallory knew she would never return to the Lucky Cat Newsagency, but she would send Jin and Helen a nice large flower arrangement for the counter.

But now, the exciting part would be announcing her good fortune and celebrating with John. She could drip-feed hints to see if he picked up on anything or was even listening. What fun it would be. *John, I'll have to cancel the dentist because I'm off to Monaco for the Grand Prix,* or I could wear a knuckle-duster diamond to breakfast. Perhaps I'll ask him to help put the Sold sign on that Georgian mansion I've always fancied down the road, or to suggest what shade of catamaran would match our two new Bentleys. Not that she disliked her current house at all or ever felt inclined to go sailing or drive a flashy car – it was just that, when there was an alternative, those possibilities suddenly had a sexy, carefree appeal. Even if only for a short time of mental indulgence.

There would still be so much money to spend, Mallory suddenly realised. $1 million would have been plenty to fulfil her dreams. Unexpectedly, she remembered a news item about a girl called Nerily from Newcastle who had not spent a cent of her $16.5 million winnings, opting to donate the entire amount to the Animal Anti-Cruelty Fund. Mallory's heart thumped against her chest as she tried to fathom the implications of having so much money at her beck and call. She'd never wanted to be a 'beck and call' person and felt the stirrings of a certain kinship with Nerily. Who knew there would be so many emotions associated with being rich?

But she could almost hear the roaming violinist in St Mark's Square, taste the chianti as they enjoyed a romantic Italian dinner along the Amalfi coastline, smell the expensive fragrances from the giant flower arrangements in their ritzy palazzo suite as sheer curtains blew gently onto the balcony. Mallory took another deep breath and tried to settle her excitement before sharing the news with her husband.

John's car was parked in the driveway, his early arrival home a possible sign of an anniversary surprise. Mallory parked in the street and quietly let herself in the front door, a smile tweaking her lips. Maybe her news would put a spark back into their stale marriage – nothing else she had tried had worked. Her plan for their anniversary dinner had been to prepare his favourite meal of rare beef with lashings of mushroom gravy, roast vegetables, and apple pie; in the back of her mind, Mallory had presumed he wouldn't book a nice restaurant. Or any restaurant for that matter. She paused as she reached into the fridge for the bottle of champagne, noting the prime rib eye she'd bought earlier still sitting there.

If he couldn't remember their anniversary, why not keep her win to herself a little while longer; tell him tomorrow.

The rumblings of her husband's voice came from the back room. Having decided to see how the evening panned out and hopefully tell him, Mallory tiptoed to the kitchen door with the champagne; John could swap it for his beer when he was ready.

Words coiled their way through the doorway and around the bottle of Jansz.

'I've told Mallory I have to go back to the office, so I'll meet you at the Hilton. Then I'll ring her later this evening with an excuse to stay in town. We can have one of our nights.'

Mallory froze as a moment's ominous silence passed before John gave a groan and continued. 'Oh, don't. You're making me horny. Save that for tonight. Love you, Viv.'

Still with the bottle clutched in her hand, Mallory shuffled forward. Unable to process what she had just heard, she ran a quick mental list of possible options, all of which fell short of what was dawning on her. The smirk on John's face froze when he saw her standing there, stark proof she had heard correctly. Her head felt like it would explode at any moment.

'Geez, Mal. Why are you creeping around?' He jangled his car keys in his pocket, a habit that set Mallory's teeth on edge at any time, let alone in this sickening moment.

His voice was firm, but Mallory saw the panic in his eyes. The eyes that had once gazed into hers and promised 'I do'.

Pineapple muffin, coffee, euphoria, and now utter despair collided in her stomach. The room shifted, the overpowering scent of John's cologne making her head spin. Had he worn cologne to work or just sprayed it in readiness for his secret rendezvous? Is that what she had just heard? There was no more room in Mallory's body for anything else – she dashed to the bathroom and threw up in the toilet bowl.

No reassuring pat on the back or offered cool washer eventuated as she slumped against the wall, heavy with confusion. When she re-emerged, her husband sat in his favourite chair, but instead of the customary TV remote, he clutched his car keys. He flicked his eyes up and across her face, his focus wavering somewhere over her shoulder. Mallory couldn't bring herself to move closer to him.

'You're having an affair with Vivian?' she stuttered. Her mouth felt dry with vomit and the sad realisation her life was in free fall.

John nodded.

'My sister? You've been sleeping with my sister?'

John sighed as though he was addressing an elderly aunt. 'Oh, come on, Mallory. You know things haven't been great between us for a long time.'

He stood as if to leave, this small act of flicking her aside breaking through her disgust. John had obviously finished the conversation, with only the silence of betrayal now lingering in the room.

'No, John. I didn't know that. Yes, you've been inattentive, not present is probably more accurate, and now I know why. We need to sit and discuss this.' Her voice hitched. 'How long ...'

John moved to pass, his hand like an electric rod against her arm. Mallory clenched her jaw but didn't move an inch. The discarded champagne bottle rotated on the carpet at their feet, like a forgotten game of Spin the Bottle. She must have dropped it in her dash to the bathroom.

'Where are you going?' Stupid, stupid question.

'We'll talk about this later when we're both calm,' John said as he slid past her to the front door.

'You seem perfectly calm now, John. Why is that?' Mallory was sure her anger would kick in soon, but in that moment she felt overwhelmingly embarrassed and naive. Like a little girl who had trusted her brother with a special toy, only to find he had thrown it away. She bit her lip, hot tears finally brimming and scorching down her cheeks as her husband closed the front door behind him.

'Happy anniversary,' she whispered to his back.

Chapter Two

AS EXPECTED, helpless anger bubbled its way to the surface and stayed there. When Mallory wasn't pacing the kitchen, she lay fully clothed on her bed, staring at the ceiling, resentment spreading like tendrils across the sheets. Any thought of contacting either of the lovers brought on waves of nausea. Her thoughts became riddled with imagined scenarios of their conversations about her until all she could do was slump in the shower and sob quietly – not that there was anyone to hear her. She finally had to confess what had happened to friends when their calls went unanswered. It seemed that her husband's and sister's affair was news to everyone, which was a small concession to how irrelevant Mallory felt every second of her day.

Her new-found singleness was littered with well-meaning invitations from girlfriends and work colleagues after she took some of her accrued sick leave, but she just couldn't face the endless questions and inevitable raised eyebrows. Instead, she would stay at home, trailing her fingers across the furniture she and John had bought together. If she didn't forget to eat altogether, she took comfort in cooking, nurturing her herb garden, and sprinkling its offerings all over her favourite meals. John had hated all forms of "little green weeds"; he would choke at the smell of coriander and laboriously pick out the parsley from her casseroles, depositing them around the edge of his plate. Let him get scurvy she thought, chopping more parsley.

Such peaks and troughs of emotion were exhausting. With no word from John nor Vivian, she decided the only way to take her mind off the cheating couple was to turn to the only light in the sky, the spark on the horizon, the only positive thing in all the corny cliches she repeated to herself. Her lottery win and what to do about it.

Who said money can't buy happiness? She was determined to bloody well try.

Her first point of research wasn't that reassuring. Apparently, many big winners had managed to lose the lot. Lucy from Idaho had trusted an online bastard from Tennessee with her $210 million. Allan and Frida from Bath had invested their £50 million in some tech company in America which turned out to be Steve and his computer in Sydney. Young Frank in Macau had bought two mansions, two Ferraris, twenty hookers, and a nightclub before being bled dry of his millions by the Chinese mafia. And so it went on in the world of wealth and stealth.

Needing to be more proactive, Mallory read an online post called 5 Steps of What to Do if You Win the Lottery: Don't tell anyone, *tick*. Claim it within the timeline, *tomorrow*. Check the tax requirements, *none on a win in Australia*. Get a Financial and Legal Advisor, *soon*. Decide to take it as a lump sum or annuity, *previous point*.

Just the winning ticket, several ID details, and a bank account were all that was needed when Mallory visited

Tatts Headquarters and met with the lovely Philipa. Philipa calmly informed Mallory that she was, in fact, $20 million richer than she had been previously. She offered glossy booklets that seemed to, thankfully, back up Mallory's online research about what to initially do with all the money.

What a marvellous job, Mallory thought. To be able to inform people of their newfound wealth, to be able to offer them the opportunity to fulfil their monetary dreams. The complimentary tea and Lindt chocolates had been a welcome diversion from Mallory's growing sense of living in a parallel universe. But Philipa had most likely seen it all before; except for this winner's occasional tear because of a cheating spouse presumably.

Time was what she needed; time to get used to being wealthy, on the inside as much as the outside. Did rich people walk differently? She was sure they did but had never taken the time to really notice. Did she even have to know such things? Probably, if she was to rub shoulders in lounges of exclusive, private hotels and the pointy end of the plane. She wasn't about to race off and buy a shelf of Chanel limited edition handbags or a dozen Jimmy Choo shoes – did they even make a wide fitting? She hadn't a clue about how to invest in art or gold or purchase a Bulgari necklace. How do people learn these things? she wondered.

Perhaps there was a fancy Retreat for the Recent Rich, where they would teach you how to meditate away your new money concerns and give lectures on what charities were above board. They would surely over-charge their newly minted residents.

THE MERCURIAL DAYS continued while the world rotated around her. Calls from well-intentioned friends were met with smiles and stilted conversations smattered with, 'It's just a rough patch', 'We'll get through it', 'No, I haven't confronted my conniving sister'. But deep down inside, Mallory knew her marriage was over, that she had been discarded like the dry old teabags that sat ignored in her sink.

Peter Sarstedt's song, "Where do you go to my Lovely", was an earworm in her head as her Sleep Easy herb tea steeped and steamed. '... *both touched with a burning ambition. To shake off their lowly-born tags* ...'. She wondered why other songs hadn't come to mind: "The Winner Takes it All", "Money for Nothing" or "Mo Money Mo Problems". After all, neither Mallory nor John had been lowly-born in the backstreets of Naples; in fact, their backgrounds had been upper middle class with all those trappings and experiences, before marrying and settling down to a mortgage and future together.

The winnings were safe in her separate bank account in a branch in a different suburb. John was still being left in the dark. Mallory was determined that nothing would give her away too soon but was unsure what her next step should be. A possible solution came during a 'What jobs do your daddy and mommy do' session with one of her primary school classes. After Jack had explained the finer points of his mum's messy gardening job, and Jasmine had explained how her dad sat at a desk all day, Mallory's attention was sparked by the next little presenter.

'My dad is in Italy,' young Jeremy announced.

'What work is he doing there, Jeremy?' Mallory asked.

'He isn't working there. He works here. He's in Italy to think.'

'And what's he busy thinking about, do you suppose?' Mallory prompted.

'His life,' Jeremy had said. 'He's gone to Capri to swim and relax and decide what to do with his life. That's what he told Mum.'

'Oh.' Mallory faltered at his innocent disclosure. 'Okay, thank you, Jeremy. Well, um, perhaps we could all collect a book from the shelves and read quietly until recess.'

But Mallory's problem had been solved by the tale of Jeremy's dad. Why not go to Italy and think? After all, Italy was No.1 on her Wish List. She felt smug at the thought of taking off without telling anyone, just with a backpack and staying wherever the next train took her. The excitement of such an opportunity swirled inside her chest as though a little whirligig of adventure had taken flight. Yes! She could climb the steep hill on Capri and decide what to do with her new life, before watching an Italian sunset with a chianti, and a plate of delicious spaghetti. There might even be a handsome local to take her around the Amalfi coast on his yacht. It didn't have to be a big yacht – she was only recently endowed with millions and would be perfectly happy with his jaunty red dinghy.

The enthusiasm of la dolce vita had evaporated by the following morning. Mallory ran her muesli around the bowl, her eyes dry and prickly. It had been a sleepless night with images of a version of Jeremy's father on a boat in the Gulf of Naples. *What was I thinking? Of course, I can't just take off; I'm always over on my baggage allowance as it is, so a backpack is a ludicrous idea.*

She ran the idea past Zarni whilst coming clean about her win but had sworn her to secrecy. She had omitted the actual winning amount, and her friend had never asked.

Zarni had been hysterically happy at the news and promised not to tell a soul.

'Oh Mallory, how marvellous. You must take that trip. You just have to and if I wasn't so scared of flying, I'd come with you and leave Paul and the boys to fend for themselves for a week or two. You'll have to write a Travel Blog. You know like Hilary did when she went to Scotland.'

Mallory laughed, a certain lightness entering her soul for a moment. 'That was tedious, Zarni. All the photos were so gloomy it was like they were on the *Game of Thrones* set, and Hils couldn't remember the names of any towns they visited. A blog might be fun though. I've often thought of starting one. I'd call it Mallory's Musings ...'

'Or Hiking from Husbands Hung Up On Hanky-Panky,' Zarni snorted. 'I still can't believe it. How could they both deceive you like that!'

Mallory shook her head. 'I let the one call he's made to me go to message bank. Mind you it was only to say he'd be calling by the house to pick up his things. I resisted the urge to hide his precious golf clubs before I made sure I was out when he arrived.' She sighed. 'And what about poor Warren? He's living on the other side of town apparently, so he won't run into them. I wonder how long John and Viv will last now they're living together 24/7.' She allowed a small smirk to cross her lips. 'I hope she doesn't want the TV remote.'

'Well, this win is the universe's way of telling you to move on. Easier said than done I know, but you deserve it.'

'And you deserve this for being such a true friend,' Mallory said as she handed Zarni an envelope containing a voucher for a week at a luxury spa with all the trimmings. She didn't mention the bouquet of flowers that would be delivered every month for two years or the anonymous donation she'd made to her friend's refugee support program.

Zarni's eyes filled with tears as she hugged Mallory and showered her with thanks. 'Take the trip, my friend,' she urged.

Mallory had found it rather cleansing to pass on a large chunk of her winnings. The Royal Flying Doctor Service and several women's refuges would surely have been thrilled with the anonymous donations she'd sent. Through her teaching contacts and a registered charity, several disadvantaged children also benefited as Mallory committed to covering their educational needs for as long as they needed, whether they wanted to become an artist or doctor. As long as they were happy. Happiness counted.

She had been advised by estate planning attorneys that because she had been the buyer of the ticket, with numbers she alone had chosen over the years, and that she operated a bank account separate from John and he could meet his future needs, then the winnings would most likely be deemed hers in a divorce settlement. In the meantime, she was free to dispense donations as she pleased. She had followed the 5 Steps advice and found an honourable investment trustee.

Mallory carried on with her life and role as a teacher for the next month, ever wary of appearing richer. The ramifications of her life taking a different path were constantly at the forefront of her mind, both because of the money and John's affair. John and Vivien's affair. What if she hadn't won the money and never knew about their affair? What if she had told him, or her sister, about the win before finding out about their relationship? What if, what if …

Having money meant having choices, and she promised

herself she would make only good ones. Any eye-to-eye communication from John had never eventuated and the mere thought of either of the pair being in her world became too much.

She had moved out of their home when it went on the market, moving to an apartment overlooking the Brisbane River, and had officially retired from teaching. The parklands around her apartment in New Farm provided shaded walks along the calm river to the Powerhouse Museum, and local delis and cafes, with the nearby River Cat ferry able to take her into the city. The house had sold quickly, and her other possessions had gone into storage – for some reason, she had needed to consolidate, reduce her footprint somehow, to just enjoy the small things in life for a while before heading overseas.

Then, any further thought of taking off to Italy was squashed – it seemed the universe had other plans for Mallory Campbell. This time it came via a phone call from her father's nursing home.

Chapter Three

THE TWO-AND-A-HALF-HOUR FLIGHT had passed in a blur of mixed emotions. How quickly things changed – first the lotto win, then the counterbalance of her marriage collapse, and now she was revisiting Appletree Hill. Thank heavens several of her old girlfriends still resided there; buffers if she started to stray into melancholia. Twenty minutes after collecting her luggage (cornflower blue) and rental car, Mallory had manoeuvred away from the airport terminal for the hour's drive down the coast.

Returning to Appletree Hill and her history there probably wasn't a snug fit with making good decisions, but it had been made in response to her father Harold's ill health, in addition to an itch that she had to scratch. Several itches. She now recognised how life could spin on a dime, for better or worse, and was determined to tidy up a few loose ends and to check on her father's welfare – who knew what life held for everyone in its fickle hand.

The familiar scenery streamed past her window. Mallory frowned, not sure if the fluttering she was experiencing was nerves, excitement, or sadness. Not for the first time, she was contemplating another kind of life, but the destination and journey to get there were still a blur. Like a distant fluffy cloud that would surely float closer, clear and reveal her future.

The difference was that now she had the means to consider Peter Sarstedt's burning ambition and to answer the question, Where do you go to my lovely?

The southern Victorian air was so different from the semi-tropics at this time of year. The sky seemed lower, the wind always with a threat of a shift for the worse, but as the road followed the curve of the bay and took her away from the city her shoulders dropped a couple of inches and her breathing slowed. The last time she had made the trip she had been on her own too, John being too tied up with work; too tied up with *her*, more likely.

Mallory turned the hire car inland, to wind around and across rolling, eucalypt-studded hills. Roadside signs pointing to seasonal farmgate produce started to appear, the honour system of putting payment in a tin tied to the adjoining little shed apparently still working. Many of the vineyards had tasting rooms and cafes attached, with fancy signs and vine-covered verandas. Her car picked up speed across the hilltop ridge which offered panoramic views of more vines, various fruit trees, and contented beef cattle. It was beautiful as the shadows lengthened and a soft light fanned out across the countryside – from a distance the shire presented as it always had.

The afternoon chill tiptoed in, but thankfully her B&B was only ten minutes away, so she persevered with keeping the car roof off. There was something so carefree and Grace Kelly about it!

Thick native bushes started to appear alongside the road, towered over by gums shoulder to shoulder with golden liquid amber trees. Many had lost their leaves already, a thick tapestry of browns and rusty yellows blanketing the roadside. As she turned off onto Blueberry Lane's unsealed track, the carpet flicked away from the tyres, resettling in her wake as if any exit was being gently closed behind her. She slowed past a rusty letterbox slumped on its hinges. Vague memories of its giant hedge, which still surrounded the property, sat at the edges of Mallory's memory but she couldn't recall who had lived there, or that she had ever shown any interest. There must have been more exciting haunts to find for a young girl. She drove on a few metres to the next entry, through the open iron gate and up the crushed rock driveway.

The cottage settled quietly into the surrounding bush, its fresh grey and white timbers juxtaposed against the overhangs and darkening afternoon. Mallory had been delighted to see the house listed as a B&B and had booked it immediately. Now she sat for a moment as the car roof slowly curled shut. She affectionately ran her eye over the house, remembering her childhood visits to Vern and Doris and her nights sleeping on the meshed-in veranda. The space was now open with new boards, uprights, and roofing. The property had been called Fruit Flan back then, as a nod to the many rampant apple, pear and cumquat trees that surrounded the house. A shiny new plaque renamed it The Getaway. It had presumably changed hands several times over the years she had been absent, but she knew in her heart its original owners would be turning in their graves to think strangers came and went in their home, that no one person was there to love it day after day; and for donning it such an unimaginative name. Sadly, Mallory predicted the interior would bear no resemblance to its past either.

The key was in the safe box as the realtor had directed. Mallory took a deep breath and opened the door.

Although the interior had been swept clean of its past, her memory supplied images of her beloved old friends sitting in their favourite corduroy chairs with steaming mugs of tea as her younger self pulled out yet another well-worn jigsaw puzzle for them all to complete. She conjured the homely aromas of thick minestrone and spicy apple pies that would settle around the cottage for days. A peek into the various rooms revealed stylists' stock prints of landscapes on the walls and Ikea doonas, no longer the family portraits or crochet blankets that had once unfashionably (but lovingly) adorned the rooms. What Doris had once called her 'natural habitat' had been updated and cleansed to reflect the vibes of a stark hotel. The changes were what she had expected, but Mallory sighed with disappointment as she unpacked and prepared for an early night.

BLOODY HELL. Mallory's deep country sleep was rudely interrupted. She burrowed her head under the pillow, determined to block out the sound – was it a radio or a live guitar? Plucked notes pierced the otherwise quiet night – melodic but completely intrusive at 3:00 am. She dragged herself out of her cosy bed onto cold Aussie hardwood flooring, tugged on a pair of socks, and shuffled down the still hall. Resisting the light switch, she cracked open the back door, gasping as the icy air blew past and through her.

Maybe the wind is bringing the music from across the paddocks, she thought. No, it's close by. Cursing she hadn't put on slippers as well as her socks, Mallory eased open the screen door and padded along the veranda, hugging her useless silk dressing gown around her shivering body. It was freezing, the night air clear and bright under a starry veil. Hazy light filtered through the bushes from the property next door, obviously the site of the insomniac guitar player. She gathered her gown up from the frosty ground and sprinted on tiptoes to the fence just as a creature – possum? bat? sundry nocturnal animal flashed through the branches. The city girl in her squealed, the light next door instantly extinguished. Darkness settled around her, waiting for her next move.

The screen door slammed behind her as she ran back inside the house. A quick look out the kitchen window revealed only her haggard reflection against the black curtain of night. Soggy socks were dragged off and flicked to the side. Her cold fingers trembled as she flicked the switch for the kettle and waited for it to warm before wrapping her palms around its sides. The allure of sinking under a heavy doona won out against a green tea so Mallory raced back to the bedroom, quickly pulling on another pair of dry socks before diving into the warmth.

The rest of the night passed in thankful silence. As the magpies and kookaburras started their day and the wind rustled together the carpet of leaves, Mallory wondered if she'd dreamt the whole incident. Her still damp socks, nestled against the kitchen cupboard, told her otherwise. *I'll let it go, after all, it's not like it was All Along the Watchtower or anything too pumping.* She popped her instant porridge into the microwave before adding slippers and gumboots to her shopping list.

EXCITEMENT MINGLED with apprehension as Mallory set off for the village of Appletree Hill. She hadn't visited since her mother's funeral a few years earlier, and that visit had ended so badly she hadn't hung around to indulge in lattes or conversations, or rushed to return. Harold had hardly spoken to her and Vivien as they had attempted to comfort him, to prepare the funeral; he had only accused them of meddling when they offered to help with his affairs. Then her brother Patrick, Warren and John had got embarrassingly drunk at the wake. Her father had proclaimed they wouldn't be welcome back. Of course, she'd contacted him over the years but his resolve to remain distant hadn't weakened, even for his daughter.

In less than ten minutes Mallory had parked in the service lane of the town's narrow main street. She saw the milk bar had extended and transformed into a gourmet deli; the old butcher shop's window looked like it had its own stylist and Mrs. Bowery's dress shop was now called Emporium which 'brought the world of fashion to hinterland Australia'. Mallory frowned at the tartan gumboots in the window, imagining they would be more at home in the Scottish Highlands. She had heard the area had become a coveted weekend escape for city folk, a country retreat for the wealthy owners of hobby farms, and for young housewives hoping to open artisan studios. A glance in the real estate window proved it to be true. *Good Lord, look at those prices.*

The sound of John's scoffing hovered around the fringes of her mind. She imagined his unwarranted general opinions about 'small towns large egos', but it was still her town and occupied a special corner in her heart. Not for the first time, Mallory reached up and dragged down the shutter on his memory, trying to make her thoughts airtight against him.

The Rotary Park boasted a newly painted rotunda that squatted in its centre. It had been the unofficial town hub at one time, hosting many Christmas plays, summer concerts and winter speeches to launch a car show, but now seemed so small. It had been the go-to place for teenagers to meet in her school days, either for a sneaky cigarette or a quick kiss. Not that Mallory Pepper had ever been invited to share a Marlboro or a 'pash'; those pastimes had been for the In crowd, and her eyes had been for one boy only.

She wandered on, pulling her coat against the crisp breeze and any memories she didn't want to address. The little town had blossomed – it appeared to be the same but was nothing like it at all. Was she jealous of those who had stayed and given its future a go? No, not for all those years. Appletree Hill was perfect to the eye, but Mallory knew what simmered beneath its surface, how gossip could ignite and spread like bushfire through the undergrowth.

Desperate for a strong coffee, she was also eager to sit and absorb the comings and goings as a visitor; to get a feel for its people, its heartbeat. Perhaps main street could become the venue of her new Friday ritual, but without the pineapple muffin. The bakery had been converted into a vine-covered indoor-outdoor café. Gone were the packaged white bread, sprinkle buns and pale sausage rolls – replaced with a tempting range of home-baked cakes and crisp sourdough loaves nestled in brown paper. No wonder there wasn't a spare seat in the whole place. Disappointed, she continued to stroll down the street, past a deserted gallery and antique store, more real estate offices, and two appealing restaurants that were closed until dinner service.

At the far end of the main street sat a dishevelled nursery, like an unwanted afterthought that had been carelessly left behind. A faded umbrella tilted over a few little wrought iron tables accentuating its apparent sad neglect. 'Nursery & Coffee' was chalked on both sides of a dusty sidewalk A-frame. How the little business had escaped the gentrification the rest of the street had endured, Mallory wasn't sure. She stepped into the foliage-filled interior and was immediately greeted by a cheery good morning from behind a huge floral arrangement of gerberas and glossy sage green sprays. A young woman, maybe late twenties, poked her head around the edge as she attempted unsuccessfully to gather the bunch into a length of raffia. Her hair, nearly as red as the gerberas, was piled loosely up on top of her head, a twig of some variety poking through the curls.

'Can I do anything to help?' Mallory asked.

'No, I'll be alright. There!' she said, finally managing to tie the raffia into a knot and large bow. 'But thank you.' She lay the bunch to the side and shot Mallory a wide grin. 'Now, what can I do for you?'

'The sign said coffee?' Mallory pointed over her shoulder. She glanced at the impressive range of fresh flowers propped in tin milking cans. 'And I'd also like some daisies and a bunch of proteas, please. They don't have to be gift-wrapped, they're just for me.' *Well, one is for me anyway.*

Mallory settled herself at a table, grateful for the cushion atop the cold iron seat. The coffee was hot and strong, the apple cake delicious, and all quickly served by a slight, serious woman whose name tag said Hettie. 'Plain' would have been Mallory's mother, Stella's, description.

Thick grey hair was pulled back from her lined face which was devoid of any makeup; her eyes seemed weary as she focused on the cup and saucer. Not a skerrick of jewellery adorned her wrists or fingers, the only concession being tiny gold ball studs in her ears. Mallory peeked at her while pretending to sip her coffee. She instantly recognised the woman as Heather McMunn who had bullied and ostracised her throughout their years at secondary school. Unfortunately, their parents had been friends. Mallory used to dread their group card evenings when the McMunn family would descend and the Pepper siblings had had to entertain Heather and her sullen brother, and vice versa. The only consolation of those nights was that playing cards had seemed to lengthen her father's customary short fuse, and he had become the perfect host. He would jovially slap Heather's father on the shoulder as though they were best mates, and refill Heather's mother's glass with a repeated, 'Bubbly for the beautiful Barbara.' It hadn't escaped Mallory's notice that, where her father had transformed into Mr Personality, her mother had become tight-lipped, often escaping to the kitchen for long intervals in search of more vol au vents or cubed cheese.

The simmering memories were unsettling – she hadn't thought about the McMunns for a long time. She wondered if Alfred and Barbara had passed on but, uncomfortable under Hettie's sudden curious stare, she wasn't about to enquire. Instead, Mallory took an avid interest in her phone, her heart thumping that her long-ago adversary would suddenly recognise her. A plaintive call of 'Mum!' from inside took the woman away. Any similarity between the dour Hettie and the sunny woman who apparently was her daughter seemed to stop at their shared fair complexions.

Mallory's deep sigh blew across the apple cake crumbs. She knew her next encounter with an Appletree Hill local would not produce a 'happy to see you' greeting, but she couldn't put off the inevitable any longer.

Chapter Four

'HI, DAD.' Mallory heard the tremble in her voice as she plastered on a smile, knocked, and entered Room 6 Banksia Wing, Hillview Nursing Home.

She quickly scanned the bed-sitting room, recognising the faint residue of Glen 20. Her relief that the space was clean and neat turned to disappointment when she saw how devoid of personal charm and memories it was. It was as though her ninety-year-old father had been dropped through the roof to plop onto the beige pseudo-leather recliner. No family photos or long-adored artworks, no trinkets or travel mementoes were on show across the in-house furniture. Where was his old rugby trophy or the worn corduroy chair he had refused to part with for years? Only the name plaque on his door identified the shrunken man sitting before her. Guilt threatened to rise.

Of course, Harold Pepper could have afforded more than the original musty nursing home he had entered after his stroke Harold had always been tight with his money. On many occasions he would grandstand about how much his children's education was costing him – their home had been a pressure cooker around exam time as the children strove to prove the benefits of his outlay.

He would never know that it had been Mallory's financial windfall that was paying for his upgrade to a suite in a brand-new facility. Her attempts to get Patrick on board with their father's welfare had fallen on deaf ears, so she had taken matters into her own hands from afar. Its name said it all – atop Eliza Hill, the home enjoyed views of its extensive gardens and the lush countryside. There were even weekly spa treatments, but she presumed he hadn't bothered with what he would see as an unnecessary indulgence. A new wheelchair sat motionless in the corner. Mallory smiled at the crochet blanket draped over one of its arms – she just couldn't imagine HP being wheeled anywhere in public with his knees covered in the bright pink and orange patchwork of wool.

'Well look who the wind blew in,' he croaked. Cloudy, silver eyes, unblinking and whip-smart, held hers for a moment before returning to the TV screen. Reruns of *Fawlty Towers*.

She waited, but nothing more than John Cleese's whining voice filled the room. She gently nudged open a gap in the curtains to let in the garden view, sunlight, and a chink of joy. Her father had never been a big man, rather wiry and strong as he had to be to work the fruit orchard on his own, but now he was thinner and frailer than Mallory had ever seen him; his trousers hanging over worn slippers and pooling on the floor. His hair was as wispy as a spider web, a comparison that was probably quite apt considering his reputation as being a crafty old sod.

'Can we turn that volume down, Dad while I'm here?' She didn't wait for a reply before pressing mute. Rheumy eyes slid in her direction as she propped on the side of the bed to face him. A stroke had put him in care, ongoing mini seizures and the progression of cancer kept him there.

'How are you?'

'How do you expect me to be, stuck in here? I haven't had my cup of tea yet.' There was a slowness and slight slur to his words, an echo of the stroke.

As if on demand a trolley cluttered to a stop at his door, and in bustled a jovial carer, cup in one hand, a plate holding a small lamington in the other. 'Oh, you have a visitor. Would your visitor like a cuppa, Harold?'

'No,' came the terse reply. Mallory grimaced at the woman and shook her head. Anything for peace.

'Can I help you with that, Dad?' she offered. His once strong hands now shook, his skin mottled and paper-thin with age. Mallory was unsure if he hadn't heard or if he was just ignoring her. *Nothing changes.* Her nerves jangled as the tea was noisily slurped and coconut scattered like dandruff across his knees.

Mallory moved across to the visitor's chair and forged ahead. 'I thought I'd let you know that I'm staying in Appletree Hill for a while. I've rented Fruit Flan; you know Vern and Doris Peeling's old place. Except now it's renovated with a new name.' She paused, hoping for a reaction but none came. 'Anyway, I'll be around ...'

'So you said. What do you want?'

Mallory bent to pick up his napkin, blinking back tears. But then what had she expected? For her father to skip in jubilation if his old body had allowed it? To enquire about her health, her life? It was tempting to make up something preposterous if only to fill the void, but she knew her father wouldn't have reacted either way. Not even to the news of $20 million having come her way. Rarely had he ever shown any excitement or love towards family members – except for her brother, Patrick.

The ping of room alarms echoed along the nursing home's corridor, the tea trolley's jangle fading in the distance. HP gazed blankly out the window and across the wedge of green hills. A sudden surge of sympathy, or was it pity, welled inside Mallory as she studied his sagging profile, his mouth loosely applying itself to the cake. It must be awful to be in here all day, every day when your life had consisted of being in the open air, of social events and being in charge. Mallory started to question her visit, despite his time left being limited. The nurse had said as much when she had notified Mallory of the latest blood results. She had always been torn between feeling empathy and rage towards her father, so she needed to focus on the reasons for her visit.

When Patrick had ensconced himself in the family home years ago, 'To help out', he'd said initially, Mallory and Vivien had been relieved. After all, the sisters hadn't the time to visit from interstate very often, and their father made it clear he was happy with that.

Mallory had returned to Pepper Farm many times, mainly to see her mother. But it had always been a chore to have to gather her nerves at the back door before the jolt of negativity greeted her within. When Stella had died suddenly, Mallory had returned for her mother's funeral. Stella's wake had been held in the refurnished loungeroom – where the antiques had disappeared to was anyone's guess and it hadn't been the appropriate time to probe Harold of their whereabouts. The changes to their family home had come as a shock – ugly air conditioning units had been installed throughout, the house's interior had been repainted a dull pale blue, and the solid kitchen replaced with shiny splashbacks and coastal tiles. But the worst of it was that Patrick had made himself comfortable in the main bedroom with their parents relegated to single rooms at the rear of the house.

Vivien had joked that Patrick's latest girlfriend, Stacey seemed to know where more things were kept than they did. 'Don't stress the small stuff, Mallory. Patrick can live in the house and keep an eye on Dad. It'll all pan out later in the will when Dad passes.'

When Harold Pepper had suffered a stroke, an email to Mallory and Vivien from Patrick alerted them to the fact that 'Dad has passed on his wishes that I take over the house and property, in thanks for my ongoing help to them after his daughters had left.'

John had been livid at the thought that an inheritance had possibly been snatched from them – he had made no secret of his desire to become a country squire in his retirement.

'You've been passed over, Mallory. Why didn't you put something in place? Some kind of Power of Attorney?'

'For heaven's sake, John. It doesn't mean Dad has left the whole thing to Patrick. He hasn't said that. It doesn't mean he is the only recipient should something happen.'

'Well something will happen, won't it. I mean the old man won't live forever. He's already been ousted to a nursing home because of a stroke, which I'm sure he hates every second. If Patrick has managed that then who knows what else he has manipulated.'

The sisters had discussed the ramifications of Patrick remaining in the house, and then Vivien had withdrawn her interest, preferring to trust in her brother and the system. But a sick feeling had remained in Mallory's stomach, just like the sour crab-apple pain from her youth when she had overindulged on the bright little fruits. What if it had, in fact, been Patrick who had chosen the tawdry nursing home, and not penny-pinching on her father's part? Mallory's lottery win had led her, with Bridie's help, to find the best nursing home in the area. The only response from Patrick had been to make it clear he wouldn't be contributing to its cost, followed by a few questions as to how she could afford it. They'd gone unanswered. But now, with their father's health failing, she was back and knew she would be the target of more questions.

Harold had slumped forward, a deep snore vibrating around the walls. Apparently, the stroke made him tire easily – another side effect of old age that HP would find abhorrent. Sighing, Mallory collected his cup and plate and wandered into the corridor. The trolley was nowhere to be seen; in fact, no one was to be seen. Hearing voices from the carers' station she wandered along the hallway, trying not to glance through doorways into others' private spaces. Televisions blared. She felt tired and incredibly sad, emotions that mingled with relief that she had returned to the town. A tiny lady appeared, shakily carrying her own rose-patterned cup. She was like a fragile hummingbird.

'Oh, let me take that for you,' Mallory offered.

'Thank you, dear. Happy birthday,' she said before shuffling away.

Mallory slid the crockery onto a counter and turned to leave.

'Is that you, Mallory?'

Mallory's heart, dull from her visit, kickstarted at the familiar voice. Frowning, she followed the question to the corner lounge suite. 'Gosh, hello Stuart.'

Instantly, she was transported back through the years to snuggling deep inside a parka, her fingers frozen but her heart warm as she watched Stuart Forbes play football; back to when they'd meet after school and stroll the country lanes, stopping to steal kisses behind the hedgerows; back to when he had looked at her with such yearning, she could hardly stand it. The Stuart Forbes gazing at her now was an older version of his eighteen-year-old self. He was still as solid and handsome as he had been in his teen sports gear, whether it was cricket, football or rugby. His once unruly black hair was short and styled, now more dove-grey than blackbird. Mallory's heart raced as it recalled how his green eyes used to sparkle and dance, always quick with a cheeky wink. Now, the age lines accentuated those eyes' handsome depths, and something else that Mallory couldn't quickly decipher. A heaviness? They regarded each other for a moment, almost frozen in time. She wondered how he saw this older version of herself that stood before him.

Mallory flicked her eyes to where an old woman, stooped and frail, slumped in a wheelchair beside him. She was literally a whiter shade of pale, her legs like toothpicks sticking from below her nightgown. The woman stared ahead, lost in her thoughts and world. Mallory hoped it was a happy place.

Stuart gently released the limp hand he was holding and stood. Tentatively he took a couple of steps to peck Mallory on the cheek.

He was a good head and shoulders taller than Mallory. She glanced up into his face; the face of the boy who had stolen her heart, with whom she had shared laughter and dreams, with whom she had tenderly taken the path from virginity to making love all those years ago. From another time.

Mallory took a step backward, turning her attention to the old woman, who she realised was Stuart's mother.

'Hello, Nellie. It's Mallory Campbell; I mean Mallory Pepper.' But there was no recognition, no response.

'What are you doing here, Mallory?' Stuart asked.

Mallory pointed back over her shoulder. 'My dad is here. As is your mum obviously. What a coincidence.'

He nodded. 'How is he?'

After all the angst Harold Pepper had given the young Stuart about dating her, Mallory would forgive him for not really caring. She ran her hand through her hair, trying to be diplomatic. 'Well, you know Dad. Never one to miss an opportunity to let you know about life's shortcomings. Oh, excuse me, I shouldn't have said that. I haven't seen him for a while and kind of wished for a friendlier greeting than the one bestowed on me.'

Stuart nodded, seemingly unsurprised. 'It's hard being in here, but you know what. They are in a safe place with safe people. That's how I look at it.'

'Oh, I hope so,' Mallory replied.

Nellie's legs started twitching. Stuart frowned as he returned to his mother's side.

'She doesn't like to be away from her room for too long and gets agitated. I'd better take her back.'

'Yes, of course.' Mallory hesitated as Stuart flicked off the wheelchair's brake and adjusted his mother's knee blanket. He paused as if about to say something but instead gave her a nod of goodbye before wandering off up the corridor. Mallory waited for him to glance back over his shoulder, but he turned into a bedroom doorway without so much as a wave.

THE NURSES at the floor desk told her everything they thought she wanted to hear as Mallory arranged her gift of proteas in a vase. 'He's such a dear.' 'He's coming along well with his exercises.' 'We haven't needed to increase his medications yet.' Then, 'No, we haven't seen his son visit for some time.'

A quick peek into HP's room showed Mallory he was still asleep. There was no point staying any longer.

Bumping into Stuart Forbes had surprised and, for a moment, caught her off-guard. He hadn't seemed too keen to stay and chat or to find out more about "The Recent Life of Mallory Pepper", but then he was being very dutiful to his mother. Mallory had always been jealous of how close the Forbes family had been, compared to her own, and it seemed little had changed. He had probably driven down from the city for the day and was already locked and loaded to return to his life there. But then she couldn't claim to know anything about his life, so why should he care about hers.

The fresh air was welcoming as she strolled back to her car, but as the door slammed shut, any joy she had felt quickly evaporated. In the cold light of day, sitting in a silent nursing home car park, she acknowledged that her father would never open his heart to her. Hot tears pricked Mallory's eyes, misting the manicured hedges and rose bushes.

Zarni had warned her of course. 'Mallory, honey. Don't get me wrong. I've never met your father but from what you've said over the years, and what hasn't been said I might add, I just hope you aren't getting your hopes up. Why would anything be different now?'

Mallory had shrugged. 'Doesn't he realise that his children are the only family he has? That he needs me?'

'Why would he think he needs you? You've often said any help you've offered over time has been ignored or thrown back at you. Excuse me, I don't mean to criticise your dad, but ... Anyway, from your stories, I'm sure he has your brother on a short string.'

Mallory had scoffed. 'I doubt it. Patrick suits himself. I know Dad has never welcomed my visits, but I can't ignore him, can I, particularly after the home called to advise his cancer's progressed. I just wish it wasn't always such a drama.'

A family drifted out of the building, a young girl leading a fluffy dog, her parents chatting as they pushed an elderly man in a wheelchair. Before she knew it, Mallory had reversed out of the car park and steered in the direction of her old family home, as if tugged by a giant magnet.

PEPPER FARM HAD NEVER BEEN a farm exactly, but its name had been one argument that Stella Pepper had won with her new young husband, Harold. She had insisted on a distinguished name for their beautiful, rambling old red-brick house that sat amidst a thirty-acre apple fruit orchard. Harold had won the discussion about where to live and Stella had won the argument about its name.

As they grew older, Mallory and her siblings had escaped the stifling atmosphere that seeped into every corner of the rooms, preferring to roam the property, picking apples during the season, playing hide and seek, and climbing the gnarled old branches. But progress soon found Appletree Hill and the neighbouring properties had started to be subdivided and sold off. Then, some twenty years ago, developers had circled with very lucrative offers to sell. The

Peppers had refused but much to her parents' horror a neighbour had sold his land to a golf course developer. All the temper tantrums and vitriolic letters from Harold had made no difference to the local council, and their home had become exposed to a fairway.

However, the clearing for the golf course and the fact that Harold had refused to spend money on planting any kind of treed barrier, had opened up stunning 180-degree views of the bay, which Stella grew to love. Not that that had placated Harold. The house had also become visible to tourists who risked wayward golf balls as they slowly drove along the narrow road that ran between the greens, fairways, and view-soaked clifftop. Even more unwelcome were those who ducked across the course to accost a family member if they were on the grounds with questions about the area.

Now, it was Mallory who pulled into one of the roadside car parks dotted along the ridge. It was a popular spot for hang gliders to launch, but none were tempted to test the gusty winds today. Mallory turned her attention across to Pepper Farm. A warm smile tweaked her lips at how old and breathtakingly beautiful it was.

The properties on either side of Mallory's childhood home had been re-sold several times, their original farmhouses knocked down to be replaced by modern, soulless bungalows – all black concrete, glass windows, and clipped, rectangular hedges. They were gin and tonic houses, whereas Pepper Farm had remained, for the most part, a large cabernet – robust and a little rough around the edges. Even at a distance, Mallory saw the orchard was finding its own will in Harold's absence. She licked her lips as though she could still taste the crunchy sweetness of the fruit she and her friend, Bridie, had often picked during the long summer school holidays.

The house had remained unchanged as she grew older, making memories easy to access; doilies scattered over dark, dustless wooden furniture, a lingering silence except for her mother's humming as she religiously set the dinner table at 5:00 pm. The aromas of roast lamb and fried onions had stained the dining room's curtains long after the meal had been quietly consumed. The heavy timber floors were always cool, even in the height of summer, except in the main hallway where a frayed runner had spread for decades. She and Vivien had secretly hidden their Minties wrappers under it until their brother had threatened to dob them in.

But they were childhood memories. Patrick and Pepper Farm could soon expect an adult visit from Mallory, especially now that it seemed their father was no longer king of his own castle.

Chapter Five

'MALLORY, I'm so glad you're here. What say I pick up a lasagne and salad and invite myself for dinner at Fruit Flan?'

Mallory liked that the locals still referred to The Getaway by its original name. It kept a little slice of history alive while the world seemed to be constantly upgrading. Bridie was the touchstone of her own history in Appletree Hill; the bestie throughout childhood, with their little town the common thread as they aged. The friends only caught up in person when either was in the other's town, but frequent emails and photos happily filled the distance.

After their school years had finished, the girlfriends had set off to travel briefly before moving on to teachers' college together. Mallory had grabbed the opportunity to leave Appletree Hill and her overbearing father, but Bridie had felt the tugs of country life too strongly. Not to mention those from her old boyfriend, Rodney who had remained on his family's horse stud, studying accounting by correspondence. They had met at one of the surf carnivals during high school and, apart from Bridie's stint at college, hadn't been apart since. Now, Rod remained the trusted accountant for a handful of clients, whilst Bridie admitted to being content with her garden club and interstate visits from their children. Mallory knew that there was more to her friend than just planting seeds – she was President of the Appletree Hill Agricultural Show, ran the district's charity kitchen, and had even organised reluctant locals to march on Parliament House in a recent climate change rally.

Bridie was a loyal, down-to-earth woman whom Mallory adored and was grateful to have as a lifelong friend. After prolonged hugs and exchanged 'Don't you look great' compliments, they now sat on Mallory's front veranda, a glass of local chilled pinot in hand, feet propped up on a bench, and the dinner heating in the oven. Mallory slid a little lower in the cane armchair, content to while away the evening with light chatter and gossip. The nighttime country noises of crickets and possum scuffles added to the relaxed, bush ambience.

'Who lives next door?' Mallory tilted her glass toward the side fence.

'I'm not sure. I think it's vacant or an interstate owner, so no one is permanent. Mind you, this village has grown so much that I haven't a clue who half the people are anymore, and you can imagine how much that frustrates me! Why?'

'Oh, I just thought there was music coming from over there the other night.'

Bridie gazed around her, grinning, her attention having flicked past any musical neighbour. 'Who would have thought we'd be sitting on Fruit Flan's veranda after all these years. It's a shame the house is so different though.'

Mallory nodded. 'I thought that when I first pulled into the driveway. Doris's garden and kitchen table were my saviours when I needed to escape the boredom of home. There are still small signs of its previous glory if you know where to look.'

Bridie let out one of her laughs, so deep it sounded like it came from her Blundstone boots. 'Glory? Hardly. Vern was always patching something instead of just buying a new replacement at McWinter's hardware store.'

Mallory laughed. 'True.'

'You can still see the notches in the doorway where Doris used to measure me. "Growing like a mushroom" she used to say. They've been painted over but the impressions are still there. And in the back bedroom, someone has shabby-chic'd the little old bookcase that used to sit under the window in the lounge room. There are even a couple of Doris's cookbooks with her notes in the margin advising to add more salt or a cross through a recipe she apparently didn't like.'

'No leftover copies of 'Daisy's Dreams'?' Bridie joked.

'No. As John said at the time, "It was your heyday, Mallory. Move on."' They both laughed at Mallory's attempt to imitate John's scoffing tone.

Between teachers' college and comfortably settling with John, Mallory had been very successful. Her 'Daisy's Dreams' series of children's books focused on fun 'what if' moments as dreamed by a little girl named Daisy. It had become a big seller on the domestic and international markets.

Mallory had floated through her writing success, planning to return to it after having children and working in their conference business. Unfortunately, neither goal had been successful. It hadn't been a conscious decision not to have children of her own; she had accepted the two miscarriages as meant to be and hoped for other opportunities that sadly didn't eventuate. Then Warren had bought into the business and, as so often happened, a partnership had changed the dynamics as John increasingly interacted with his new partner. It hadn't helped when Mallory's sister had set her sights on Warren – the fellow didn't stand a chance. From that day onward Mallory had felt like the spare wheel.

She had left the business to pick up her writing and teaching degree again. There had been a spike when a publisher had picked up her 'Daisy's Inspirational Quotes for Kids' books, but sales had slumped with the glut of similar titles and their complementary bookmarks and merchandise.

Then time had just flitted by and before she knew it the opportunities for further publication or having children had passed. John never understood why her young students didn't fill the void, so she had never discussed that absent space in her soul. It was an uneasy outcome she often regretted.

The two women sat in comfortable silence, sharing the beauty of the misty countryside. Finally, Bridie glanced sideways and breached the unspoken. 'So, Mallory. Don't feel as though you need to talk about it if you don't want to but, speaking of John. Has he ...' Seeing Mallory bite her bottom lip, Bridie leant across and placed her palm on Mallory's arm, and waited.

Mallory shook her head and smiled. 'It's okay. Our marriage was certainly on shaky ground, but I was trying to keep it together. He was very quick to inform me of his apparent boredom and how Vivian understood him and his needs more than I ever had. Something about her younger outlook on life.' She sighed and gazed into the distance.

'Ugh, what a toad. It's sliding doors though, isn't it? I

mean, what if you hadn't overheard John talking to Viv? Would you have ever learnt about their affair? And, even if you hadn't, you may not have stayed with him anyway. Who knows.'

'There are too many 'what ifs' right there, but I can assure you I've gone over all those possibilities a million times. And now any conversation has been reduced to sickening one-liners. I know our marriage had lost its, well, lost its everything really, but it hurt so much more knowing there was a third person involved.'

'Let alone that the third person was your sister!'

Mallory nodded before sending Bridie a quick glance. 'The completely silly thing is that I won some money in the lottery, and I was going to surprise John with a trip to Italy the very same night my marriage self-combusted.'

She was interrupted by Bridie clapping her hands to hear about the win. 'Oh, that's wonderful. How much? Does he know that you won something?'

Mallory laughed, intending to skate around the first question. She still felt uncomfortable with the large sum of her winnings. 'At the last possible moment. It came up as part of the property settlement, but things were in my favour, thank heavens. And Zarni knows. Truth is, I haven't had a chance to get my head around my good fortune apart from making a few charity donations. Maybe things turn out the way they are meant to.'

'Do you believe that?'

'No. Maybe.' Mallory bit her lip again to silence the anxiety that hid below the surface of her smiles. Coming back to Appletree Hill had unnerved her more than she could ever have predicted. Was she meant to return? Perhaps she was searching for something other than helping her father.

Mallory cleared her throat and took a deep breath 'Both, and together I guess. I was sorry that the business folded, for Warren's sake, but how could it continue after his business partner and so-called friend was having an affair with his wife.' Mallory sighed. 'Remember when Viv first saw Warren? She latched onto him before he could take a breath. I can't help wondering – because I don't know anything about how their affair unfolded – did she do the same with John, or did he instigate things? Apart from that, I'd always presumed that the four of us would continue through life together. In business and as a family. What a joke.'

'Well, if you've come into a bit of money and it didn't all go in the settlement, you could always hire a hitman,' Bridie said with a grin. She softened her tone before continuing. 'I know you caught up with Warren; have you seen him again?'

Mallory shook her head. 'I doubt I will.'

She had left several messages for Warren over the days following John's exit. When he had finally returned her call, she hadn't recognised the exhausted, quiet voice at the other end of the phone, let alone his appearance when they had finally met.

They must have looked such a sad-sack couple as they slumped over coffees that went cold, both sniffing their way through a conversation that didn't go anywhere.

'So, you had no idea about their affair, Warren? You were in the same office, surely something must have given them away,' Mallory had prodded.

'Well, 20/20 hindsight is great, isn't it Mallory? He was your husband, and she was your sister, so why didn't you catch on?'

She had reached across the table, and placed her hand

on top of his. 'I'm sorry, I was too blunt. It's all such a shock. Will you be okay, with the business side of things?'

He explained how he hadn't thought too much about their business, had just been putting one foot in front of the other day by day. He was fulfilling existing contract orders, but not taking on any more jobs or following up on queries.

'John hasn't even approached me with any idea how it will all pan out.' He shrugged. 'Maybe he's high on love. Maybe he expects me to just walk away, but I won't. I'll fight for what's mine. Which could mean lawyers and more financial outlays.'

Mallory had presumed he meant the business, not Vivien. What did she have to fight for? Her future, yes her future.

She had sat a little higher in the chair at that thought and although she still felt sick every other minute, the words formed a fork in the road. They had to. And another fork in the road had led her back to Appletree Hill. She turned her attention back to Bridie.

'And Vivien?'

Mallory sighed. 'No, I haven't spoken with her. The thought of my sister deceiving me on so many levels is so, so … I don't know. Like she's put me in a jar, slammed the lid then shaken it, watching me. A part of me really, really hates them, and I did struggle with an unbridled rage that they could deceive me like that. But I've focused on moving past that stage; it doesn't do anyone any good, does it.' She shuffled her feet. 'I can't help feeling humiliated though.'

Bridie placed her wine glass on the floor and faced her friend. 'The whole thing is bullshit, Mal. How dare they! Snakes in the grass, that's what they are.'

'Zarni heard they're living together in some swanky apartment on the Gold Coast.'

'So be it – they've taken every scrap of your trust with them,' Bridie declared.

'I doubt either of them care about that.' Mallory shrugged. 'I don't know why but it feels odd being back in Appletree Hill. I mean it's wonderful in many ways but so much is unresolved. I thought I'd come back for a while, make sure Dad was okay, visit Patrick and the house, and then go back to sorting out my future and what I want to do.'

'And?'

'I just can't make any decisions; I keep doubting where I think I should be heading. Or rather, where I want to head. Instead of each drama having its own box, they're all in one big simmering lump of lava. Thank heavens for the windfall which I am deeply grateful for.'

'Well as always, if the decision is being happy and having money or sad and having money, we'd all choose the former. So here's to happiness.' Bridie took a sip of wine, squinting past Mallory as though the answer lay in the lavender bushes that lined the front fence. She popped a fat green olive into her mouth, chewing and thinking.

'But getting back to what you just said, maybe you're mixing up the two. You've got enough time here to hang out with wonderful people like me, to sleuth around Pepper Farm and Patrick, and check on your dad. Then you can sit down and have a good hard look at yourself and work out what you want. It's still early days in a lot of ways. You've resigned from teaching, so your future is free.'

Mallory nodded. 'I was just treading water, but I guess you're right. Maybe I'm trying to clean up too many messes at once. Speaking of which, I can smell our lasagne, so I'll get organised before *it's* a burnt mess. Inside at the table or a tray on our laps outside?'

'It's getting pretty chilly, so let's eat inside.'

As Mallory tossed the fresh, green salad, Bridie brought the deep-dish beef lasagne to the table to settle for a few minutes. 'Yum, look at that bubbling cheese. Who cares how many calories are in each slice.' She started to rattle through the drawers in search of servers as Mallory found paper napkins.

'Cheers,' they said, grinning across the table at each other. 'It's been too long,' Bridie added before they each tucked into their meals.

'Guess who I saw in the village?' Mallory teased. Bridie shrugged, so she continued. 'Heather, oh excuse me, Hettie McMunn.'

'Was she at the nursery café? She's had that business for a long time but her daughter seems to run it. Weren't your parents close at one stage?'

'What? No, just family card nights. She never really liked me. Then there was that whole debacle with Stuart.'

'I have no idea why I thought there was more to it, to be honest. Gawd, is this Alzheimer's? Just the way she spoke about you once I thought you may have been friends, but lost touch after she hit on Stuart. We haven't crossed paths for years. Anyway, you did look a bit like each other in school with your pale skin and reddish hair.'

Mallory choked. 'Oh, nonsense. Just because you were the coconut oil queen!'

'And didn't I pay for those attempts at being a bronzed goddess.' Bridie inspected several patches of stitched skin along her arms. 'Anyway, back to Hettie McMunn. She left suddenly, when she was in her early twenties, and came back a few years later with a toddler. Olivia. Said her husband had died but we all knew that she had left Appletree Hill to have the baby. Not that it mattered but even now she won't come clean. No one knows who the father was but odds on it was Banjo Carruthers.'

'Really? What happened to him? He was quite a bit older than us.'

Bridie shrugged. 'He left the town and never returned. Who knows.'

'So, Olivia is the young woman I met in the café? She's lovely. So unlike her mother, I have to say, except she's got the red hair.'

'Olivia is great and apparently is giving the café a go, despite its outward appearance. Not quite up to 'village standards'.' Bridie hooked her fingers to emphasise the obvious expectations of the new breed of visitors.

'Good on them, I guess,' Mallory said.

The friends turned their attention back to their dinner, scooping more salad onto nearly bare plates.

Such a long time ago. So many changes, yet some things stay the same, Mallory thought. Was that a good or a bad thing? She had left behind Appletree Hill without a backward glance, eager to start another life in another place and mend her broken young heart. At the time she had doubted it would ever heal, but it had. So many laughs and happy days and years within her marriage had followed, as they should. Then came John and Vivien's deceit. Out of the blue, she wondered if Patrick knew about his youngest sister's affair with his other sister's husband.

And now here she was, back in Appletree Hill escaping from the city life she had once fled to. How ironic that one of the first people she bumped into, Stuart Forbes, was a contributor to why she had left in the first place.

'I went to see Dad at the nursing home,' Mallory said, taking a sip of wine.

'How is he?' Bridie asked, a slight frown appearing on her forehead.

'He's definitely on the decline ...'

'And?'

'Why can't I just accept that he's a cranky old man who enjoys being mad at the world? I really don't know how Mum put up with him. She was always the mediator between Dad and us girls, protecting us against his criticism as much as she could. I feel guilty speaking of him like this when he's not well, but standing in front of him brought back so many memories, Bridie. He still manages to strip me of all the steps forward I thought I'd made.' She shook her head in disbelief.

'That you *have* made,' her friend corrected.

Mallory shrugged. 'It was like I was a schoolgirl again.' She poked at a shard of burnt cheese stuck to the lasagne dish.

'You're still his daughter. But Mallory, go easy on yourself. You always said he never contacted you in all the years after you left Appletree Hill, not even a phone call of congratulations when you were a bestselling author. It was Patrick who let you know when your mum died. It has always been you doing the giving and filling in the gaps. Remember that Harold is in a lovely home thanks to you and no thanks to his other two children.'

Mallory nodded. 'That's what Zarni said too. I'm lucky to have such wise friends.'

'Wise?'

Mallory smiled. 'Well, how about irrationally well-intentioned? At least you're both on the same page with the advice.' She let a minute go by before taking a gulp of wine and then glancing at Bridie. 'I saw Stuart Forbes at the nursing home too.'

'What!' Bridie spluttered. 'Gawd, you've only been back in town a nano-second and it seems you have a magnet hung around your neck. What happened?'

Mallory welcomed the laugh that bubbled through her lips. 'He was there visiting his mum. Poor Nellie. Anyway, we chatted briefly and then he left. End of story.'

Bridie watched her friend as she stood and brought across a candle. The evening had darkened, the small dining nook dimly illuminated by the kitchen lights.

'You know he doesn't live around here anymore, don't you? I mean I've lost track of what he's been up to, but he did spend time in America. May have married there? He did something to do with building. I could do some of my own sleuthing though,' Bridie offered.

Mallory shrugged. 'Everyone has moved on although I must say he has aged rather well. He's obviously kept fit, and his hair has these little grey ...' She laughed at her words.

'His hair has these little grey what, my friend?' Bridie's giggle joined Mallory's.

Her hands waved away the comment. 'It doesn't matter. I've got enough on my plate with Patrick and Dad. Ugh, I wish I'd just clear my head and work out a clear path on how to deal with them.'

Bridie leant across and gave Mallory's arm another squeeze. 'Some families aren't as emotionally connected as others; some people like your dad just aren't put together with a lot of love glue.'

Mallory chuffed. 'Love glue! I'd forgotten that phrase. But that's your family, isn't it Bridie. Glued together with love. I wish it had been mine.'

Chapter Six

THE LOCALS KNEW that a southerly wind was a sign of change. It brought with it a sudden biting chill as it whipped leaves from the trees and carried them across the farm fences before they had a chance to settle. It was a warning to pack away hammocks and to air out scarves and jackets; to make sure the woodpile had started to mount and was dry.

It was also when the back door to the cottage would rattle against its frame, a whistle of wind curling its way underneath and across the kitchen floor. It was an invisible force that no owner, nor new door had ever been able to outsmart. Mallory, wide awake from her fun catchup with Bridie and the wine they had consumed, listened to the whirling gusts as they blustered around the house. Seeking solace in a comforting green tea, Mallory dragged a spare blanket around her shoulders and plodded to the kitchen.

The beat of music began as she moved to the rear of the house, its deep bass thumping against the windows. She presumed she must be downwind of whoever was playing, otherwise the neighbourhood would all be shouting for silence. What neighbourhood, and could they actually 'shout for silence'? A sprinkling of houses adrift on varying acreages didn't make up a neighbourhood. She sighed as her mind pinged against dozens of thoughts and grabbed a mug.

Beyond the window sprawled the deep blackness only experienced at sea or in the country. It was almost tangible. Yawning, Mallory poured the boiling water over a teabag. As the music had again infiltrated the cottage walls at such an early hour, she knew the rocker would have to be confronted. But not now, not when setting foot outside would mean being carried away by the wind like Mary Poppins.

Instead, she searched the cottage for a draught snake, but there wasn't one to be found. Perhaps it's too uncool these days to use the homemade psychedelic fabric rolls that she remembered Doris using to block the gap under doors. A rolled bath towel pushed against the draught would have to do. She emptied the untouched tea into the sink and headed back to bed, pulling the bedroom door firmly behind her. As her eyelids closed, she wondered if she should have brought the cane setting in from the front veranda.

That same thought was uppermost in her mind when she woke to a still, quiet morning, soon realising she must have slept deeper than she thought. Easing open the front door she was greeted by what looked like the remains of a mini hurricane. The table and chairs lay upended but intact on the driveway – how they had arrived there she couldn't imagine considering the wind direction. It must have swirled around the house from all sides. Mountains of leaves and spiky tree branches covered the veranda and damp ground. Her car had escaped any damage other than there being a thick drift of gravel and twigs and gumnuts mounted against the wheels. Her morning would now be spent in clean-up mode, then a visit to her elusive, noisy neighbour.

***

'HELLO? ANYONE AT HOME?'

Mallory had walked a short distance down her driveway, moving aside fallen branches as she went, when she saw a break in the shrubbery. A small track disappeared towards an old gate, forlorn and hanging off its hinges. She'd carefully made her way through the undergrowth, squeezed around the drooping gate, and headed for the neighbouring driveway. She couldn't imagine why the properties would be connected in the first place. The musky smell of peaty soil and damp leaf cover hadn't changed since her childhood days at Fruit Flan when she had invented her own adventures; when she had happily roamed across the pastures until Doris called for her to come inside. Her shoes would be wet through, her arms scratched from thorns and spiky twigs, but there would always be hot chocolate and bandaids at the ready when she re-emerged. Sometimes Doris would phone Stella to say Mallory was staying the night, at other times Vern would drive her home.

'Hello,' Mallory called again, but no reply came. Perhaps they had left before morning. As noisily as possible she crunched across the gravel path, up the cracked front steps, and onto the front veranda. So much debris had accumulated that her shoes left a snail trail across the timber deck as she walked to the front door. The sharp sound of the brass knocker echoed within as she rapped it a couple of times, then a couple more. Dark green, or was it brown, velvet curtains were pulled tightly across the windows which sat on either side of the weathered wooden door, no doubt to keep out prying eyes. Peeling cream paintwork around the window frames, cracked render, and thick cobwebs added to the house's plea of feeling abandoned and unloved. She had no recollection of ever visiting the house in the past.

Was that scraping sound from inside? She slowly followed the veranda around the corner, her ears peeled for any indication of occupants. She noted the house's original concrete would have been grey, typical of old farmhouses, but had been rendered at some time with a sickly ochre that had also faded. The garden had overtaken the roof in places, tendrils and long leafy fingers trying to prise it off.

Mallory called out half-heartedly as she approached the back screen door, or what was left of it. It was open wide, too rusty to swing in the wind. She cupped her hands around her face and peered through the slit between the door frame and timber boarding. Puddles of light highlighted a pale green kitchen, a clean diamond patterned lino floor, and a square timber table and chairs. Mallory frowned. If this old place was as deserted as it appeared from the outside, then why was a tea towel neatly folded next to a new kettle and a plastic-wrapped loaf of bread; was it a cat or a dog who drank out of the shiny blue bowl on the mat beside a pair of seemingly new gumboots?

She wasn't about to hang around until the musician appeared – it could be hours. She should have brought a handwritten note to slide under the door, politely asking to keep the midnight recitals to a minimum. Would that be too rude, considering she had just arrived? Deciding to give whoever it was a bit of slack, she turned and wound her way back to the front of the house. This time she headed down the curved driveway, noting along the way the gnarled, overgrown, apple orchard to her left. Stopping, she turned to gaze back at the house and smiled. It would have been beautiful in its day, simple but sturdy; and what a stunning outlook over the surrounding rolling hills. She glanced at the rusty letterbox as she passed it, but there was no nameplate to help work out the property's history. She'd have to ask around town.

IN CONTRAST to the previous evening, the night sky was clear and scattered with stars, all signs of the storm having passed. Mallory snuggled on her front veranda, two layers of clothing, thick socks and a mohair blanket protecting her from the chilly air. She was surprised at how much the temperatures had dropped within the last few days. A warm coffee was clutched in her hands, its steam fogging her reading glasses. Her book, a political drama from an author she usually enjoyed, lay unopened beside her. She felt restless, unsure of why she was staying in this town. What was she hoping to achieve? Her father obviously didn't care where she was which added another complicated level to her grand plans of mending their past grievances. She had put off visiting Patrick for another day, only leaving him a voice message to say she was in town and would call by soon. He hadn't responded. Her coffee tasted bitter but welcome as a distant town's halo of light wavered across the edge of the horizon, making her feel even more on the outer.

Her phone beeped with a message from Bridie: An invitation to dinner at Peggy and Martha's home on the weekend. Mallory smiled and immediately replied with a thumbs-up emoji. It would be wonderful to catch up with the couple, who she hadn't seen in person since their wedding nearly two years earlier. They had sent a heart-warming message on hearing of her split from John with an open-ended invitation for her to stay at any time – true friends knew when to prod and when to back off.

She scrolled through her phone to open their wedding folder, bracing herself for John's handsome face to appear. But there were surprisingly few, even less of the two of them together. Had she missed something in their relationship then, had the affair with Viv already started? Mallory spread her fingers across the screen, enlarging his face as she searched his eyes for tell-tale signs of boredom or secrecy. Or hatred. He looked just the same as he always had. No, the same as she had become accustomed to him looking.

It didn't help to go over it all again, to keep questioning the why and where, let alone how long they had been seeing each other. More than 'seeing each other' – what a stupid simple phrase. They'd been having sex, being intimate. Her husband had been happy in the early days of their marriage, even in the middle. She just knew it. She turned her phone off and tossed it onto the book.

Mallory had loved him despite his frustrating ways. That had fragmented like a shattered mirror as she had listened to him whisper how much he yearned for her sister.

'What now, universe?' she asked into the wide open sky. But the Milky Way had no miraculous answer.

Chapter Seven

AFTER LOADING her groceries into the car boot, Mallory discreetly scanned for any sign of Hettie. It was a glorious, clear Saturday morning, perfect for sitting outside at the nursery. How the little cafe survived during the long, wet months when there was no cover, she had no idea, but its rustic quaintness and homemade cakes somehow appealed to her more than the other cafes along the strip.

'Hello again,' came Olivia's greeting. Perhaps Mallory wasn't as invisible as she had assumed.

'Hello. A flat white, please. And one of your blueberry mini muffins,' Mallory said. 'I also need a large bunch of flowers to take to friends. Maybe a mix of natives and ... Oh, I'll leave it to you.'

It was relaxing to sit behind her sunglasses and people-watch. Locals with well-behaved dogs bustled up and down the footpath, stopping to greet and hug friends; visitors dawdled past the shop windows, many with takeaway coffees in hand.

'There you go.' Olivia set down the coffee and muffin.

She shuffled from foot to foot, apparently wanting to chat. 'So you're visiting, are you? From the city?'

'Brisbane actually, but I'll be here a while. I've rented The Getaway – do you know it?'

Olivia shook her head. 'I keep to myself really.'

'It's just up the road a few kilometres. Beside an old house with a large hedge.' Mallory's prompts only produced a blank expression on Olivia's pretty face.

'It's just that my mum thought she knew you. From the other day?' She flicked at non-existent crumbs on the tabletop.

Mallory took her time blowing across her coffee and nibbling her muffin. 'Oh? This is so good. I'm sure if I'd had the large one, I would have eaten the whole thing by now. Do you make them yourself?'

Distracted from her question, Olivia's face lit up with a wide smile. 'Thank you. Yes, me and my friend Alice make all the cakes for the café; like a small business, you know? You've got to plan your life early and work hard.'

Mallory spluttered. Hadn't she been told that exact advice herself, but by whom? 'Well, that's interesting. Who gave you that advice?'

'Oh, my mum has always said that. I'll be right back with your flowers.'

Mallory watched the girl as she raced back into the store. Maybe she was misjudging Hettie, but after what Bridie had shared about their school friend, it didn't sound like something she would say. Olivia quickly returned with an oversized bouquet of wildflowers, large leaves, and native sprays in an explosion of autumn tones, wrapped in a swatch of hessian and tied with the nursery's trademark orange raffia.

'They're perfect, thank you,' Mallory said.

'I put a few extra sprigs in at no charge, b'cos I appreciate you coming back.'

So, Heather had recognised her. Mallory mulled over the implications as she sipped her delicious coffee. It would only be a matter of time then until she said something – Heather McMunn had never been shy of saying what was on her mind.

'OH, THEY'RE GORGEOUS,' Peggy cooed as Mallory handed over the bouquet that evening. 'Come in, come in. Martha is just fixing drinks. Bubbly or a dirty martini?'

Mallory returned Peggy's bearhug enveloped in her signature fragrance of Pears soap. She glanced around the large open entrance hall, at the many framed photos of horse races, her shoulders relaxing in the familiar surroundings. As a girl, she had loved visiting this messy ranch-style home that had belonged to Peggy's parents. Its large rooms had always been shambolic, with riding boots sprawled in one corner and dog cushions dumped in another, bags packed for the weekend race meets piled in the hallway. A bookcase reared opposite the entry, each shelf heavy with trophies from the family's successes at the track. Peggy's family had been the go-to horse trainers in the area, a talent their daughter had clearly inherited. The mustiness of those days was replaced by the lovely scents of beeswax, a large vase of white lilies, and the rich aromas drifting from the kitchen.

Peggy took Mallory's coat and then held her at arm's length, peering deep into her friend's eyes. 'It's so good to see you, but do I sense you are thinner? That's probably the fallout from everything you've been through with that man.'

She held up her hand as an oath. 'But, tonight is for old friends to catch up and have fun. You can share, cry, laugh or dance naked for all we care – whatever takes your fancy.'

Mallory laughed, pulling Peggy into a hug again. 'I'm sure you wouldn't want to witness the latter but thank you anyway. I'm getting there.'

'We're in here.' Bridie's voice filtered through the doorway.

'You go in while I find a vase for these beauties,' Peggy urged.

A step down into the loungeroom and Mallory was greeted with more hugs from Bridie. Stoic Rod gave her a quick one, mumbled something along the lines of welcome back, and Martha beckoned her with a raised champagne flute. She looped it behind Mallory's neck while planting a large kiss on her cheek.

They chatted over pre-dinner drinks, no one sitting for too long as they refilled glasses or recounted childhood stories for Martha's benefit. She had been working at Rod's family's horse stud when Peggy had swept her off her feet a decade ago, the two quickly forming a business and romantic connection.

'So as the girls' accountant and client, who claims this as a business dinner, Rod?' Mallory teased.

'They're the best trainers around here so they can have this one,' he said.

'Then why aren't we stinking rich? This business is a money pit,' Peggy said, mock accusation in her tone. 'Not to mention the wear and tear on these old bodies. We're thinking of cutting back our number of clients even more, so you'd better come up with some snazzy tax loopholes to bolster the funds, Rod.' Their laughter was silenced by an unexpected loud knock at the front door.

'Who on earth...' Peggy muttered as she put down her martini glass. They overheard friendly conversation from the entrance before Peggy reappeared with a long mailing tube in one hand and a guilty look on her face. 'Guess who's coming to dinner!'

Martha rushed forward, unaware that Mallory, Bridie and Rod were too shocked to move. 'Who have we here, Peg?'

Peggy's lips trembled with mischievous glee. 'Well, the others might remember Stuart Forbes. Martha, Stuart is from the Melbourne firm who is building our new stables and office. I just didn't know that it was *the* Stuart Forbes from our youth. He's in the neighbourhood, obviously, so got the job of dropping off our latest plans.' She glanced around the group. 'Wasn't that nice of him.'

'Thank you, Stuart,' Martha said. 'Did I hear you're staying for dinner because there's plenty to spare.'

Say no, please say no, Mallory urged silently as she pretended to load up a cracker with a wedge of cheese. From the corner of her eye, she watched as he tilted his head forward slightly and scratched the back of his neck. It had always been a sign that he was nervous. *Then say no!* His eyes quickly travelled from one guest to the next, settling on her for a second longer then back to his host.

'Pleased to meet you, Martha. I'm sorry to intrude. I thought I'd catch you before dinner time.'

'Oh, we eat early, don't we, Peg? Early mornings at the track and all that.'

Rod leant forward to shake Stuart's hand. 'Stuart.'

'G'day, Rod. Hello, Bridie. Lovely to see you again. And unexpected.' He turned to Mallory. 'Mallory. Twice in the last few days. Now that's a coincidence.'

'Hello, Stuart. Again.'

Peggy stepped in, obviously trying to relieve any awkwardness, although her smirk showed she was rather enjoying the banter. 'Well, whilst Martha sets another place and Rod fixes you a drink of some sort, why don't you escape with me to the kitchen so we can sort what you like and don't like. Gawd, you're not a vegetarian, are you?'

Stuart laughed in denial and followed Peggy's raised martini glass out of the room.

As Rod went to fetch Stuart's beer, Martha grabbed Bridie and Mallory's elbows. 'Okay, spill it. What's going on? I realise his visit is a surprise to us all, but why are you two standing there like stunned mullets?'

Bridie raised her eyebrows at Mallory.

'Stuart and I were an item once. He broke my heart, he left town and that's about the end of it,' Mallory said. 'Ancient history.'

'For a big-time author, you don't tell a very engaging story,' Bridie teased. She turned to Martha and lowered her voice. 'Mallory and Stu were a tight item through high school – she was the brains, and he was the sports star. Do you want to tell what happened, Mallory or should I give a quick version?'

Mallory shrugged, pretending she didn't care, so Bridie continued in hushed tones.

'Long story short, Mallory was sick the night of the school formal and didn't go. Stuart Forbes was her handsome boyfriend and her date. Well, Mallory's father saw Stu in a corner with another student, Heather McMunn, and drew all the wrong conclusions. Heather said Stu had cornered her and wouldn't leave her alone. She said all sorts of mean things and it all blew up in a huge mess.' Bridie leant across and hugged her friend to her side.

'He seems so nice,' Martha whispered.

'He was,' Mallory and Bridie said in unison before Mallory continued. 'It should have all just gone away but the rumours sort of snowballed and everyone took Heather's side. Stuart said he was just making sure she was okay because she was a bit of a loner, but Heather inflated her story and his reputation was badly damaged; he didn't make the graduate footy team while it was investigated and, um, it caused us to split. Dad was the main person who pretty well ran him out of town, ranting for days about how "that boy had done the wrong thing by his daughter".'

Martha winced. 'Oh.'

'It's part of our childhood histories, I guess. Bittersweet for me because of what Heather implied Stuart had done, but at the same time it was a moment when Dad actually stood up for me for a change.'

Mallory may have tried to sound flippant but her mind was in overdrive. What did it matter that Stuart Forbes was here? It would have been worse if they hadn't already bumped into each other, if she hadn't gotten past that heart flutter at seeing him again. Wouldn't it? They had both moved on many years ago, got married etcetera. What was his etcetera anyway?

'Please sit up at the table, everyone,' Martha announced. 'Mallory, why don't you come here next to me.'

The gulp of champagne tasted good as Mallory moved to the dinner table. Having Stuart in the same room posed no problem at all – it was a long time since they were silly teenagers.

Chapter Eight

HAVING NEVER KNOWN STUART, Martha obviously felt she would play devil's advocate, to ask all the tricky questions that the others were avoiding.

'I'm rather pleased that we decided to go with a building firm that has past connections to the town,' she began. 'Do you miss living in the country, Stuart?'

Stuart gave her a small smile, obviously on to where her subtle questions may be heading, then turned to the large tureen of thick beef and mushroom casserole in front of him. Carefully, he spooned some onto his plate, the rich aroma curling its way around the table. Waiting for his reply, the others kept busy serving themselves green beans with bacon and crunchy baked potatoes. Peggy passed a wooden board holding warm sourdough to Mallory. Their eyes locked, Peggy's twinkling with amusement, Mallory's with a question of how-far-will-she-go?

'I do, but I visit quite often. In addition to delivering plans to a particular client, I have to visit Mum in the nursing home. Well, I don't *have* to, I want to. She isn't doing too well lately.'

Peggy nodded in sympathy. 'I remember Nellie. She was such a gracious lady and I wish her well. Where are you in Melbourne, Stuart? We don't often get up to the big smoke anymore, do we, Martha?'

'We're in Richmond.'

We're, Mallory noticed. Or was he referring to his office?

'This meal is so good,' Rod said, helping himself to more beef, but probably in an effort to ease the interrogation.

'Well, save some room for the lemon tart,' Peggy said. 'Over to you, Mallory. How long are you in town?'

'I guess we're all at the same stage, aren't we, as I've come to check on Dad. I also need to have a chat with Patrick about a few things that I'm not looking forward to. Nothing changes.'

'I've seen Patrick a few times when I've ventured into town from over the hill,' Bridie said. 'And Stacey. Although they never return my wave.'

Rod asked, 'I presume you weren't invited to stay at Pepper Farm, Mallory?'

The thought almost made Mallory choke on her crusty bread. 'Good lord, no. I settled in before contacting him. Not that any invitation would have been issued; there's no way he wants me poking around the house. I'm staying at the old Fruit Flan property, which is now The Getaway B&B, but I still call it Fruit Flan. Thank heavens the estate agents have someone looking after the gardens as that storm the other night spread every possible piece of countryside across the driveway. I've raked some of the leaves into piles but it's an endless job. I need some of your gardening expertise, Bridie, to know if I should trim anything.' Mallory could hear herself rambling, but no one had mentioned Vivien, and she didn't want to give them any opening.

Bridie laughed. 'Just make sure there aren't any large trees that have been damaged and might topple over. We had a giant spruce get uprooted and crash last winter.' She paused. 'Turning to gentler forms of beauty, where did that gorgeous bowl come from, girls? I can't take my eyes off it.' They all turned towards where Bridie was pointing, to a large multi-coloured and gold-flecked glass bowl which sat in pride of place on the sideboard.

Martha sent Peggy a tender look. 'We bought it from Murano in Venice when we were on our honeymoon. We were silly newlyweds, weren't we, Peg.'

'We were,' Peggy replied. 'It was so expensive but we thought, hang it. We're two old broads in love, and you can never have too much colour in your life. We waited and waited for it to arrive, hoping we hadn't been scammed by the very handsome young Italian, or is it Venetian, at the glass factory; but here it is safe and sound. It's always been in the study, so that's probably why you haven't noticed it before.'

'I was supposed to go to Venice,' murmured Mallory, a little louder than she intended.

'Were you, when?' asked Rod before being sent a warning glance from his wife. Stuart spoke before Mallory needed to reply.

'Venice is definitely on my bucket list with its amazing architecture and history. I've been to Milan and Rome but there seems to be something so unique about a city on water, wouldn't you say? If I ever win the lottery I'd move to Italy for a while and rent a villa in Tuscany and welcome friends on a rotation of visits. We could all jaunt up to Venice for the weekend and stay at one of those outrageously expensive palazzos.'

Bridie laughed, flicking a glance across to Mallory.

'That's on everyone's list, I'd say. Now can I help clear all these plates, Peg? That lemon tart is beckoning.' Her attempt to change the subject fell on deaf ears.

'Would you share that you'd won?' Peggy asked no one in particular.

Martha held up her glass, slowly rotating the red wine. 'I'd tell you, my love. Actually, I had a friend once who won a year in France travelling to all the different wine regions. He'd entered one of those competitions on the tag attached to a wine bottle where you have to say in twenty-five words or less why you should win.' She took a long sip. 'I wish I knew what his entry said, but let's just drink up anyway.'

It was the perfect conversation for Mallory to fess up about her win to the girls, but Stuart's presence made the opportunity slip by.

As Rod was bringing her up to date on recent real estate sales, Mallory could just overhear Stuart entertaining Martha about his time in America but she missed most of the detail. By the time she listened properly, Martha was asking him about American Quaker barns. The conversation continued to be rapid and friendly throughout the rest of dinner and as they moved fireside.

'Do you still write, Mallory?' Stuart had lowered himself onto the couch beside her. He sat side-on to give her his full attention, one ankle propped on the opposite knee, balancing his coffee cup in his lap. Subtle fragrance notes of his sandalwood cologne wafted across to her.

Mallory laughed. 'No, that was so long ago. It was good while it lasted. The publisher wanted more but ...'

'But?'

'Oh, I don't know. Life got in the way. I was sidetracked helping with my husband's new conference business which quickly took off, so I was needed there. Publishing and writing aren't easy to return to once you stop, with plenty more great writers ready to take your spot on the bestseller list.'

'That's a shame. My wife and I used to read 'Daisy's Dreams' to our kids all the time. Guy particularly liked the one about Daisy joining the circus with her pet emu. I wouldn't have thought you'd be one to give up on something you're obviously good at.'

Mallory bristled. Stuart Forbes had no idea about *her* life or *her* decisions.

'I went back to teaching. Maybe that was my outlet for children's books – reading rather than writing. I've retired now. Gosh, that sounds so old, doesn't it. I live in Brisbane and now have the flexibility to travel more, visit Appletree Hill, and catch up with good friends.'

'And how's ....' Stuart began.

Mallory knew he was heading towards asking about Vivien. Of course, he had known her whilst they were growing up, but she wasn't sure she could make up a good enough story about her sister without cracking with bitterness. He would hear it in her voice immediately. She glanced at her watch. 'Excuse me, I really must get going and I'm sure Peg and Martha are ready for bed if they have an early morning.'

Mallory jumped to her feet and headed for the kitchen. She stood in the doorway, quietly watching her hosts. Peggy had her arm wrapped around Martha's waist as Martha's head rested gently against her partner's shoulder, her hands full of washed cutlery. Peggy's face was tipped slightly as she smiled down into Martha's eyes. They both appeared to be so strong together, yet vulnerable. The closeness of the two women was enchanting and Mallory hoped all was well in their world.

They turned as Mallory cleared her throat, not wanting to intrude any longer on their private moment. 'I'll be off after a wonderful evening. Thank you both.'

'Well, it wasn't without surprises, but there you go.' Peggy grinned. The three embraced, promising to catch up again soon. Bridie, Rod and Stuart were waiting with thanks at the front door.

'Oh, I didn't mean to break up the party,' Mallory said as she shrugged on her coat.

'We'll take a look at the plans and get back to you, Stuart,' Peggy said. Without glancing at Mallory, she added, 'Are you hanging around Appletree or heading straight back to the Melbourne office?'

'I'm doing a few things for Mum, so will be around for the next few days,' he said. 'Thanks for your last-minute hospitality. It was good to see you all.'

Mallory said a quick goodbye to the group and headed for her car. It had been a welcome panacea to catch up with her old friends again, even Stuart. His banter and humour reminded her of why she had fallen for him – quick with a joke and a dare, but soft as a marshmallow beneath the bravado. She knew in her heart he hadn't attacked Heather McMunn. He had had a few secret beers and admitted he had tried to tug her back to the group of classmates but that was all. If only Heather had backed him up. It had been Harold's rare protectiveness of Mallory that had warmed her heart.

DURING THE EVENING, she had enquired about who might be the musician next door to Fruit Flan but no one shed any light on who it could be. Peggy thought the owner lived interstate, which left the unknown resident either as a squatter or a ghost.

'Oh,' Mallory had frowned. 'Did someone die there?' No one knew that either, which surprised them all seeing as Appletree Hill was a small town. 'Feathers I could handle, ghosts I'm not so sure.'

'I overheard a lady in a florist shop in South Melbourne once,' Bridie said. 'She was talking about the shop's beautiful mural which she had painted and described the butterflies and feathers hidden in the branches to represent "her ghost". So I guess they're not all scary.'

They concluded that it was a squatter, so Bridie volunteered Rod to accompany Mallory on any further visits, just to be on the safe side.

The property next door was steeped in darkness as Mallory parked the car and let herself into the cottage.

Chapter Nine

IT WAS time to confront Patrick, despite his not responding to her texts. Mallory would like to give him the benefit of the doubt and think he may have gone away, or at a stretch be busy visiting their father, but her instinct was that he was avoiding her. Or just didn't care. The sight of Pepper Farm's narrow entrance and rustic driveway – easy to pick out amongst the surrounding modern homes with their solid fences and forbidding gates – brought a happy lift to Mallory's mood.

The original front door had been on the other side of the house, but when the golf course was built Mallory's parents had adopted the narrow back laneway as their more private main entrance. Expecting to see an empty driveway, she was pleasantly surprised to see what she presumed was her brother's car parked under the row of pine trees.

Mallory scanned the area as her car idled in the turning circle, taking in the garden which was overgrown but still hinted at enchanting bones. Tendrils of snow peas washed over the wire side fence, scattered field flowers and native grasses nodded gently in the breeze underneath long-established camellia bushes. In contrast, the corner where she and her mother had established a thriving strawberry patch had been stifled under a pair of ugly water tanks. She had been saddened to see the tanks whilst at Stella's wake, but now they were covered in a thin coating of brackish dirt. It was all blanketed in broken branches and, because of the time of year, piles of autumn leaves. And of course, there were what remained of the rows of stately old apple trees, the rest of the initial working orchard out of town having been sold as Harold had aged. 'Bloody government takes what it wants in taxes anyway,' he would always complain, but he had a point.

Under the back stair had become the depository for Mallory's muddy gumboots and a multitude of 'treasures' found on her nature and beach walks She stared down at its emptiness, regretting not having a pocketful of sandy shells to scatter. She took a deep breath, rapped loudly on the green timber door, and waited. When the door finally flung open, she didn't know who got the greatest shock; her brother to see her standing there, or her because of Patrick's shabby appearance. It would seem he was recovering from a heavy cold, or perhaps a late night out. Who knew?

'Mallory!' He hurriedly raked his fingers through his tussled hair, yet it made little difference.

Mallory plastered a wide, friendly smile on her face. 'Sorry, I did leave a few messages but, well, I was down this way so thought I'd chance you being here.' She flicked her eyes behind him, urging for an invitation to enter.

'Oh, sure. Come in. Sorry I didn't get back to you. Forgot all about it.' Patrick stepped to the side. 'Coffee?'

'Yes, thanks. You look a bit worse for wear. Are you okay?'

'Yeah, sure. Stacey and I had a late night that's all. She's headed to work.'

'Aren't you working today?' Mallory took a few steps into the large kitchen, wincing again at how it had been blandly modernised. She reached for the coffee mugs in the cupboard they had nestled in for decades but found only glass jugs – a stark reminder of being a stranger in her old home. Patrick shuffled forward to make a coffee for her, obviously aware that she was still waiting for a reply.

'No. I've cut back my hours at the Council. Lots to do here as you can see. And someone must greet the tradesmen. Actually, a landscape guy is due any moment for us to go over a few ideas I have.' He jerked his thumb back towards the snow peas.

Mallory nodded, refusing to be put off. She hugged the lukewarm mug to her chest and, unasked, wandered through to the expansive lounge room. The stunning panorama that lay beyond the large square pane of glass always caught her breath. Manicured fairways, grassy roughs and emerald putting greens flowed to the clifftop road where she had recently parked. The deep window seat beckoned so she relaxed into its corner. Patrick dropped onto a leather couch before proceeding to impatiently brush random crumbs and fluff off the seat and onto the carpet. Her eyes roamed the room, appreciating that no matter how many modern embellishments Patrick might add, the house would always have an old-world charm to her – solid like a good friend you could always count on. Her attention came to rest on the window and what lay beyond.

'I never tire of how beautiful this view is,' she whispered. 'What a shame Dad never fully embraced it. It would have been nice for him to see out his days here if he'd been well enough.'

'Have you seen Dad?' Patrick's tone was sharp, accusing.

'Of course, I have. It's the main reason I'm here.' Mallory paused. 'How long since you've visited him?'

Patrick didn't answer immediately, obviously weighing up if Mallory already knew the answer, that Harold Pepper hadn't seen his son in a while. 'I called in recently. I still don't know why you're bothering to pay the exorbitant fees his nursing home charges. The other place was fine, and it was only a mild stroke he'd had. They looked after him with no problem. How can you afford it anyway? Old John must have left you a good sum in your divorce settlement.'

Her jaw clenched but Mallory held his gaze. She had texted him a note about the divorce with her change of address details but obviously he didn't have enough interest to enquire how she had meandered her way through the upheaval. He didn't mention Vivien so she let the ignorant settlement comment slide.

'Well, I'm glad our father is getting better care despite our differences over the years, and so should you. He's suffering from progressive cancer too don't forget.'

Patrick shivered as though the mere mention of an ailment caused him angst, but his mind was still on the costs. 'I only signed his transfer from the other home because you were paying.'

There was that dig of superiority again. Mallory continued. 'I would like to know though, what you have planned for Pepper Farm whilst you're its, what? Caretaker?'

Patrick quietly placed his mug on the coffee table, his deep frown a sure sign she was on dangerous ground. But if the past year had taught Mallory anything, it was to speak up when needed. Particularly if there was a shred of doubt that something wasn't right. She was sure it was just greed and laziness that was motivating Patrick, but she had to make sure. 'The *three* of us are Powers of Attorney, remember.'

'Either/Or I believe the phrase is, Mallory. Individually or together. Or is that 'was'?' A smirk passed across his face. 'No need for you to check but I think you'll find that Dad changed his wishes to me having sole power.' He shrugged. 'I was here, my sisters haven't been for some time. I'm the one taking care of Pepper Farm, paying the rates ...'

'From Dad's account, not yours.' A cold shard shot through Mallory as she wondered what else Patrick was charging to their father's account, what cash withdrawals were being made. She needed to see some bank statements and visit the solicitor. She tried to muffle the deep sigh that escaped her lips – she didn't want to down the track of bickering over the estate, particularly as Harold was still alive and well.

Mallory stood, although standing over Patrick had little effect on her confidence. 'Does Vivien know what you've done?'

He stretched back on the couch, lazily shaking his head. 'No, communication with either of my sisters hasn't been top of my agenda. I knew you'd both come sniffing around when Dad got sick and, wow, look who's turned up. Although I would have bet Viv would have beaten you to it.'

Mallory was speechless. Had her family come to this? It obviously had.

'Thanks for popping in, but I have quite a few things to do today. Perhaps we could catch up for a coffee in the village before you head home,' Patrick said, rising to his feet.

Mallory had been patronised enough in her life to

recognise the underlying tone in his words as he hustled her out the back door. It closed on her heels. She would have liked to have wandered the grounds of her childhood home for a while, to breathe in its history and be told she was welcome, but anger was simmering dangerously beneath the surface of her whole body. Instead, she strode purposely to her car, all too aware there would be a pair of narrowed eyes watching her every step.

RAIN MISTED the car's windshield as Mallory drove into the only remaining car park at Hillview Nursing Home. She wavered in her mission as the rain got heavier, but decided 'in for a penny in for a pound' and turned to the back seat for her umbrella. A flash of greying red hair caught her attention.

She gasped to see Hettie McMunn run through the downpour to a car parked a few spaces along. It was all Mallory could do not to slink down in her seat as though she was a trespasser. Instead, she kept still as Heather reversed. *She's obviously visiting someone, or dropping off flowers from the nursery.* All the same, she waited until Hettie had driven out of sight before fetching her umbrella and making a dash for the entrance.

Harold Pepper was propped amongst cushions on his recliner. He seemed startled as Mallory entered, glancing behind her briefly and then back to her face. He flicked his head toward her like people do when passing a neighbour in the street; as if they want to acknowledge knowing someone but not well enough to stop and chat.

The room was stuffy despite the cool day and the air conditioning humming its contribution. Mallory moved to edge the sliding door open a fraction and tugged back the curtains. Surely he'd like a little more natural light.

'Leave those. They're fine,' Harold barked. 'Bloody raining again.'

'Okay. Sorry. How are you today, Dad?' Mallory asked as she closed it again and cursed herself for the inane question. No doubt he wasn't wearing his hearing aids so she pulled a guest's chair closer in an effort not to yell. 'I was hoping to chat with you. About Pepper Farm.'

Harold's eyes flashed, alert. 'What about it?'

Mallory scrambled. Why was she here exactly? She certainly didn't want to make a personal claim on it, as her father suspected. It was more to make sure he wasn't being taken advantage of, by Patrick and Stacey. Mallory knew her mother would turn in her grave if her children had not shared Pepper Farm at the end. Her intentions were truly honourable; but how to go about discussing that?

She softened her tone, cutting out any accusation from her words. 'I just called out there to visit Patrick and was surprised to see how many changes have been made. Did you know about them, and that you're paying for it? I know a few had been started whilst you were living there, like the re-paint, but where has all the furniture that belonged to you and Mum gone?'

She paused but her father's face remained as emotionless as a block of stone. Mallory bit her tongue, realising how she was throwing too many questions at him. 'I guess I just wanted to make sure that you're okay with everything Patrick is doing.'

Harold continued to sit and stare blankly over Mallory's shoulder, not volunteering anything to the conversation. The silence was tangible as Mallory waited – perhaps he needed time to sort his words, she thought. But when her father did reply, his voice was measured and firm.

'The house isn't yours.'

'I know that. It's yours.'

'Damn right.'

Mallory moved a hand to rest on the recliner's arm. Perhaps she would make more headway if they were on the move, a tactic she'd used with students. 'Do you want to go for a walk around the corridors or down to the lounge?'

Harold closed his eyes in dismissal. 'No, I'll just wait here for the girlie to bring my tea.' Instantly he was asleep, soft snores drifting around the lingering tension.

Frustrated, Mallory stood to leave. She noticed that the native flowers she had brought on her last visit sat on the small table under his television ... next to a takeaway box marked with a Nursery Cafe sticker. Mallory checked her father was still dozing before gently lifting the lid. A fresh apple slice, her father's favourite cake, sat untouched inside. Could Hettie McMunn have dropped it off? Mallory's heart rate arced up a notch as she contemplated the implications of that possibility – her father wouldn't have ordered it, so why had she brought it, and how did she know it was a favourite?

Her father's lined face looked serene and gentle, his chin resting on his shirt which was moist with dribble. Again, she was torn by their ongoing strained relationship and how her father had withered to an even grumpier old man. She gently eased a tissue under his chin and left his room.

OLIVIA HAD JUST FLICKED the café sign to "closed" when Mallory pulled into a car space, despite it only being mid-afternoon. Foregoing a coffee, she headed for the rotunda in the nearby park, figuring some fresh air might help to sort through increasing concerns about her father, and brother. For a moment the need to talk to Vivien, to confide in her sister that all was not well within their family, flicked around her but was replaced by a bitterness that wouldn't go away. Could she put aside Vivien and John's relationship for that conversation? No, never.

The rotunda provided comforting shelter as silent, gentle rain filtered through the surrounding gardens. She could almost hear each autumn leaf soaking up the raindrops, their crispness becoming soggy in moments. A bit like Dad, Mallory sighed. She saw the underlying spark of sarcasm was still there, but he was slower in its execution, perhaps due to the stroke or the pain he was in. Mallory had seen him wince several times. Or had his brashness always just been a defence mechanism that he wasn't bothered with anymore?

Shoppers started to reverse their cars out from their spots, no doubt wanting to be home before the rain grew heavier. A figure ran along the park's path leading to a back track, then diverted toward the rotunda, the face shielded by a spread newspaper. A moment later, Stuart Forbes stamped up the steps and tossed the sodden paper onto the opposite bench. He gave his arms a shake, rain droplets fanning out like when a dog shakes himself off.

'I thought it was you, Mallory. Just wasn't sure with all the damn rain on my glasses,' he said. With a beaming smile that tugged deep within her, he added: 'Exiled on main street.'

Mallory laughed at the reference to an album from his

all-time favourite band, the Rolling Stones. 'You don't know how true that is.' She nodded at his takeaway cup from the bakery. 'The nursery café down the street has great coffee although it just closed. Have you tried it?'

'No, I haven't. Can I go get you one from the bakery?' When Mallory shook her head, he settled himself at the other end of her bench, wiping his wet glasses on the tail of his shirt. 'Can't say I've even noticed it despite my regular trips into town after seeing Mum.'

The physical distance he had put between them didn't escape Mallory's notice and she wondered if it was intentional. 'It could use a bit of a push in its exterior styling but the flowers are lovely and the cakes are delicious. And you'll never guess who owns it.'

Stuart shrugged.

Mallory let her comment hang in the air. She knew she was teasing but wanted Stuart's full attention.

'Heather McMunn! But she calls herself Hettie now, and it's her daughter, Olivia who runs it. I gather Hettie doesn't keep the best of health.' Mallory watched Stuart as he frowned into his cup.

'Well, based on history, that's probably a good reason for me to keep getting my caffeine and carb hits from the bakery. How do you know all this so soon after arriving back in town?'

Mallory nodded to herself. She admired his matter-of-fact tone, keeping the past in the past. 'I recognised her, and Bridie filled in a few gaps too. Her daughter, Olivia, said Hettie did recognise me apparently, but she didn't say anything at the time.'

'Your parents and hers were friends, weren't they? I remember your father used to drive Heather's brother Ian, Patrick and me to footy. Barbara would sit up the front with him in his old car and he'd bullshit all the way home after the game. He knew nothing about football.'

Mallory started. 'Really? Why would he do that? Why would he drive everyone to something he had no interest in? He played rugby in his day.' It was just another example of his own daughters being left out.

Stuart shrugged. 'That's the extent of the memory. Sorry, but keeping Harold Pepper in my memory bank was never a priority.' He slapped his hands on his knees and looked into the distance, seemingly ending the conversation.

The wind started to pick up across the park, swirling around the rotunda and flicking spits of rain under the roof. A chill settled under her coat, but Mallory fought the need to leave, instead edging out of the spray closer to Stuart. The heat from his body was like a welcome, soft radiator.

'It's amazing we keep running across each other. How long are you in town? I mean …' She stumbled, hearing her words as just echoes of Peggy's earlier probes.

Stuart's sparkling eyes held hers, a slight frown creasing his forehead. 'You don't have to keep tabs on what you say, Mallory. As I'd mentioned, I intended to stay long enough to check on Mum and wait for Peggy and Martha's reaction to our plans, then head back to Melbourne. Which is a long answer to your short question.'

Mallory nodded.

Stuart obviously caught her hesitation. 'How *is* your dad anyway? Are you still treading on eggshells around him as well as around Patrick?'

'Gosh, you make it sound like I'm second-guessing myself with everyone,' Mallory said before realising that he was probably right. Her shoulders slumped. 'But, yes. My visit just now wasn't particularly high on the father-daughter love scale.'

Meeting Stuart's empathetic expression, she continued. 'You must know what it's like. Your mum is old and frail too and I guess I just presumed, hoped, to build a few bridges with him, you know? But they get so impatient despite our best intentions.'

'Harold has always been a difficult man, desperate to be the grand patriarch who wouldn't listen to anyone who questioned him. Including me, remember? He was of an era when wives and daughters were told what to do.' He paused. 'Maybe you're expecting too much after all this time and need to ask yourself exactly what you want from him.'

'I don't want anything from him. Well, that's not true. I guess I do want him to acknowledge me. He was the same with Vivien but she doesn't care. About anything really, including me, but Patrick could do no wrong. And now, I'm the only one looking out for him. He was in an old, musty nursing home before I had him moved to Hillview. Sorry, Stu, I'm rambling.'

'What do you mean about Viv? Aren't you two close any more?' Stuart asked, flicking away her apology.

Mallory looked into his face, his intelligent countenance searching hers just like he used to do when they were young. Her heart would pound as she waited for the next step she knew was coming – he would gather her into his arms, making sure she felt safe. She would love a hug now, but probably not from Stuart. Those days were long gone.

'No,' she replied. 'But that's a tale for another day. Life's complicated.'

'Only if you make it so,' Stuart said, gently. He waited but when it was obvious Mallory was going to be true to her word and not discuss her sister, he ventured on.

'I heard Patrick and his girlfriend are at Pepper Farm.

That must hurt, but it's years since you've lived here, and hopefully he's maintaining it. The legalities are okay aren't they?'

Mallory shrugged. 'I'm not so sure about that anymore either.'

Weak sunshine tried to nudge its way through the drizzle. Mallory's spirits lifted when she noticed a beautiful, vibrant rainbow arcing its way above a band of tall magnolias.

Stuart followed her gaze. 'There you go. New tomorrows.'

They sat for a moment, the drip-drip of raindrops falling from the eaves and shoosh of car tyres on the wet road, the only sounds. Mallory had nowhere she had to be, and wondered what Stuart's excuse to stay was. She needed to fill the space, the silence hinting at a slight intimacy she hadn't expected.

'Peggy and Martha are great, don't you think? It can't be easy running that business, and keeping it afloat. Oh, excuse the horse pun!' Their soft laughter danced around the rotunda.

'So, tell me about you. Is it your own building company?' Mallory continued.

'I'm a partner in it. I don't hit the tools so much anymore, but I enjoy the customer contact and fulfilling their briefs. Life's good. Well sort of good.'

Mallory told herself to keep quiet, not to rush in with some silly comment or diversion.

Stuart glanced at the fading rainbow, then back at Mallory. 'Cassie and I separated a couple of years back and the divorce came through at the end of last year. Neither of us was in a hurry really as we still get on well. We'd just drifted. Then she met someone, so it was time to make it all official. Which has caused a bit of friction between me and my son, Guy. He lives with me in Melbourne. He's become very anti-establishment for some reason, wants to give up his job blah blah. His mum says whatever makes him happy, for me to give him more money until he finds himself.'

'And that's not going to happen?'

Stuart shook his head. 'He said, and I quote "I should support young entrepreneurs more". He doesn't pay any rent but he seems to have gone through the money his grandfather left him somehow. So, maybe there is some truth in your "life's complicated" statement.' He shot her a cheeky grin. 'Anyway, I just don't like being told what to do.'

Mallory smiled and nodded in return; even the young, Stuart Forbes didn't like being told what to do, whether it was on the sports field or in the classroom. It was partly why she had been surprised, and she had to admit disappointed when he had seemed to bow to those wanting him to leave Appletree Hill all those years ago.

'Well, I'm sorry to hear your marriage didn't work out. You mentioned the other night you have more than one child. A daughter?'

'No, another son, Tim who lives in The States. He's okay with us divorcing thankfully, he likes Cassie's new fellow and just gets on with his own life. That's not to say I don't deposit money into both of their accounts regularly. Gosh, sorry all that makes me sound like money is the decider, but it's not I can assure you.'

'I guess you never stop being a parent. Children never eventuated for my husband, ex-husband, and me.'

'Ex-husband?'

Mallory shrugged. 'And that's yet another story for another day.'

'How many other secrets are you hiding Mallory Pepper ex-Campbell?' Stuart's expression was mischievous as he leant across and whispered. 'What say we go for a drive around the 'hood tomorrow and see why all these people are paying such silly prices to live here? What's your number so we can text with a time that suits us both.'

Mallory hesitated. She wanted to move forward with her life, not go back down the rabbit hole that was memory lane. She bit the inside of her lip, then reached for her phone as a gentle warmth spread through her. 'It beats visiting the nursing home.'

Chapter Ten

4:00 AM and Mallory lay awake trying to remember a remedy she'd read about for dark circles under eyes. She would need it in the morning after being awake for over an hour already. The deep beat of the music was being carried on a strong wind from across the fence and dumped into her bedroom.

Flicking the lights on and off as a clear person-trying-to-sleep signal hadn't worked. She'd rammed her head under the pillow, and even tried tying a woollen scarf around her ears. It was the base that disturbed her, the constant thump thump that seemed to keep pace with her heartbeat. After her earlier inspection of the neighbouring house, there was no way she was going to make a late night, no, early morning, visit on her own to see who the squatter was and tell him to tone his entertainment down. Even if he did fold his tea towel neatly and cared for a pet. She realised suddenly it may be a female, one of those cutely tattooed band types that wore Doc Martens and sported pointy fingernails dipped in black polish. She still wasn't going to venture across in the dark alone. She'd have to hold out until the first sign of daylight and hope that someone would still be there.

Stuart wasn't due to collect her until mid-morning. Attempting to pinpoint why she had agreed to go on his magical mystery tour was a good distraction to the uninvited concert, so she let her thoughts meander. He obviously didn't want to go over ancient wrongdoings and misunderstandings, and she'd been pleasantly surprised that she hadn't either. They'd been kids after all. And now, they shared the traumas of an aging parent, broken marriages, and a comforting knowledge of each other's youth. They didn't have to ask the inane questions that need to be asked when not knowing someone's family or history; where and how they'd grown up, the impact of their schooling, or whatever. They both knew about each other already, so a pleasant friendship whilst he was in town would be all there was to it.

As the bedroom filled with Carlos Santana vibes, Mallory's hands slowly found their way across her stomach. She grimaced to be wearing a brushed-cotton top and baggy pants, but they were the only pyjamas that kept her warm. Slowly she undid the buttons on the top and slithered the pants down and off over her socks. Shivering she reached into the bedside table for the small tube of gel that lay inside. If she had to lie there until daybreak, she may as well enjoy herself.

AFTER A STRONG COFFEE and a warm shower, Mallory decided to drive next door rather than walk. She didn't want to appear to be sneaking up on whoever was inside the house, and the car would provide a quick escape if needed.

She purposely did a little skid on the gravel, then slammed the car door, making as much noise as possible. Even so, her heavy knocks on the front window and door brought no response. She was tossing up whether to leave when sharp barks cut the air.

With her friends' warning echoing in her ears but ignored, she set off, pulling up short as she turned the corner of the house. A stocky grey Staffordshire Terrier had seen her first and was turning itself inside out, barking and leaping. His lead was tied loosely around a veranda upright; not very well apparently as it suddenly unravelled, and the dog barrelled toward her. Mallory stood stock still, her eyes closed, steeled for any attack. But all she felt was the heavy thud of paws against her legs and a wet tongue slathering her hands – he seemed overjoyed to see her.

The back door slammed, followed by a brusque male voice. 'Rooster! Rooster, come here now!'

Instantly the dog took off back to his master, the lead snaking behind him. The fellow, perhaps around thirty years of age Mallory guessed, retied his pet and stood peering at her. Cautiously she approached down the veranda.

'And you are?' he asked, frowning. He quickly glanced through the window back into the house.

Is there someone else here too, for backup? Mallory paused and took a breath. 'Hi. My name is Mallory and I am living next door.' She shot out her arm in the direction of Fruit Flan in case he had no idea there was a house on the other side of the thick bushes. 'And the thing is, I've been kept awake a couple of nights from really loud music. And I think it's coming from here.'

He didn't reply.

'Is it coming from here?'

'Well, you tell me. Is it a problem?'

'Of course it's a problem. I'm here to relax and soak up the countryside but am being bombarded by music at some ungodly hour. What's your name anyway, and are you supposed to be here?' Mallory cringed at how old and grumpy she sounded, like she had suddenly become an overzealous Neighbourhood Watch warden.

'Well, that's a relief,' he said, smiling but giving no explanation. 'I'm, um, Keith.' He flopped onto an old cane chair and pulled Rooster to him, scratching a large white patch of fur on the dog's chest. 'I'd offer you a chair, but I don't think there's another. You're welcome to grab one from the kitchen while I hold Rooster.' He nodded towards the room that Mallory had earlier spied through the crack.

She shook her head. 'What's a relief, Keith?' His name tripped awkwardly over her tongue; it seemed too old for him.

'Oh, I figured you'd come to get me to "vacate the premises".' He hooked his fingers around the last words.

Frustrated at his continuing lack of details, Mallory steeled her voice. 'Why would I be doing that? Apart from the noise.'

He shrugged. 'This isn't my house. Is it, Rooster. I mean we're living here for the time being, but I don't own it or anything. In fact, it's deserted. No one apart from you knows we're here so I'd appreciate it if we kept that bit of info between us.' He tapped the side of his nose with a finger.

'We?'

'Rooster and me.'

'So, you're squatting?' Mallory asked, partly impressed

by the young fellow's layback attitude. His appearance matched the image – a faded grey T-shirt emblazoned with some band's tour dates from five years earlier fell over baggy green track pants that trailed across the tops of his bare feet. His build was on the small side, but it was a bit hard to tell from the oversized, built-for-comfort clothing. Black, wavy hair curled around his face and edged the T-shirt's neckband.

Keith squinted at the sky, obviously considering her question but not worried by it. 'I think squatters trash places, don't they? We don't do that, in fact we've tidied the old girl up a lot, added to its value probably. I've just got a few things to do in town then I'll be gone, until the next visit.'

Mallory crossed her arms, the warden vibe still hovering. 'Well, I seriously doubt the 'added value' notion, and are you saying you've done this before?'

'Sure. Whenever I need to come and see, um, a particular person in Appletree Hill, Rooster and I stay here. It's great. Supremely quiet.'

Mallory stared at her cheeky neighbour, her mouth open. He really didn't see a problem with what he was doing. She scanned around them and had to admit that there was a lot of evidence that the garden had had work done. She remembered the neatly folded tea towel. Who was she to say he couldn't be there?

'Who does own this house?' she asked.

Keith shrugged. Whether he knew or not wasn't going to be revealed.

'So why do you play at such odd hours?' Mallory asked, ignoring the not-another-question look of exasperation on Keith's face.

'I just find that's when inspiration hits. I've never been a big sleeper and I guess it's a good opportunity to use that time while I'm here.'

'How long *are* you here for? I mean can we come to some arrangement? You keep the music down and I won't say anything about you being here?' Mallory placed her hands on her hips hoping to appear in control.

Keith pressed his lips together as if her request needed deep and considered thought. 'I guess that's fair. I mean I didn't realise the sound carried so far. The last thing I want to do is alert anyone important that I'm living here.'

'As opposed to a tired neighbour?' Mallory retorted, not feeling very important at all. 'It's a deal then.'

She turned and walked away, feeling his eyes on her retreating back and imagining his amused reaction to an uptight older woman. Rooster offered a short bark of farewell. It was only when she reached her car that it dawned on her she had agreed to an arrangement that had been her deal in the first place. 'Cheeky boy,' Mallory whispered as she drove back down the driveway, turned right, and into her own entrance.

'ANYWHERE IN PARTICULAR you'd like to check out?' Stuart asked, his fingers paused on the car's ignition button.

Mallory smiled to herself. *Actually, Stuart Forbes I was just checking you out.* His casual low-key kit of worn jeans, RM Williams boots, and sloppy designer jumper was very sexy in a country kind of way. When tossing her jacket onto the back seat of his SUV, she had noted a heavy Driza-Bone coat, adding to the image.

She shot him a smile. 'No, let's just meander around the back roads and see what's changed. When I was here for

Mum's funeral, I was bound to family duties and returned to Brisbane straight after, but you'd be up to date with all the changes if you come back regularly.'

Stuart flicked on his sunglasses as they drove out of Mallory's driveway and onto the side road. 'No, not at all. I'm usually pretty pushed for time as well. I go to the nursing home and then head back to the office, but having this barn design job for the girls might mean I can stay longer.'

Appletree's palette of greens, browns and golds flashed past the window as Mallory settled into her seat and gazed out over the pastures. 'I'm sorry to see that she's so frail, Stuart.'

'So am I but that's to be expected I guess, at her age. And your father's age too.'

She glanced across at Stuart.

'Time for one of those long stories?' he asked, a smile tweaking the corners of his lips but his eyes remained serious.

'Maybe over lunch,' she replied.

They had turned off onto the track leading to the coastline's popular blow-hole. It had been a popular spot for as long as Mallory could remember, but she hadn't been back since moving away.

'Remember hiking down here on hot days? We'd stand on the edge, trying to balance against the on-shore wind, and wait for the water to whoosh up and spray us with cold water. It was such fun.'

'Let's do it again for old time's sake,' Stuart proposed as he parked the car.

'It's hardly a hot day,' Mallory protested, wrapping her arms across her chest, but his challenge sat in the air. Sighing she reached behind for her coat and opened the door. 'Whoa, that's icy,' she gasped, quickly zipping up the coat and draping its hood down around her face.

With heads bowed against the blast of the wind and hands deep in pockets they marched the short distance towards the cliff face. A higher balustrade had been built around the blow-hole, warning signs not to climb over placed every few feet. Mallory was disappointed, feeling the structure took away from the stunning view that lay just beyond it. She was about to voice her reaction when a sudden surge came from below and cold jets of water shot into the air. Carried by the wind the spray drifted over them. Laughing, they both turned their backs to the spray at the same time, huddling together as another wet jet erupted behind them.

Stuart dipped his head so Mallory could hear him through the wind. Little drops of water hung from his black eyelashes, others rolled down his face and dripped off his chin. The jagged scar, white against his tanned skin, remained along his jawline; the result of a dog bite when young, she remembered.

'This is definitely a summer outing,' he joked.

He didn't need to say anymore and as one they scurried back to the warmth of his car. As Stuart tossed their wet coats into the car boot, Mallory quickly lowered the mirror. Her face was flushed with cold, her hairline damp, but there was a certain spark behind her eyes that she couldn't ignore. Was it the force of nature that made her feel so alive, or the proximity of an old boyfriend?

Stuart jumped in beside her and handed her a clean cloth. 'Don't you just love nature,' he quipped, perhaps answering Mallory's question.

Silence swirled around them as they dried off as best they could. 'Good lord, look at that,' Mallory said, pointing through the windscreen to a distant hillside. The smooth green surface was pockmarked by several huge rectangular buildings that resembled bunkers. 'Is that a factory?'

A snort came from Stuart as he started the car and they drove back to the road. 'It's an enclave built by one family. A holiday house I might add.'

The cluster was still visible as they drove away from Appletree toward the next little village. 'It's won a few awards apparently, but I feel it's a shame they cleared the whole area then built concrete blocks you can see from the moon.'

'I can understand why all the glass because those ocean and hinterland views are stunning.' She tilted her body toward Stuart. 'What would you have designed?'

'Well, I haven't been on the site to truly get the feel of the contours and outlook but ...' His face creased with a slight frown as he flicked his eyes across to the structures. 'I would certainly have kept all the vegetation and trees, but surely they'll replant because they must get pretty fierce on-shore winds. I'd like a more interconnected, softer look, certainly not that pale grey concrete; with the houses nestling into the landscape much more, with sheltered pockets to the rear.' He paused. 'That's what I love about the design process – the opportunity to create for a particular space to produce a one-off, beautiful result. Actually, I'm hoping to win the contract to build the new tasting rooms and restaurant for a local winery.'

'That would come with a few side benefits, I imagine,' Mallory said. 'Speaking of which, how about we find somewhere for lunch and a warm coffee?'

'Fancy or homely?' Stuart asked.

When Mallory opted for the latter, Stuart winked and did a quick U-turn. A few minutes later he slowed onto a dirt side road and through open double wire gates, bringing them to a stop in front of The Back Paddock Store and Restaurant.

Autumn-toned grapevines crept out of large oak barrels and made their way across the roof of the surrounding deck and appealing but deserted outdoor dining area. A garden overflowing with healthy coastal rosemary shrubs and thin wire reed sculptures ran the length of the restaurant's frontage before disappearing around the corner to where an artisans' studio offered locally made pottery.

'You won't need your coat; they'll have an open fire going. And they have the best homemade flaky sausage rolls on the coast. What have you found there?' Stuart asked as he reached her side of the car.

Between two fingers she twirled a large heart-shaped leaf which had sat beside her foot when she got out of the car. She laughed at the memory of how she and Vivien would madly collect them as children, allocating each with the name of a boy they would marry. 'I used to love these leaves,' she replied, now a little embarrassed. She let it drop back to the path.

A gentle hum of conversation and laughter drifted through the air as they entered and Mallory excused herself to the bathroom. When she returned, Stuart was seated at a table by the window; he half raised out of his chair as she approached. Always the gentleman, she thought warmly.

'Gosh, it's busy isn't it,' she said as she took her seat and picked up the menu. 'I know you're tempted by the sausage rolls, but I'm opting for the lamb shank and lentil soup and sourdough.'

'I'm not sure about the lentils but the lamb part sounds hard to pass up,' Stuart agreed. They ordered a glass of local Riesling each and two bowls of soup.

Stuart leant forward and sighed. 'This is nice. Cheers.'

'As is this,' Mallory replied taking a sip of wine. 'I can't believe I'm back in Appletree. I must say the memories are coming thick and fast.'

'I know what you mean. I went and watched the Badseeds footy team play at the local oval the other day. Just perched on the railing with a pie and yelled directions that no one was interested in. The game took me back to training in the fog and braving Dad's anger once when he realised I'd borrowed his car to get there.'

Mallory laughed. 'Only once? Lord knows I wasn't allowed near Harold's pride and joy. Mum was lucky to borrow his car to go shopping half the time.

'Mostly good memories, though, for you?' Stuart asked.

She thought for a moment about that. 'Well, better than I expected. I'm between things, a lot of things, and being here is forcing me to take stock of where I am and to make some hard decisions. Not to mention the whole drama of Dad and Patrick.'

Stuart didn't take his eyes off her as their meals were placed on the table, hearty aromas from the steam curling between them. 'You didn't mention Vivien in that little family reference. You always seemed to be close when you were young,' he prompted.

Mallory met his gaze, then quickly looked away and into the open fire crackling nearby. Her shoulders dropped, feeling relaxed in his company and somewhat comforted by his sincere interest. She tore off a chunk of sourdough and then placed it back on the plate, willing the deep breath she drew in not to shudder with emotion on its way out.

'I have so many memories of looking after my younger sister through school. Then we didn't miss a beat as we both headed to college and travelled. When John wanted to move from Melbourne to Brisbane to expand the conferencing business, I was thrilled when Vivien moved up a couple of years later. She married Warren, John's business partner and we had a great relationship.'

'But?' Stuart spooned some soup and gently blew across its surface, allowing her to answer in her own time.

'You know that John and I separated. Well, um, unbeknown to me he had been having an affair.'

Although Mallory pretended to focus on her bowl, she saw Stuart's spoon pause on the way to his mouth. Was he waiting for her to confirm what he suspected?

She nodded at the unspoken question. 'He had been having an affair with Vivien.'

'Shit,' Stuart whispered. 'Oh, Mallory I'm so sorry. Vivien!' He placed his hand over hers. 'What did you do?'

A small chuff of relief escaped Mallory's lips at his response, but she hoped she could hold on to her dignity as words tumbled out. 'What could I do? It was so, so difficult. Particularly as I found out by accident; it wasn't as though any guilt led them to confess. I stayed in the house for a while, but his ghost-like presence was everywhere so I put it on the market. When the house had gone too I was feeling, um, displaced I guess you'd say. I bought a lovely apartment but then Dad got sick. I'm still not sure where home is, but for the moment I'm back in Appletree.' She shook her head. 'I'm sure there will be some degree of mockery from Patrick when he finds out about their relationship, so I appreciate your reaction.'

'I would never mock you,' Stuart replied gently.

'I know. Anyway, I'm not here to expose my marriage to a brother who doesn't care about his sisters anyway. I haven't even spoken with Vivien. The thing is I don't want to hate anyone. That doesn't mean I'm brimming with forgiveness or haven't wanted to sew a couple of voodoo dolls to stick pins into, far from it but, oh I don't know ...'

Stuart's attention hadn't strayed from her for a second. 'Well, they say that love and hate are two sides of the same coin.' He laughed. 'Phew, where did that come from? You're clearly a good influence on my attitudes and my use of English,' Stuart said, beaming.

'I can't imagine you hating anyone,' Mallory said. She meant every word of it.

The soup was delicious when she finally tasted it, warming her body and her heart as it went down, as did Stuart's next comment.

'Well, old Harold is lucky to have you.'

'Thank you for saying so. There are plenty of other things in my life that I'm very grateful for so I'll get through this. Tell me more about you; I'm sure it's a much more exciting story,' Mallory said, settling back in her chair.

She watched him as he recounted his career and the slight back injury that forced him to turn to design, which proved to be a blessing in disguise. The irrepressible sparkle in his eyes when he spoke of what excited him hadn't diminished over the decades – his focus used to be his sport, but now it was his job and his sons.

The server arrived to take dessert and coffee orders, but they opted just for coffee.

'I imagine it's tricky being a parent as your children become adults,' Mallory said. 'You obviously want the best for them and don't want them to fail or be unhappy but at the same time they're adults with their own responsibilities and decisions to make. I don't have kids so haven't experienced all the ups and downs.'

Stuart nodded. 'I try to just give options that I can think of. Unfortunately, Guy sees them as objections.'

Mallory laughed. 'Like his father then? Won't be told what to do?'

Stuart gave her a cheeky 'I don't know what you mean' look as he signed the bill.

Mallory smiled across at him. 'Thank you for listening.'

'Well, it hasn't been much of a tour, but it has been very enjoyable. I'm back in Melbourne tomorrow for the week.'

On the return drive, Mallory had been about to tell him about meeting her neighbouring squatter, then remembered her promise to Keith so had faltered. Stuart slowed his approach to Fruit Flan, obviously wanting to say what was on his mind. She noticed his hands tighten on the steering wheel.

'Mallory, don't take this the wrong way but I've been thinking of the whole John and Vivien thing. How crushed and, well, deceived you must have been. I hope you don't compare that relationship with what happened between us all those years ago.'

She stiffened. 'What do you mean?'

He sighed as he parked the car. 'I think you know what I mean; that in both instances you were the one hurt, you know? I hope that we have got past all that, that you realise I wasn't like that, am not like that. Oh, by the look on your face I shouldn't have said anything.'

Mallory stepped out of the car before he had a chance to do the same. She leant down to look across at his frowning face. 'Don't be silly. I doubt first lovers are meant to be forever lovers. As you said, life is meant to be explored. It was a different time and what you and I had was long ago. Thank you for the lovely tour.' She quickly paced to the house and let herself in.

She was standing inside the cottage, her back pressed hard against the closed door. That was the second time

Stuart's comments had caught her off-guard, and she wasn't sure why it mattered. Perhaps she hadn't swept away the dust of her childhood as neatly as she expected, or perhaps she just refused to be thought of as a victim. As Stuart drove away, she remembered her coat was still in his car.

Chapter Eleven

THE COTTAGE certainly needed some TLC after the recent high winds. Dust, dead bugs and shrivelled leaves had found their way under doorways and across every interior surface. It felt good to roll up her sleeves and tackle it room by room, to redirect her frustrations with everything Appletree was throwing in her path. Mallory decided to think through one at a time as her friend had suggested.

Her father was being cared for, even if he didn't want to live at Hillview. His temperament and attitude towards her hadn't changed but she was now satisfied she had done the right thing to move him to a better facility. Before his stroke, he must have frequented the nursery café, although Mallory could hardly picture him sitting having a cappuccino at one of their little tables. The delivery of his apple cakes to his room was still a mystery to be considered later.

There was an issue with Patrick. His superior attitude toward her, and the fact that he had taken over Pepper Farm irked her, but really, how much did it matter long term? Her memory of Pepper Farm spoke of a connection to the bricks and mortar and her mother, not to her actual childhood growing up within its walls. She refused to be warned off, knowing she had every right to hunt down the legal documents to check exactly what her father had put in place. Hopefully, her brother had been bluffing about the Power of Attorney and hadn't persuaded Harold to change his will away from an equal split between his three children. Then, the claws really would come out. Vivien would materialise for her share, Patrick would refuse to move and Mallory ... well, she wasn't sure what she would do.

For one silly moment, she considered if winning the lottery had to be 'earned' in some way, that such good fortune had to be balanced out elsewhere in her life; that she had to lose one thing to gain another. Surely not. She let that thought float away with the dust mites.

The vacuum rolled across the same spot as it had for the last several minutes as Mallory's unchecked tears free-fell and splashed onto the floorboards. It was the thought of her mother, Stella, that had prompted the outpouring. Mallory flicked the machine off and leant on the stem. Closing her eyes, she whispered, 'Oh, Mum. I loved you so much. I wish we had been closer; but Dad was always in the way, wasn't he? I don't know what I want, what I need to do.' Mallory shook her head against what felt like an insatiable loss. Had she felt that throughout her marriage?

And then, bloody hell, there was the issue of Stuart Forbes.

As if her resolve to shift her mind into easier areas had projected across the pastures of Appletree Hill, her phone buzzed in her back pocket with a message. It was Bridie, suggesting they tour the farmers' market together the next day:

Bright and early. I'll meet you at Charlie's Coffee Van.

Possible storm tonight so wear gumboots. Due to clear by the morning. x

Mallory shot back a thumbs-up emoji, grateful for the timely show of friendship, then headed through the kitchen to empty the vacuum bag. The screen door was swinging on its hinges, caught in the strengthening wind. The gusts whipped around her as she ventured outside to the bin, making it clear that her spring clean had probably been a waste of time. An eerie light hovered. It was rather pretty in fact, as if a watercolour brush had added a layer of soft pink to an already dove-grey canvas. She strolled to the front yard in time to see a willy-willy as it circled across the driveway, sprigs of flowers and grass cuttings unsettled by its presence. Mallory squinted up at the tips of the giant pine trees which swayed deeply to and fro, always an early warning that a storm was on the way.

It was late afternoon before Mallory finished a round of baking. That too was probably somewhat ambitious she realised as she removed a tuna bake from the oven and set it beside a cooling chicken casserole – no doubt she would be filling her basket with home-cooked treats at the market, but she was determined not to scrimp on eating proper meals. Her purchases could always be of the sweet variety. The cottage had grown gloomy as the approaching storm clouds seemed to get lower by the hour, but no rain had fallen as yet. She poured herself a glass of wine, wrapped a blanket around her jacket, and settled safely on the front veranda to watch what nature had in store.

Thunder rolled in the distance; an earthy scent laden with the promise of what was to come hung in the air. Thin streams of lightning stabbed horizontally along the tips of the distant hills. Perhaps it would all go around her, she thought, somewhat disappointed. But when a crack of thunder shook the ground and the lights inside the cottage flickered, she knew they were in for a few wild hours. The wild winter storms of her childhood had always settled a tense fear in her as Patrick would make up horror stories and howl like a werewolf outside Mallory and Viv's bedrooms, scratching on their doors. She hadn't minded the summer storms nearly as much and had welcomed the release of fat raindrops onto the hot roads after a steamy day.

By the time she had gone inside to fetch a working torch, the wind was gusting again and bright flashes of lightning lit the driveway.

The bush and garden beds, so golden during the day, had taken on tones of khaki and dirty brown as though someone had dropped a camouflage net across them. Another crack of thunder, then something else. Within seconds there was a bark, then another. Mallory sat upright, unsure where it was coming from but it sounded so close.

She peered toward the bushes and along the fence line where she had scrambled only days earlier. Flashes of lightning in quick succession lit the undergrowth. Was that a patch of white and grey she had seen, or just rain being flicked from the foliage? More frantic barks shot from the trees like gunshots.

Mallory threw the blanket aside, grabbed the torch, and rushed to the edge of the garden. 'Rooster, it's okay. Come here.' She was drenched in an instant. Even above the wind, Mallory heard the dog thrashing around, obviously terrified. She swung the torch in an arc, squinting to find where he had gone, cursing Keith for not thinking his dog may run away with fear. A sudden yelp just ahead of Mallory urged her forward.

'Rooster, where are you?' A small whimper, desperate,

led her to the broken gate between the properties. She blinked rapidly, trying to make out what had happened but all she saw through the glistening curtain of rain was a blur of green with a mound of grey in the centre. Quickly she squatted next to the terrified dog, just as Keith came thrashing through the undergrowth.

'He's snagged on that wire! Hold on boy, it's okay.' Keith turned to Mallory. 'Take the torch so I can see ...'

The clear panic in her neighbour's voice wiped out any earlier opinions she'd had. Rooster obviously meant the world to him. Mallory held the torch as still as possible despite her cold, shivering body, and gently stroked the panting dog. Keith eased the tag of skin off the jutting wire. He lifted Rooster into his arms, and then by the beams of the torches they pushed their way through the gap and headed to the well-lit house.

'Sshh, it's okay boy. You're safe,' Keith whispered as he lay the heavy and exhausted dog onto the giant cushion which sat in a corner of the kitchen. As he knelt beside him, Mallory kicked off her mud-caked shoes, shrugged off her sodden jacket, closed the door firmly, placed the torches on the bench, and soaked a nearby tea towel with warm water.

Keith took it and gently dabbed at Rooster's wound. 'It isn't deep, but I'll put some cream on it and take him to the vet tomorrow. Thanks ...'

Mallory gasped as Keith turned his head toward her. Blood seeped from a gash across his forehead, mixing with trickles of water from his drenched hair and running down his cheek. 'You've cut your head.' She retreated to the kitchen, flicking open drawers in search of another cloth.

Keith chuckled as she handed him some paper towels to wipe his face. 'You don't look so good yourself.'

Puddles pooled on the floor around her cold feet, little

rivulets spreading towards the walls. Her pants were drenched, the knees muddy from kneeling next to Rooster. She felt her hair plastered down like wet spaghetti, her cheeks tingling with what she presumed were tiny scratches etched from flying branches. The musty smell of wet clothes and dog, mildew, and dirt took her back to the hallways of primary school – of soggy raincoats and squashed bananas left in school bags.

'If Rooster is okay, I'd better go,' Mallory said. She frowned through the window at the silver spikes of rain beating the window, at the trees bent over in the howling wind. 'Damn.'

'There are a couple of towels in the bathroom along the hall you can use to dry off a bit. I'll grab some blankets. I've got the fire going so I'll bring Rooster in there and we'll just wait it out. Okay?' Keith glanced away, as though embarrassed to tell a woman old enough to be his mother what to do.

Mallory hesitated but she was cold and wet, so did as he directed. The house was draughty, the wind finding every crevice to whistle through. She found the bathroom, quickly noting how clean and neat it was like the kitchen, but not taking too much time away from the warmer part of the house.

Rooster was alone, lying snuggled in a blanket close to the crackling fire when she returned. He was panting heavily, obviously still not happy about the storm or being caught out in it. Mallory couldn't ignore the dog as he rolled his eyes toward her, seeking reassurance.

'You poor thing. You were so frightened weren't you, but it's okay now.'

She stroked Rooster until Keith squatted beside her and passed her a black coffee.

'Perfect. Thank you,' she said as she shuffled across to the worn couch. It felt odd to only have a blanket wrapped around her bare legs, but she tucked them up onto the couch and figured she would just go with the flow.

'Sorry, no milk. But I do have chocolate Teddy Bear biscuits,' he said, offering a nearly empty pack. 'They're my favourite so there aren't many left. I'll clean up and get changed and be back in a minute.'

Mallory huddled back into the sofa, her hands wrapped around the hot mug. She glanced across at a mattress and pillow, bulging backpack, guitar and speaker that lay against the far wall. A laptop was open on the floor, the screen showing paragraphs of words set like poetry, but at a distance Mallory couldn't quite make them out.

Rooster jumped as a wind gust chased the cane chairs across the rear veranda, the scraping suddenly going silent. 'Sounds like those chairs ended up in the garden,' Keith said as he strode to the computer and closed the lid. He dropped to the floor and stretched his legs alongside Rooster's agitated body, balancing his mug on the hearth. He dabbed at the scrape on his forehead, but it seemed the cut hadn't been deep enough to cause much injury.

'Country storms are different to those in the city,' Mallory said. 'They kind of envelop you, make you feel like you're a part of them.' She took a sip of coffee, an excuse to pause before her question. 'Do you live in Melbourne, Keith?'

'Yeah, I'm a city boy. Rooster belongs to my girlfriend. My dad doesn't like dogs, but Mum's okay with him. I've brought him away with me for a few days to give him a bit of a run.' Keith laughed and massaged the dog's ears. 'Didn't mean it to be that much of a run though, boy.' He dropped his eyes away from his dog and searched Mallory's face.

'Thanks by the way, for helping tonight. He just shot out of the kitchen door when I was checking out what was happening and wouldn't come back.'

Mallory waved away his gratitude. The coffee tasted deliciously bitter as she watched her young neighbour through the steam. He had appeared so confident when they had met earlier, but now with the worry of Rooster embedded in a frown, and his lack of smart comments, she realised he may not be as bold as he tried to appear. Which brought her back to why he was living in this, apparently abandoned, house.

Mallory tossed the biscuits across to Keith and nodded. 'Of course, I'd help any animal that needed it. I remember when I was young ...' *Gawd, Mallory you sound like an old bore* '...um, I used to visit the cottage I'm staying in next door and every season there would be little birds falling out of their nests. It broke my heart. I even set up a sort of net to catch them, but Vern, the owner, told me I had to let them be. To let nature take its course. I always felt guilty about that, so have made donations to Wildlife Rescue ever since.' She didn't divulge that the total of her recent generosity to animal welfare centres was more than $200,000.

Mallory was surprised to hear a hiccup of suspicion in Keith's voice when he spoke.

'Then you grew up here? In Appletree Hill.'

Mallory nodded.

'So you'd know all the people in the town then.'

What was he getting at? 'No, not really. I mean I haven't lived here for a long time. My dad is still alive, and my brother is here too but it's changed a lot. A couple of friends from school live in the area ...'

Keith unfolded his body from the floor and stretched to take her mug from her hand. She hadn't quite finished the coffee but let it go. He towered above her and, although Mallory didn't feel in the least threatened, she knew it was time to leave.

'Well, thankfully there seems to be a break in the rain so I'll head home,' she said, glancing at the kitchen window. She gathered the blanket around her body and padded to the bathroom, shuddering at the thought of having to change back into her soggy pants. In under five minutes, she had patted Rooster, said good night to Keith, and was on her side of the fence. She hadn't had the chance to ask him about his life or why he was here but somehow, with his defences so quickly raised, she doubted his answers would have been near the truth anyway.

Chapter Twelve

'MALLORY, OVER HERE.'

Mallory gave Bridie a quick wave and headed to the farmers' market's most popular coffee van. She had taken Bridie's advice and arrived early to secure a car park close to the entrance as well as wearing gumboots, which was just as well as the showgrounds' red dirt had turned to sludge after the heavy rain. It hadn't deterred the crowds though. The market was bustling with shoppers and, judging by the many circles of friends all talking at once, those there just to socialise. Everyone was rugged up in puffer jackets, beanies, gloves, and boots. Most were armed with large open-weave carry baskets more akin to a French summer picnic than an outing to the cold Australian countryside.

'Oh, what happened to your face?' Bridie gently ran a finger across Mallory's cheek.

'I'm fine. Just a few scratches earned last night during the storm.'

'Oh, no. There are some organic skincare makers here who will have something to put on that, or perhaps some aloe,' Bridie suggested. 'Did the storm damage the house?'

'No, it's a long story but suffice to say my squatter next door has a dog who got spooked and made a run for it through the bushes. I ended up going on a search and find mission through the undergrowth, hence the scratches, but he's okay and it all ended well.'

Further questions from Bridie were interrupted by the arrival of Peg and Martha, their concern making Mallory go through the explanations again. Apparently, they had all suffered a little storm damage but the area was largely left unscathed.

Loaded with coffee and fresh croissants, the friends gathered at a large, sheltered table. 'So, who is this mysterious squatter? The ghost of some late great band member?' Bridie said.

'Oh, let it be Prince,' Martha said, bringing her palms together.

Mallory laughed. 'Definitely nobody so famous. He's just a young fellow staying a few nights. He's looking after the place and we made a pact that I won't be a snitch if he won't play loud music into the wee hours.'

'I still don't think you should go over there on your own at night,' Bridie said.

Mallory laughed. 'Has she always been so protective and mother-henish since her kids left?' she asked the others.

They all nodded in unison.

'So, what's our plan of attack for the stalls?' Mallory said, rubbing her hands together.

At once, Bridie suggested the plant and flower section, Peg suggested the locally made crafts and Martha opted for the bakeries.

'Well, it sounds like we need to divide and conquer. I'm happy just to meander in someone's shadow and meet back here for a refill in a while. Does that work?' She scanned the row upon row of stalls which seemed to cover most of the showgrounds. 'The market is a lot larger than I anticipated, and from the gorgeous alpaca scarves I saw on the way in, I think I might be going to do some damage to the credit card,' Mallory said.

Bridie gave a thumbs up. 'That's what we want – lots of support for the local artisans and economy.' She paused. 'Oh, Mallory, take a quick look over Peg's shoulder. It's Patrick and his girlfriend Stacey. Over there. She's wearing a rather mud-splattered bright pink and white check raincoat.'

Mallory heard the barely concealed amusement in her friend's words. She peered at the couple across the lip of her coffee cup. 'Damn, they're coming this way.'

'Those leather boots would have cost a fortune,' Martha muttered. 'Should I ask where she bought them?'

'You'll do no such thing, Martha,' Mallory spluttered, knowing full well her friend was joking. 'It is a sign to move on though and check out the goods.' As Mallory gathered the empty cups and paper bags, she sensed Patrick hesitate. He had seen her. She tossed the rubbish into the bin, turned, and caught up with Bridie.

There was always the chance of running into Patrick whilst staying at Appletree Hill; it was his home after all. But, after his rudeness at Pepper Farm, she wanted to dig a bit deeper into their father's affairs before confronting him again. And there was the John/Viv issue she desperately wanted to avoid. She tightened her scarf and turned her mind to much more pleasant endeavours, such as the amazing birdhouses swinging in front of her. Put together with old timbers, tree branches and metal straps, they ranged from single to multi-level, with tiny ledges and hollows for birds to enjoy.

'Either of these little cuties would look great hanging in my garden,' Bridie enthused. She held aloft a birdhouse in each hand. 'The one with the rusty wire gate or the one with the vintage key above the door? Yes, the key one I think. I'll need to take it back to my car, Mallory so I'll catch you up.'

The buzz of conversation and the faint sounds of a bush band swirled around Mallory as she strolled the aisles. The delicious scent of barbecuing sausages (gourmet no doubt) and onions drifted in the air. She hadn't visited a country market in years – Brisbane's Southbank market along the river just didn't compete with these truly original products and relaxed atmosphere. She hung her new wicker basket over one arm and idly filled it with purchases – a punnet of late raspberries, a bottle of local apple cider, some jams and chutneys. She plucked a hand-crocheted tea cosy from a selection of brightly coloured crafts – it was shaped like a giant strawberry, ridiculous but a must-have.

When she stopped in front of a trestle table of tussic mussies tied with orange raffia, Mallory flicked her eyes up ready with a greeting for Olivia McMunn. Hettie stared back at her.

'Mallory. I thought it was you the other day,' Hettie said briskly. She slapped her hands together, obviously trying to keep warm.

'Heather, Hettie. Hello.' Mallory said, unsure how to respond to the woman's frosty greeting. 'Um, these all look nice.'

'We don't need your charity here or at the café. We do alright. Considering.'

The open-ended sentence hung in the air. Mallory fingered one of the little posies as a customer paid for a glass jar of Anzac biscuits and a spice cake. The crowd thinned, distracted by a roving magician, leaving the two women facing each other.

Mallory took a deep breath. 'Considering what?'

Hettie didn't break her thinly disguised gaze of impatience nor expand on her comment. 'Are you moving back then, or just here to make sure old Harold is still around?'

Why would she bother unleashing at the first opportunity, and what a presumption she was taking about Harold. Mallory was lost for words, not that Hettie McMunn seemed to notice.

Hettie drew in a sharp breath and then continued. 'True country folk look after their own, you know. Choofing old people into homes is not the way it's done. You of all people should know what Pepper Farm meant to your father, and to wrench him away from it was criminal.'

Mallory's head spun with possibilities for the woman's ridiculous outburst. Maybe her parents had suffered in a nursing facility. Bridie had mentioned Heather had had a few rough years; maybe she had been ousted from her own home.

Despite Mallory's wish that someone would approach with 101 questions about the lamington cake, no one did. There was nothing for it but to confront the woman.

'Heather, Hettie … I really don't see what business it is of yours, but Dad had a stroke and needs proper care for several ailments I'm not going to go into. Have you had a run-in with Patrick or Stacey or something, because I'm at a loss here as to why you seem to resent our family so much?'

Hettie crossed her arms, her lips pressed together, but no words came. She turned and gave a broad smile to a woman trying to push past Mallory. 'Ah, Sylvie. Your cupcakes are on the way. Olivia has just gone to help Alice unload them from the van.'

Fearing she had lost the woman's attention, Mallory waited before lowering her voice and continuing. 'Is that why you're delivering cakes to Dad, because you feel sorry he's in a home?' Fumbling, she continued, 'Why do you even care?'

That seemed to stop Heather in her tracks. Her eyes squinted back at Mallory, her hand holding a tray of vanilla slices starting to shake.

'Are you alright?' asked a man who had materialised from the neighbouring stall. He placed a hand on Hettie's arm and shot an accusing glance at Mallory as if she was the cause of the distress.

Mallory gently replaced the little bouquet of herbs and edged away from the table; her space being quickly filled by more customers. Laughter and fragmented conversations buzzed around her, now more like an annoying mosquito than a pleasant ambience. She tried to take an interest in the other offerings, but her heart was no longer in it. By the time she caught up with the others, Mallory was ready to end her market visit and find some peace and quiet at Fruit Flan. As a light rain started to fall, the others agreed. They shared quick hugs and headed for home, unaware of their friend's encounter.

Mallory sat in her car, the engine idling. What on earth had Hettie been so bitter about? Given their history, it was Mallory who should have been the one to hold a grudge, but that was so long ago and they were adults now, for heaven's sake. A car skidded on the muddy exit road in front of her, a flash of pink and white check in the front seat evidence it was Patrick and Stacey, and in an obvious hurry to leave.

Mallory sighed – was everyone in this town angry at something?

IT WAS some time later that she noticed several missed calls on her mobile. She had returned from the market and tossed her phone onto the kitchen counter as she unpacked her purchases. She regretted not having circled back for the wool scarf but had completely forgotten about it in her rush to leave. Then it had been an afternoon taking out her frustrations by weeding the flower beds. Doris would have hated seeing them in such a mess, so Mallory had decided to set things right for at least one person from her past. It was only when she went inside for a warming tea that she played the message:

'Mallory, it's Catherine from Hillview Nursing Home. I'm so sorry to leave this message, but your father Harold has passed away. Your brother has been here and we have advised the funeral directors, but hope you can contact us as soon as possible. Again, my apologies for leaving such sad news.'

Mallory's breath caught in her throat, the rasp echoing around the kitchen walls as her cup clattered onto the counter. She needed space, and air, soon finding herself slumped in the cane chair on the front veranda. She squeezed her eyes shut and then open, the hills and sky remaining sodden with her sudden salty tears. She tried to focus on the blueness above, the whiteness of the thick clouds as if Harold Pepper should be sitting there. The lump in her throat made her cough, but there was no one there to hear it, to hug her, or lend a shoulder to cry on.

They'd come, she knew, but at that moment Mallory had never felt more alone.

———

'WOULD you like me to come with you?' Bridie asked gently.

Mallory had phoned her friend from the car as she set off for the nursing home. After checking in with the home to say she was nearby and learning that Harold was being moved to the funeral parlour, she had taken time to have a shower and sift through the tip of her emotions.

'No, but thank you,' Mallory replied, her voice flat. 'I suppose my brother will be there. He knew, Bridie. He must have got the call at the market and sped straight to Hillview. I don't know yet how things unfolded; whether Dad had another stroke and, um, lingered or what. Oh, I feel so bad I wasn't there.'

'Oh, hon. You weren't to know and hopefully it was quick. Just call me if you need me and walk away from Patrick if he gives you an iota of trouble. It's time for your energy to be with Harold now, not centred around Patrick's whims. I'll let Peg and Martha know.'

Catherine, the directress of Hillview, greeted her with a double handclasp and her condolences. It had been as their message had implied with Harold having suffered a massive heart attack. A carer had been getting him ready for a walk around the grounds when it happened, his death sudden and painless.

'Your brother arranged for Petersham's to come, and as we couldn't contact you straight away, Harold has been moved to their crematorium in nearby Rosalea. They're waiting to hear from you as to whether you'd like to see him. You are welcome to visit his room now if you like.'

Harold hadn't been a noisy man, but it was a different kind of silence that enveloped Mallory as she stood in the doorway of his room. A solid silence. 'Oh, Dad,' she whispered, then moved to take a seat in the visitor's chair. An air freshener sat on the shelf, emitting thin mauve streams of a pleasant cedar scent. The space had been tidied. Mallory knew Patrick would have checked the drawers and cupboards, and collected any jewellery, wallets, or important items that their father had kept with him. They would need to discuss clearing the few pieces that remained and donating them to a local charity if good enough – by the look of the worn slippers that sat empty under Harold's bed, most would probably be discarded.

A small photo frame sat between Harold's spectacles and a packet of unopened peppermints on his bedside table. Mallory reached for it and stared into the smiling face of her mother. 'Together again. I'm sorry for what is about to unfold between your three kids, because I have a horrible feeling it's going to get nasty, and you wouldn't have wanted that.'

The world was growing dull and grey outside, the normally green gardens now heavy and sad. Just like Mallory's heart.

Chapter Thirteen

AN EMAIL WAS how Patrick alerted his sisters to Harold's death. Mallory's phone calls and voice messages to him had gone unanswered. She had heard the ping of an incoming message late the night before, had quickly checked and read it, and then lay awake for most of the night wondering what would happen next. At first light, she made herself a cup of tea and opened a Reply All email:

Patrick, Vivien. Hillview Nursing Home contacted me yesterday after Dad's passing. I met with the directress, Catherine, who told me he was at Petersham's Funeral Parlour in Rosalea. Patrick, I'm sorry you didn't take the time to call me and am at a loss as to your reasons. I would like to know what you took from his room but will, no doubt, never know. Mallory sighed and deleted the last sentence.

What am I wanting to achieve with this email? Her legs felt heavy as she dawdled to the toaster and popped in two slices of bread. She turned and leant back against the bench, staring at the cursor on her computer screen. I want, she said aloud, 'I want for no drama. I want Patrick to do the right thing by us all. I want Vivien ... no, I don't want anything from her.' Mallory's stomach clenched when she realised she would have to see her sister, and be in the same room. To speak with her. Would John come to Appletree Hill too? Surely not.

'So, I guess what I want is for the funeral to be a fitting farewell. We'll celebrate his life as it should be remembered. Then, I want the next step to be resolved quickly and amicably.' She gave a little sniff of suspicion at that wish. The toast popped but was left to go cold.

Feeling a surge of confidence and purpose, Mallory returned to her computer and added: *I will be visiting Petersham's later today to see what arrangements, if any, Dad has in place and then we can all get organised to have those wishes fulfilled. Mallory.* She pressed Send and swore she could hear her carefully thought-out words pinging across the skies to her siblings.

It was just as well Mallory started her day early – Fruit Flan was inundated with visitors from mid-morning. First came Bridie and Rod, followed by Peggy and Martha, all laden with fresh coffees, calming teabags, cakes, and floral arrangements already arranged in vases.

'They're beautiful, thank you,' mumbled Mallory through tears as she accepted a huge bunch of foliage and dark pink roses from Bridie and a delicate spray of wildflowers from the girls. Bridie admitted to having contacted Zarni when a box of various white and cream flowers was delivered accompanied by a card covered with kisses and hugs. Mallory knew her friend would call to check on her soon.

'How wonderful that you saw your father before he passed,' Martha said. 'I understand you have had your run-ins with him but...'

'... as everyone in Appletree Hill has,' Peggy added.

'Don't look at me like that, Martha. I'm sure Mallory would agree that HP was not an easy man to both grow up with and live with. I'm not speaking ill of the dead.' When Martha's glare hadn't shifted, Peggy added, 'Sorry if I offended you, Mallory.'

'No, it's true. Dad was always difficult, but I used to think that he rather liked having that reputation. Unfortunately, that didn't make life easy on his family, and he certainly didn't appear to welcome me back with open arms. But, you're right, Martha, I'm grateful I saw him.'

She glanced through to where the frame holding Stella's photo sat beside a small lit candle on the side table. She had been unable to find any photos of Harold but made a mental note to check those taken at Stella's wake. Surely something would crop up on her phone's gallery as well when she had the time to search. 'I still have some lovely memories,' she said to no one in particular.

While Rod chatted to the girls, Bridie leant across and whispered, 'Have you spoken to Viv yet?'

Mallory shook her head and shrugged. 'It's only time I guess.'

As if on cue, her computer pinged with a message. 'Excuse me, I left the computer on in case the funeral home sent anything. That might be them now. I'm heading over this afternoon to sit with Dad for a little while.'

The email was from Patrick. Mallory gasped and clutched the edge of the table.

'Mallory, is everything alright?' Bridie asked, rising.

'It seems Dad's arrangements are already in place. This is an email from Patrick. To quote him, *No need to visit the funeral home, Mallory.* She turned to her friends, eyebrows raised, then continued, *According to Dad's wishes, an advertisement will appear in the local paper advising of a gathering to pay respects at Petersham's Funeral Home on a date to be decided. On this occasion, I will say a few words, the Lord's Prayer is to be read then anyone who would like to share a memory, can do so. Dad requested that anyone who would care to, can proceed to The Appletree Central Pub and raise a glass (no funds provided for this). Harold Pepper is to be cremated privately, his ashes scattered in the Pepper Farm apple orchard according to his wishes.*

'Well, there you have it,' Mallory said softly.

'Maybe he's trying to come across as very efficient, the older brother thing, you know,' suggested Martha. 'So that you won't feel you have anything to worry about.'

'Such attempts to control everything would only make me more worried,' Peggy muttered. 'But it's up to you my friend, what you do.'

Of course she would still go to the funeral home, despite Patrick's patronising instructions. She slumped into her chair. Peggy re-boiled the kettle.

Chapter Fourteen

THE MORNING AIR WAS CRISP, just as Mallory needed it to be in order to walk and clear her head. She pulled her jacket hood around her ears and set off down the lane, in the opposite direction to the village. The thought of running into Hettie, Patrick or Stacey pushed her blood pressure beyond safe limits. A sudden thump against her leg stopped her in her tracks.

'What? Oh, Rooster it's you. Hey, buddy....' Mallory bent over to give the excited dog a good rub whilst peering to check Keith wasn't far behind.

'Hi, Mallory. I called out but you didn't hear me. Good thing I've got my backup with me, although he nearly bowled you over. He must know it was you who saved him the other night. Thanks again for that.' Keith shifted from foot to foot, obviously unsure if he should turn back.

'I'm sorry I haven't been in to enquire how Rooster's cut is, but he seems to have recovered.'

'Yep, the vet said he's a tough little thing. Until the next thunderstorm anyway.'

'Why not join me – I'm not sure how far I'm walking,

but it's a gorgeous, fresh morning and too nice to be inside. There's more head space out here.'

'Still not sleeping?' Keith asked as he shot Mallory an amused sidelong look and fell into step beside her.

Mallory kept up the joke. 'The local band seems to have taken a break in their sessions so, no, it's not that.' Unexpectedly she found herself blinking hard, fighting tears. She turned aside and rummaged in her pocket for a tissue. 'Gosh, this cold air has made my nose run,' she sniffed. She gave her head a shake and replaced the tissue. 'That's better.'

Keith, slowed, peering at her. 'I don't think so. Want to share?'

'Nothing like taking a nice country walk with an emotional older woman,' she joked before her heart told her to give up the pretence. 'My dad has just died, here in Appletree actually so it's good that I'm here but, you know ...' Tears slid down her cheeks as she bit into her bottom lip.

Genuine concern etched across Keith's face as he stopped in his tracks. "I'm sorry. Do you have people here to be with you, to help?'

Mallory nodded. 'Good friends.' She chuffed as they fell into step again. 'And not so good family. But anyway, you are too young to bear the brunt of family woes.'

'Oh, come on. You heard some of mine – I'm living with my dad who is divorced from my mum, I can't seem to be able to talk to him without him bringing up the fact that I gave up my *real* job as a rising marketing executive and he can't seem to forgive a few mistakes I've made. Well, a lot of mistakes really, but I just couldn't hack the corporate life anymore.'

Normally, Mallory would have stepped in and offered help or advice, but she knew that at that moment she could only offer an ear. There was no room in her for anything more. 'I'm sure you'll work it out. You seem like a smart fellow.'

Keith whistled for Rooster to stop sniffing for rabbits and walk to heel. 'Tell me about your dad then.'

Mallory looked to the heavens. What to say? 'Well, he wasn't an easy man by any means. He was, however, a man who worked very hard his whole life. He loved being outdoors, his home, his apple orchard, and his privacy. And his son. Probably more than his wife and daughters despite him never admitting to it. I don't mean for that to sound bitter, it's just a fact.'

Keith nodded – Mallory wondered if he was reflecting on his relationship with his own father.

'I'm sorry he couldn't live at our family home, Pepper Farm, until the end but in a way it was no longer his home as he knew it, and the nursing facility took good care of him. He was in quite a bit of pain.'

'So you think aged care places are okay?' Keith asked. His question interrupted the soft tune he had been humming.

Mallory nodded. 'So long as they're reputable and are dedicated to those living under their duty of care. I'm sure we all say we want to stay in our own homes as we age but I've seen the trauma that can cause a person in need. Not to mention those trying desperately to look after them. It's such a personal decision and a very difficult one.' She wasn't entirely sure she agreed with her statement – would she be so willing to go into care when the time came? How much easier it would be to have a devoted partner who helped make that decision with you.

'I disagree,' Keith said, abruptly. 'I've also seen someone I love who is in a nursing home and, to be honest, it makes my skin crawl. There's no independence, no privacy, no creative buzz.' He sighed. 'No nothing really.'

'But is that person capable of making their own decisions, feeding himself, working out the right medications?'

'No, I guess not,' he mumbled into his scarf.

'Life's a gamble in so many ways,' Mallory muttered. She kicked at the small stones that were scattered across her path.

They circled back toward their respective houses, each deep in their own thoughts, accompanied by Keith's renewed pleasant hum. Rooster leant in for a final rub before chasing after his master, a welcome balm for Mallory and her melancholy.

WHEN STUART'S contact number buzzed on her phone, Mallory stopped short at her front door. It was silly not to answer. She flopped onto the veranda steps, pulled out random wisps of grass that were poking through the boards, and pressed the button. 'This is Mallory.'

'Mallory. It's Stuart.'

She registered his pause.

'Hi Stuart. Sorry, I've just come back from a walk and am a bit breathless.'

'I just got a call from the girls approving the barn plans and they told me about Harold. I'm sorry, Mallory.'

Once again, she bit her lip and looked to the clouds. People's condolences reminded her of when her mother had passed, but this was different. Although she hadn't been as close to Harold as she had been with Stella, she was feeling the full force of having now lost both parents.

'Thank you ...' She had run out of words, the flatness she felt like a soggy weight in her stomach.

'Has the funeral been arranged?'

The shaky sigh came out louder than she had intended. 'Yes, Patrick has that in hand. It's on Monday as everything had been arranged, then a private cremation and a few beers at the local pub according to Dad's instructions.'

'Have you heard from your sister?' he asked, concern echoing in every word.

'No, but I presume she'll be coming. Hopefully without John.'

'Well, I'm thinking of you. I, um, hope it goes well. I'm unexpectedly in Sydney now, otherwise ...'

'No, no. Don't be silly. Thanks for calling, Stuart; I appreciate it.' She pressed end and let out a long breath she hadn't realised she'd been holding.

Chapter Fifteen

AS HAROLD WAS ALWAYS one to be swayed by the weather –moody if raining, quiet if sunny – Mallory smiled at the irony when Monday dawned overcast with a blustery, cold wind. At least there would be no graveside vigil on a windy hill for Harold Pepper's funeral. Bridie and Rod had offered to drive her to the service and home again after the farewell, but Mallory wanted to make her own way through the day. First off, she intended to visit the funeral home and see what flowers had been arranged. Once again, Patrick had been out of contact so she only had his email to go by as to what he had planned.

'Would you like a few moments with your father?' Tony, the funeral director asked as he ushered Mallory into the quiet reception.

'Yes, that would be nice thank you. Oh, my goodness these are all beautiful. It looks like no more flowers are needed.' Large urns of glossy green leaves interspersed with yellow roses were arranged in the corners of the reception and through to the service room. She glimpsed a further bowl of yellow roses in front of the podium beside a closed beech coffin topped with three white roses and lavender.

'They were all delivered this morning for your service,' Peter said as he gently eased the door closed.

Mallory wandered down the aisle. She didn't intend to stay long. She had said all she wanted to say to her father in memory of their life together, both when he passed and when gazing at the stars in the night sky since then.

'Goodbye, Dad,' she whispered as she placed a hand on the coffin. The tips of her fingers nudged a small card tucked under the lavender, *Never forgotten* handwritten across its corner. Could Patrick have found some speck of compassion in the end?

'We'll all raise a glass to you as you requested, I promise.' Mallory gave the lid a last stroke then left.

AFTER A QUICK TAKEAWAY coffee and change of clothes, Mallory arrived back at the funeral home as Peggy and Martha, Bridie and Rod were parking their cars. Her stomach was surprisingly settled, nerves at the thought of being with Patrick, Stacey and possibly Vivien shelved. Her focus was on HP and how he would be remembered by those who were now filing inside for the service.

'Should I go and sit down or greet people?' she whispered to Bridie. 'I don't even know how many will come.'

'I doubt it will be standing room only,' Bridie said. 'There was supposed to be an announcement in the papers, but I didn't see it and Harold kept to himself in recent years. Here are Patrick and Stacey.'

Mallory turned to greet her brother, stunned at the

sombre dark grey suit and tie he was wearing. Stacey was also dressed much more formally than Mallory's chosen tailored black pantsuit with an ice-blue shirt, although Mallory did wonder if Stacey's bright red and white ensemble with stilettos was appropriate. She shrugged the impression away and leant forward to give them both an air kiss. In return, Patrick rubbed his hands together and commented on the welcomed warmth inside and Stacey referred to the roses smelling like one of her favourite perfumes.

'Are they left over from another funeral, honey?' Stacey asked Patrick.

'I doubt it. Mallory probably paid for them,' he replied. 'Come on, let's sit down.'

With the mystery of the flowers playing on her mind, Mallory trailed behind them, followed by a dozen or so people she didn't recognise. She watched an unfamiliar couple join Patrick and Stacey in the front row, leaving no space for her so she moved to the vacant row on the other side of the aisle. Bridie quickly scooted to sit beside her, sending Patrick a withering glance. It only served to settle Mallory more, her brother's farcical actions now more comical than insulting. Was he aware of his acute rudeness or was it just a sense of ingrained self-importance?

Patrick's contribution to the service was fulfilled in under ten minutes. He thanked people for coming, uttered a few words about Harold's love for Pepper Farm and Appletree Hill, how he had raised his children here, and his dear late wife Stella being buried here. Nothing personal or that the gathering wouldn't already know. At one point he squinted at the back of the room and faltered, but then continued with reading the Lord's Prayer.

The sound of some of the guests shuffling to their knees

or their feet prompted Bridie to lean into Mallory and whisper, 'Harold wasn't religious, was he?'

'I thought the same thing. It's an odd choice but so be it. Mind you, the pace that Patrick is cracking through the service doesn't leave much time to contemplate anything, does it.'

After murmured 'Amens' from around the room, Patrick asked anyone who would like to share a brief memory to come to the podium and do so.

Mallory smiled at his emphasis on 'brief'. She had decided not to make a speech, preferring to chat with anyone she may remember over farewell drinks later.

Patrick cleared his throat. 'Ah, a few words will be shared by my sister, Vivien.'

Mallory heard quiet footsteps approaching from behind her. She kept facing forward, glued to her seat as she felt Bridie startle and turn.

'Shit. It's okay Mallory, it's okay.' She took her friend's hand between her palms, trying to quell the shake.

Mallory regretted not having had any breakfast, the large latte suddenly threatening to rise through her empty stomach. Her deep, calming breaths helped as her eyes followed her sister's every step to the microphone. Vivien gave a little cough and looked everywhere but at Mallory whose attention remained fixed on her sister like superglue. Vivien was also dressed for a formal funeral in a black suit, mellow white bow shirt, and high heels. Her deep auburn hair was tied back in a ponytail, highlighting her high cheekbones, and large blue eyes glistening with tears.

She looks good, Mallory thought sadly. Had there been months after she'd torn apart Mallory and John's marriage that her sister had lost weight, her skin going dry with angst as Mallory's had? Who knew.

'I do recognise some of you here today and thank you for coming to pay your respects to our beloved father. I was devoted to him and will always regret not having been able to visit more frequently during the last year.'

Mallory muttered, 'Oh for heaven's sake. What is she planning now?'

'But life gets in the way doesn't it, as only Harold Pepper would appreciate. He was such a hardworking man. In fact, one of his favourite sayings was "You've got to plan your life early and work hard." It's advice I try to live by every day. Rest in peace, dear Dad.'

Vivien stood to the side, smiled at Patrick then walked back up the aisle. Bridie turned and watched her go, reporting to Mallory that her sister had actually left the building and was nowhere to be seen. 'Like Forest Gump, she just kept on going,' Bridie muttered in an obvious attempt to lighten the moment.

Where have I heard that saying again recently? Mallory hadn't moved, remaining fixed in her seat, just staring ahead as her mind buzzed. Something was flitting through her memory. She just couldn't take hold of it, but knew she had to. Something told her she had to remember, to lift it to the surface and study it.

Peggy's voice filtered through to her. 'You're as white as a sheet, Mallory. Do you want to take a moment or need a glass of water? I think we should drive you; you look spaced out but no wonder when bloody Vivien turns up dressed to the nines.'

Mallory turned her attention to the concern etched across her friends' faces, at Bridie fending off community well-wishers. 'No, I'm fine. Really. I don't need to stay for the cremation. I'll meet you all at the pub and hope Vivien won't be there.'

With a last glance at the coffin and a smile at the two attendants standing on either side of it, Mallory trailed behind the group as they made their way out of the room. A generic funeral tune played softly in the background. She eased a long-stemmed rose from an urn and smelt its sweet aroma.

Neither of her siblings was to be seen outside which she was grateful for. Who would have thought Vivien would show up in such dramatic form.

It was only when she paused at her car, still deep in thought, her fingers rotating the flower stem, that Mallory saw Hettie and Olivia McMunn. They were walking across the car park, their arms looped together, heads bowed. Hettie wiped away a tear. Mallory frowned – it had been Olivia who had quoted Hettie as saying "You've got to plan your life early and work hard."

Mallory's heart beat hard against her chest. She hadn't realised the two women had been at the service and for a moment thought how sweet of them to attend a customer's funeral. When she looked down at the rose, and back over her shoulder at the overflowing floral arrangements in the funeral home, her thoughts started spinning like a whirligig, not landing anywhere.

THE MAIN BAR at Appletree's pub was noisy with those wanting to raise a glass to the memory of Harold Pepper; in fact, there seemed to be more at the pub than had attended the service. Mallory welcomed each one with "Thank you for coming" before both parties were happy to move on for a drink with closer friends. Martha slid a bowl of nachos beside Mallory with a shrug of apology, together with a tall glass of water and a small tumbler of whiskey. The friends clinked glasses and then raised them to the heavens.

'Well, that went well, I think,' said Patrick as, uninvited, he added his much larger whiskey glass to the salute. Stacey had settled into the cubicle to join the couple they had sat with earlier but made no effort to extend her condolences.

'Who are they?' Mallory asked, tilting her empty glass towards the group.

'That's Stacey's sister and husband. They were passing through the area and thought they'd join us.' As Bridie nearly choked on her drink, Patrick knocked back the last of his as though attending an unknown person's funeral was the most natural thing for someone to do. 'So, Dad's ashes will be ready for collection in a couple of days.'

Mallory steeled her voice, and tilted her chin up a little so there would be no misunderstanding. 'I need to know when that is, Patrick. I want to be there when we scatter his ashes at Pepper Farm. In fact, why don't I collect them from the funeral home.' A statement, not a suggestion.

Patrick shrugged. 'Sure, if you want to.'

A small wisp of relief that she had control over something, even if only a sliver of something, glimmered within her. Without further comment, Patrick sidled over to slip into the cubicle with Stacey, laughter at a private joke soon erupting.

Bridie smoothed her palm across her friend's hand. 'Well said!'

Mallory thought for a moment before nodding. 'The send-off was what Dad had requested, it was well attended by locals and all his siblings ...' At those words she shot a glance towards the entrance on the lookout for another surprise appearance from Vivien. 'And here we are toasting to his life. Thank you all for coming. I'm so glad you were there, for him and me.' She chuffed out a breath before continuing. 'Who would have thought Vivien would have just rocked up like that.'

'And appeared so heartbroken,' Bridie scoffed. 'She's obviously on the prowl for something.'

'Maybe someone else's husband.' Mallory said, her hand shooting to cover her words. 'Sorry. Maybe a whiskey on an empty stomach wasn't such a good idea.'

Martha raised her hand at the barman. 'More nachos piled high with extra cheese here please.' Her commanding tone, so out of character, broke the moment's tension and they all laughed.

Guests started to filter out into the sunlight to head home or back to work, pausing to wish Patrick and Mallory all the best. Several handed her envelopes, obviously condolence cards, which she appreciated.

As Mallory stacked them on the bar, Grace the town's pharmacist approached and handed her two more. 'I'll miss old Harold,' she said to the group. 'He used to give us all at the chemist a real run-around. Even when he moved to the nursing home, he'd find his way into town with a carer, ready for a chat or mostly a complaint. You know how he was.' She scanned the room. 'I hoped to catch Olivia McMunn here. I missed her at the service and just wanted to thank her for dropping some lozenges out to Harold the other week.'

A small frown creased Mallory's brow.

Oblivious, Grace continued, 'I did catch Vivien though. She said she couldn't make it here but asked me to pass this on. Anyway, lovely to see you again, Mallory, and my condolences.' She turned and left.

As they all stared down at the silent envelope, Mallory

tapped her finger on her name which she now saw was written in Vivien's neat handwriting.

'It's a wonder old Harold could ever get a word in with Grace around,' Bridie said drily. 'She always was such a gossip.'

'Can anyone see if Patrick has a matching blue envelope?' Mallory whispered. They all turned at once but Patrick was engrossed in recounting a story and didn't notice the attention.

'It doesn't look like it and Grace just waved to his table on her way out,' Martha reported back. 'Mallory, I think we should all head home. We can stop by Fruit Flan if you'd like us to of course, but I suspect you'd like some space.' She flicked her eyes to the blue envelope again.

Mallory hopped off her stool and gave them each a long hug. 'Thank you again, my friends. I'll be fine.'

'Call me if you need me and I will come straight away,' Bridie whispered into her ear.

They gathered their jackets and set off for their respective cars. Mallory sat for a moment, the car's heater taking the chill out of her bones – she'd need to get her coat back from Stuart soon. She had been truthful when she'd said she was pleased with how Harold's service had gone. Nothing fancy, just like he'd lived his life. She needed a moment to mentally rummage through the two surprises that had emerged though – The McMunn women, obviously upset, attending the service but not the drinks, and of course Vivien and her ridiculous speech. Mallory knew it had been for her benefit but why? Maybe the three women had now gone off somewhere together to bond over some unknown memory of Harold – no, not possible.

By the time Mallory arrived at Fruit Flan, her mind was ricocheting like a squash ball, but with no plausible outcome. A pot of tea and a sandwich were needed. She jostled her key, the condolence envelopes, her bag, cardigan, and the rose, nearly missing the little posie of wildflowers and folded paper propped on the windowsill. She flung open the door, deposited her belongings on the lounge chair, retrieved the posie, then wandered through to the kitchen.

She unfolded the paper. *I heard your dad's funeral was today. Hope all went well. Keith and Rooster* were written neatly. Mallory smiled at her young neighbour's gesture, although how he had heard about the funeral she couldn't imagine. The wildflowers and trimmed yellow rose looked pretty in a glass jam jar she found under the sink then placed on the kitchen table.

The blue envelope was like a magnet. It was hidden under her coat and in amongst the other cards, but it called to her with neon lights flashing. In the end, after setting herself up at the veranda table, Mallory retrieved the pile and took them outside. Several cards were the same, showing an old apple tree on a hilltop with a bird flying into the clouds. One by one, she read *Sorry for your loss* – it seemed HP's network was long on compassion but short on words, but she was touched by their sincerity.

Finally, Mallory slit the blue envelope open and took out two sheets of standard lined paper. 'Here we go,' she murmured to herself.

Mallory. How sad that we have lost our father, but you'd agree that he was very good at keeping his distance from us. Patrick seems to be in control and well ensconced at Pepper Farm and, again, you'll agree with me that could present a problem. I think we should stick together on this so that what is rightfully ours from Dad's estate comes to us all equally. This does raise the question of who should be able to access such proceeds – as you did come into some lottery money, I would like to think you'd consider this when the time comes to split the estate. I was deeply hurt that you took it upon yourself not to share that windfall with me but obviously the timing wasn't in my favour.

I will be in town for the next day or so, then need to go to Melbourne. I'll be back when we hear that the Death Notice is finalised to see where his affairs are at. I have spoken with the solicitors, and they confirm the three of us remained powers of attorney, but since Dad's death, they now take over the execution of the will. Hopefully all is above board.

You'll agree that we should meet sooner rather than later, just to go through a plan in case Patrick had already persuaded Dad to leave us out. I trust that the other matter between us can be put aside. John tells me that he has explained how unhappy he was in the marriage for some time and that surely you are relieved he is with someone who cares for him. I hope that you are happy for me too, as your sister.

Give me a call with where/when we can chat. Viv

Chapter Sixteen

AS THE NIGHT cooled and the hoots of owls and sounds of scurrying possums welcomed the stars, Mallory tossed and turned, no closer to putting her emotions in a place where she understood them. Her friends would be at her side in no time, but surely she would work this out herself; then the morning dawned and she was no closer to knowing what to do. Plus, her unanswered questions about the McMunn women still prickled her mind.

Her anger had been building since reading her sister's letter the previous day. At first, Mallory laughed and exclaimed, "What! You've got to be joking", but then Vivien's audacity hit her and the ripples rose from her stomach to her chest. No matter what she decided to do next in her head, it changed a moment later. No matter how many times she re-read the pages, reading between the lines for something missed, the result was the same. How dare Vivien justify their affair in such a way. How dare she turn up at their father's funeral, present mourners with a few fake, showy words then leave, with a promise to return to see "where his affairs were at". To find out what the will contains would be more accurate.

Mallory needed exercise and knew the perfect companion. Moments later she was pacing outside her neighbour's kitchen door. If Keith didn't answer in two seconds, she would walk away without Rooster. A lovely mellow tune whispered from inside the house, almost lulling her into a calmness she didn't want to feel. When rich vocals joined the guitar, she knocked harder on the screen door. A moment later, the door opened.

'Mallory. Are you okay?'

'I'm fine. I'm about to go for a walk and wondered if Rooster would like a run. I'm sorry to interrupt if you have company.' She scuffed her shoes, trying not to grind her teeth behind an attempted smile.

Keith must have noticed her thin cotton shirt. 'It's pretty cold. Did you bring a jumper?' He reached behind the door.

Mallory glanced across at the morning dew. 'I've left my coat somewhere. Oh, the other reason I'm here is to thank you for the flowers. So thoughtful of you but how did you know ...'

Keith waved away her thanks and passed her the jacket, a signal for Rooster to jump like a spring around her feet. She attached his lead and was instantly dragged along the veranda and down the unkept driveway. It would appear dog training had never been a priority.

All the same, she missed having a dog. It seemed with just one sniff, snortle or pleading look they extinguished any heavy feelings that might be simmering. Mallory's heart lightened as she made her way along deserted hedged laneways, constantly tugging her companion to heel and wishing she'd brought some treats as bribery. After a time of sniffing every blade of grass, Rooster started to tire and trotted happily beside her, but she still kept him on the lead, not trusting his overt interest in foreign smells or rabbits. It was a clear day, which made for chilly air and a welcome brisk pace.

Vivien's letter had been the trigger, the catalyst for all of Mallory's pent-up emotions from the past year to explode. "You'll agree to this and you'll agree to that" her sister had presumed, as though she had been taking lessons from Patrick. What was that about; actually, no Vivien I don't agree with any of it.

Despite the time that had passed, and the various emotional stages she'd confronted, Mallory had yet to grieve the end of her marriage – partly because of its deceitful end, partly because it was exhausting, but more directly because she had been in disbelief. How does one go about processing such actions by those you loved, as well as keeping an iota of self-esteem? How had she and Warren missed signs of the relationship between John and Vivien? Mallory still wanted to pin Vivien down, to rant and rave and fling accusations and questions at her. A meeting in Appletree would need to be somewhere private, but there was no way Mallory would invite her sister into her space at Fruit Flan.

She breathed deeply and scanned the immaculate pastures. *So beautiful.* Rooster gave a sudden lurch towards rustling in the grass, possibly a field mouse; Mallory knew it was too cold for snakes to cross her path. The road was uneven, potholed in some spots from the recent rain, prompting her to keep her head down so as not to trip.

A couple strolling in the opposite direction slowed, obviously wanting a chat but Mallory gave a friendly wave and a smile and tugged Rooster on their way. She had no idea where she had wandered but would give the walkers a bit of distance then head back the same way so as not to get totally lost. When Rooster squatted by a shrub, she used the time to catch her breath, to remind herself of all she had in her life, rather than what she had lost. She could boast of good health, supportive long-term friends, and opportunities to work or travel if she desired; so why did she feel in such limbo? She was both relieved and happy to be a lottery winner, to be independent with a glittering road of options spreading out in front of her. But ideas to put anything into practice just spun like unmatched pictures on a poker machine.

Where had that carefree girl and young woman gone – the one that would snort when she laughed, skip when she heard good news, or cry with emotion during sad movies? Even when money wasn't plentiful. How could she possibly have written such whimsical, motivating kids' stories at one point, then ignored the satisfaction it had brought? When would all that joy and silliness magically return, or had it vaporised along with her sex life? Could you even put a price on a feeling, a desire – where had she heard that love is currency? At that, she did burst out laughing, presuming for a moment it was Bridie. No, it had been Stuart back when they were teenagers, exploring their love for each other.

'I'd pay anything to keep you by my side my whole life,' Stuart had said as he had drizzled sand into her navel. 'If love was currency, I'd be a rich man.' He had nodded seriously, obviously impressed by his borrowed words, when she was the English Dux.

It had been 'firsts' for them both, within a sheltered sand dune on an unseasonably hot weekend. She had laughed nervously, glancing around to make sure no one was within sight. Stuart had spread out his beach towel and then looked deeply into her eyes as he'd untied her bikini. They had kissed and fumbled, making sure each was ready. His suntanned skin had been warm against her ivory body as they had come together, trapped granules of sand leaving marks across her stomach. She had run her finger across them that night as she'd stood under a hot shower, reliving each spine-tingling moment. He had held her tightly afterward, had kept asking if she was okay. She had never been happier. The afternoon had floated by as they wandered lazily hand-in-hand along the beach and through shallow rockpools, before cooling off in the clear waves, and making love between quick naps.

The ensuing tender hours and days they stole for themselves had been full of desire, with no hint of what was to come at the upcoming dance.

'There you go, Rooster. Love and fortune don't necessarily go together.' Mallory bent down to unleash Rooster's lead as she turned into his driveway, surprised to feel the sting of tears. She was unsure what her next step would be, but one thing she did know was that Vivien's letter had left her feeling stupid and naïve, old and incredibly sad.

Like an athlete out of a starter box, Rooster darted up the driveway, around the veranda to the back door. Mallory knocked, refilling the dog bowl from the outdoor tap while she waited. In the end, she had to open the kitchen door to return the coat onto its hook. A different version of the earlier song she'd heard drifted from the lounge room. Mallory called, 'Just bringing Rooster home,' and wandered through.

Keith sat cross-legged on the floor with his back to the doorway, headphones on and guitar in hand. Mesmerised, Mallory watched as he sang a few lines, then made changes to sheet music which lay on the carpet at his side. Surely he wasn't composing this beautiful song himself. She edged into the room, vaguely trying to catch his attention, but wanting to listen further. She startled him. Frowning, Keith snatched off his headphones and went to stand.

'Sorry, he said, 'I was in the middle of something.'

'No problem,' Mallory held out her palm for him to stay where he was. 'That's amazing. Did you write it?'

He shrugged. 'A work in progress, but yeah, it's my composition. I'm trying to polish off a few pieces for a session.'

When he didn't offer any more details, Mallory explained that Rooster was safely returned, and let herself out. As she wandered back down the driveway, her phone rang. It was Harold's solicitor's number.

'Mallory. I'm just calling to say that we will be having a reading of your father's will to beneficiaries in our offices on Friday week. I'll send you an email with the time.'

'Oh. Is that usual? Who will be going?'

'It was Harold's request but I'm not at liberty to say who will be there.'

Well, that takes the pressure off me deciding whether to meet with Vivien or not, she thought. I'll leave it in someone else's hands, meet up with her then, and see what eventuates.

'SO, it would seem that I'm the one to make all the overtures, Mallory.'

Mallory spun at the sound of her sister's voice. She had been into town for some fresh salads to go with her mountain of casseroles and was deep in thought about which ones to deliver over to the girls, annoyed she had forgotten to add a breadstick to her purchases. She hadn't noticed the visitor sitting on Fruit Flan's veranda.

'Shit.'

'Well, that's not a very nice welcome. Do you need a hand with those bags?'

'No, Vivien. I don't,' Mallory snapped as she placed her shopping on the ground and leant against her car door. 'What are you doing here? In fact, how did you know where I was staying?' A quick scan of the property revealed a small car tucked under the trees.

Vivien had moved to the top of the steps and was leaning on the post. She shrugged. 'My letter was an olive branch, but when I didn't hear back from you, I thought I'd take matters into my own hands. As to Fruit Flan or whatever it's called now, that information was shared from your old adversary, Heather McMunn. You could have knocked me over with a feather when I went into that bedraggled nursery for a takeaway coffee and she appeared. Mind you, I think she got just as big a shock to see me in her cafe.'

The frown that had appeared on Mallory's forehead deepened – had Olivia or Hettie mentioned where she was staying, or was it that small towns still had a way of knowing everyone's business? Too many options but in the end she did know one thing for certain. She was ready to confront Vivien and the meeting date at the solicitors suddenly seemed too far away. Shaking off any hesitation, Mallory picked up the bags and headed for her front door. Vivien turned to follow her inside, just as a sharp bark from Rooster drifted through the trees.

'I'll be back in a moment,' Mallory instructed as she

closed the screen door firmly behind her, blocking Vivien's attempt to join her.

With a clear plan of where she wanted their conversation to head, Mallory reappeared on the veranda with a glass of water for herself. She swivelled the spare chair a little towards the view to focus on the countryside's beauty should she need its calming influence, but then decided to stand. It could be a sign to Vivien that she was welcome to leave at any time. Mallory turned with raised eyebrows, waiting for her to make the first move.

It didn't take long. 'I guess you got the call about the reading of the will ...'

'Let's just address you having an affair with my husband first, shall we?' Mallory said, pinning down Vivien's gaze. 'I will decide when we put this aside and it won't be before I get some answers. They're going to come from you. Now. I'm not interested in John's view; lord knows I heard enough of his views over the years and I'm not going to discuss our marriage in any way with you.' She paused. 'So, I just want to know one thing, and that's how long had you been sleeping together before I found out?'

There was more she could have said, but she needed to squash the image of them together that had wormed its way into her vision.

Vivien rubbed at an invisible thread on her jeans and cleared her throat. 'We'd been seeing each other after work on and off for a few months then, um, we'd had a few wines over lunch one day and ended up at a motel. You've got to believe me Mallory that we didn't intend for it to go any further, but then John told me how unhappy he was. He felt lost and needed to reinvent himself with someone who would support him down that road. Warren and I were going through a rough patch so it did. Go further I mean, until we fell in love.'

The words "how unhappy he was" bounced between Mallory's temples; the reference to "reinvention" too ludicrous to contemplate at that moment. She was somewhat surprised by how forthcoming Vivien was, but no doubt she knew how Mallory liked to have things in their place. Or perhaps her sister just wanted to take the opportunity to brag; to not be the youngest sibling for a change. Whatever.

'The question is the same, Vivien. How long had you been sleeping together?' Her words had picked up speed as the underlying tension started to bubble.

'About a year before you overheard us, if you must know.'

Whatever timing Vivien had put on it, Mallory knew it would still be like a hard punch to her chest. What did it matter whether it was a year or a month? But it did because she could cast her mind back over that time and pick apart each conversation she and John had had at the end of the day, in the car, while walking the neighbour's dog, over a meal; each time they too had made love. Which had become less and less frequent and, she had to admit, more and more lacklustre. She bit her lip – sleeping together would be a more appropriate description. But now she knew.

In the past, the sisters would have enjoyed sitting in silence with each other, neither feeling the need to fill the space with words or opinions. To Mallory that silence now was hollow, empty of trust. 'What happened to us, Vivien? Disregarding John, I'm really sad that you have destroyed any connection we had as sisters and friends. And so easily it seems.'

'I'm sorry Mallory, really I am.' She broke the eye

contact Mallory was holding onto and licked her lips. The over-confidence she had shown at the funeral and a few minutes earlier had gone, replaced by a look of stubbornness.

'Surely you realised it was our anniversary that night you were meeting each other at the Hilton? Everything else was bad enough, but to totally disregard our anniversary? And what about Warren; you broke his heart.'

For a moment Vivien stalled, probably digesting the fact that Mallory and Warren had been in touch, but she recovered quickly. Her hand flicked through the air as though sending her ex-husband into the sky, then she chuckled, sending a shiver of anger through Mallory.

'John mentioned the anniversary mishap when we met up, but to be honest we had both completely forgotten. Anyway, isn't it more important now to just sort out Dad's inheritance?'

'Wow,' Mallory whispered to herself, still in disbelief that her sister could be so callous. Apparently, it was all about the money now; but about Harold's or her own?

'You made your point very clear on that.' Mallory's stomach started to squirm, a dull ache spreading wherever it could find an empty space.

'And?'

Mallory shook her head. 'And what? My lucky windfall has nothing to do with anything. Particularly you.'

Vivien huffed. 'Well, we think it does. You don't know how much John felt deceived when that piece of information came up during your settlement. How much was it anyway? What? You can ask personal questions and I can't?'

'It's none of your business,' Mallory replied through

gritted teeth. 'But I can tell you that I shared a hefty amount of it with various charities.'

Astonished, Vivien swivelled to face Mallory full-on, her mouth open. 'Without telling anyone?'

Rooster's barking became more insistent from across the fence. Could he sense the sparking hostility between the sisters?

Mallory was so tempted to stress how excited she had been to rush home and share the news with her husband, to take him away on an extended holiday – only to have her world disintegrate. She wanted to give her side of the sad story, but Vivien obviously wouldn't care. *I could tell her how I would have given her some of the proceeds from my win, no doubt about that.* But Mallory bit her tongue.

'I'm not going to discuss it with you, Vivien. The lawyers made it clear that I owed John nothing – they were my numbers, and the ticket was bought by me with my money. It was always his idea to run our own bank accounts as he didn't expect my writing career to bring in anything worthwhile, so the joke's on him. I was generous with the proceeds from the sale of the house you may remember and, once again, that's none of your business either. Whether you're shacked up together or not.'

'It's just ...'

At that moment, the Star Wars theme echoed from Vivien's pocket. As the series had been John's favourite, Mallory presumed he was the caller. Quickly, Vivien scrambled for her phone and cut off the music.

Mallory held up her hand and took a deep breath. 'Saying "we never intended to fall for each other or take it further" are such tired phrases. I will never forgive either of you, Vivien. Where have your apologies been for the last twelve months, how did you think your sister or Warren were faring?'

'Love is blind, and none of us is getting any younger,' Vivien said petulantly. Just like when she was a little girl, Mallory remembered. If her sister hadn't got what she wanted she was capable of sulking for hours, holding a grudge for days.

Another short bark came from Rooster. Mallory couldn't help but let out a snort of laughter, both at Vivien's remark and the dog's timing.

'Go on laugh,' Vivien said defensively. 'You were always the clever sister, Mallory, the one good with words, the one who could have done anything. I was always the second fiddle on the achievement board of honour.'

'That's not true,' Mallory said, genuinely shocked. It certainly wasn't a sentiment she had held. 'I never believed that nor did anything to give that impression.'

'How do you think I felt coming back here, to Dad's funeral knowing you'd be looking at me, judging me? It was all I could do to stand up and say those words; I had to leave straight away. You and Patrick sitting all righteous in the front row ...'

'I don't believe you felt that for a second nor do I give a shit. Does Patrick know about you and John?'

Vivien shrugged. 'Not unless you've told him.' She paused. 'John offered to come with me you know. He wasn't sure how you'd react to seeing me, but I told him I'd be fine.'

'Well, it's good to know that you're fine, Vivien. I'll see you at the solicitors.' Mallory tossed the water from her glass into the garden and instantly regretted not emptying it onto her sister. With clenched teeth and a heart that threatened to beat a thunderous path through her jumper, she strode inside. Not long afterward, the sound of Vivien's car retreated into the distance.

Chapter Seventeen

'OH MY GOD, SHE DID WHAT?'

Mallory nodded. 'Thanks for letting me debrief. The least I could do was bring provisions to eat while you listen to me moan and groan.'

Bridie and Mallory had joined Peggy and Martha at the girls' home the day following Vivien's visit. They had been quickly ushered outside with jugs of water and a glass of wine, and instructions not to start talking until they were all gathered. Mallory trailed her fingers along the healthy potted olive and lemon trees that bordered the flagstone terrace. Complete with an overhead trellis trailing shady vines, it was modelled on a hotel courtyard the girls had seen in Milan. Perhaps I could just travel, Mallory thought. Travel and collate amazing ideas to bring back to a new home in Australia. She moved to the large concrete table – it could easily seat twelve people but was now set for the friends all at one end, so they couldn't miss a word.

After Mallory had given them a quick recount of Vivien's visit, which had been interrupted numerous times by her friends' exclamations (against Vivien) or nods of approval (for Mallory's reactions), they raised their glasses to a positive and amicable outcome at the reading of HP's will.

'You've seen and confronted Vivien now, so it's time to move on with your future,' Peggy said sagely. 'Why not write a cookbook? This is delicious.'

Martha laughed. 'We love a tuna casserole and fresh green leaf salad, even more so when we don't have to make it and it's accompanied by a good story, so thank you. We can offer chocolate tart with coffee though.'

'Well, as I say, I do appreciate it. There's nothing like a visit weighed heavy with drama, is there.'

'Said like a true writer, although hopefully not the theme for a children's book. Speaking of which, when *are* you going to resurrect your writing?' Bridie asked.

Mallory helped herself to a slice of the crusty bread she had picked up from the bakery on the way to the girls' house and dipped it into the shallow dish of olive oil.

'There's absolutely no room in this head for anything but my current obligations towards Pepper Farm, thanks to my family. They're giving me the pip.'

'You'll have to *peel* back the layers of what Patrick has been up to first,' Bridie said knowingly.

'To get to the *core* of the problem, you mean?' Peggy chipped in.

Mallory laughed, waving her hands in the air. 'Stop it, that old play on apples is just bad taste. Oh no, I didn't mean that!'

Martha caught on. 'Maybe we need to plant a few *seeds* in the Stuart direction.'

'Oh, I have missed you all,' Mallory gasped between laugh hiccups.

As the afternoon crept onward, the friends went over

their reactions to HP's farewell and retold stories from their childhood, filling in Martha with any details she didn't know. More than once, Peggy groaned that there were a million jobs to do around the stables but stayed seated and poured more coffees. Mallory heard her phone beep with several messages but let them go to message bank.

'Going back to Vivien,' Peggy began, shooting a glance across at Mallory to make sure she wasn't pushing her opinion too far. 'It must feel good to have stood up to her. She really has shown no remorse, has she? I don't remember her being that callous.'

Mallory shook her head. 'A lot has changed over the years, shifts that maybe I didn't pick up on, and I don't have the energy to sift through now. She always was a woman on a mission when it came to men, Warren being an example.'

'But not with you, surely,' Martha said.

'No. Well, I didn't think so. I was surprised to hear she still holds a grudge about some aspects of our childhood, but we were sisters and that's normal isn't it? Of course, we are still sisters but it's different and our relationship will never go back to the way it was. Sad really.'

The sound of car wheels crunching the driveway and the last words of a Bluetooth conversation drifted to the back terrace. 'That'll probably be Stuart,' Peggy announced.

'Stuart? Those seeds you mentioned sprouted quickly, Martha,' Mallory said, startled.

The group laughed as the man in question dawdled through the gate, his attention on his phone screen before it turned toward the group. His frown melted as they all greeted him as one. He rounded the table and placed a hand gently on Mallory's shoulder, his green eyes looking deeply at hers. 'I left you a few phone messages. I'm not stalking you. I just wanted to check in after Harold's funeral and to say I'm heading down to Appletree.' A cheeky grin spread across his face. 'But here I am already.'

'Oh, sorry, I missed your calls. We've been too busy chatting,' Mallory said, patting the side of her handbag.

Stuart waved away her excuses. 'No problem. I hope he had a good send-off?'

Mallory sensed he was fishing as to whether Vivien and John had appeared. 'Yes, thanks Stuart. It went well and was what he had requested with a small but lively gathering, including Patrick, Stacey and Vivien. She made quite an entrance at the service and then shot through.'

'And?' Stuart said, sensing there was more to come.

'... only to reappear at my house for a heart-to-heart.'

'Ah. And did she get one?'

Mallory thought for a moment, as she had done throughout the night after Vivien's visit. The bottom line was that she was actually pleased she'd met face-to-face with her sister at last; was satisfied she'd held her own during what was at times an emotional conversation. Time was beginning to wield its power of healing, and she was becoming more detached by the day. Suddenly aware of the silence and her friends' expectant expressions, she smiled. 'Yes. Acceptance is a long way away, but our rather stilted confrontation-slash-chat was the first step.'

'Now Stuart, hopefully that frown over your phone as you came in wasn't bad news about council approvals for our barn,' Martha said as she placed a fresh coffee and a slice of torte in front of him.

'No, no. I can advise everything's approved so we can start work as soon as possible. The text was for this father receiving yet another six-word email from his youngest son saying he was staying away another week.'

'Where is he?' Martha asked.

Stuart shrugged. 'Look, he's an adult, I get it, but I can't help thinking it's because of me that he stays away from his home in Melbourne. Mind you, he has no idea where I am on any given day anyway. We've had a few differences of opinion as to how he spends *his* days. If he's got a passion for something and he's exceptional at it, then I'd say to go for it, but he just won't open up as to what he has on his mind, or more importantly how he's going to achieve it.'

Bridie laughed. 'Oh, Stuart. You sound like you need to borrow one of Rod's spreadsheets. Life can't be put into columns sometimes, and kids must find their own way to being their best selves.'

'Maybe the apple doesn't fall far from the tree, and I'm not referring to Appletree's many orchards.' Mallory winked. 'I seem to remember a young fellow who took off surfing down the coast without telling his parents where he was. At least your son is keeping in touch.'

'I guess so,' Stuart said, his focus drawn to his dessert.

'Well, I would like to see what all the fuss is about with this barn,' Mallory said. 'Can we go see where it's to be when you've finished?'

'I'll head home,' Bridie said. 'Thank you for the catch-up and lunch. It's so good to have you back in town, Mallory. You sure do add spark to my boring little country life.'

Stuart popped the last bite of torte into his mouth, picked up his plans, and the four headed to the potential building site along a wide gravelled track, lined with swaying olive trees. Mallory scanned the property as they walked the short distance; past existing stables, corrals, and paddocks divided by white fences. Several beautiful steeds stood under the dappled shade of a row of giant spruce trees – they gave a cursory glance from large brown eyes as the group strolled past. A few neglected rows of vines made Mallory pause.

'Did you always grow vines?'

'Not really. Nothing commercial in any case. I did have high ideas of supplying small batches to wineries in the area but it became too overwhelming. Hence those straggly old girls will need to be cleared for our super-duper barn.'

'But if you're thinking of cutting back on horses, why do you need a big barn?' Mallory asked.

'Not necessarily cutting back on horses, just the training of racehorses. Martha has a bee in her bonnet about running a tandem business – maybe an agistment or something to do with providing a riding therapy centre for people with disabilities. Her nephew in Perth runs a not-for-profit along those lines after his friend was in a car accident and there wasn't anything available. She'll sort it and in the meantime she thinks that "if we build it they will come". And if they don't then we have either a very large B&B smelling of hay or we stick with what we're doing.' Peggy squinted into the distance. 'It would be good though, as neither of us is getting any younger and this kind of work takes its toll.'

Over the next ten minutes, Mallory watched Stuart as he explained his plans in minute detail. It certainly did sound like an amazing structure, simple but sturdy, squared off but complimentary to the countryside. Black walls and large sliding doors, olive green trims, and everything that the girls needed. Her heart warmed to see the spark of excitement in Stuart's eyes as he went through the big picture down to the smallest details that he had incorporated. *In fact, you're a rather handsome package all over, Stuart Forbes. From your windblown mop of curls to your tanned forearms which I can see poking out below your sloppy joe jumper, to your baggy jeans which still pull taut*

across apparent muscles when you squat in the dirt like that.
She gave a shiver.

'Oh, are you cold Mallory?' Martha asked.

Stuart grinned at her as he rolled up the plans. 'I have a
cure for that. Your coat – it's still in the back of my car. Um,
I guess you forgot to take it.'

Because I left in a hurry? Mallory met the amusement
in his eyes as they tempted her to retaliate. Mallory laughed.
'Thanks. I'll grab it then head home. We'll catch up soon
Peg, Martha. My place next time.'

As Martha and Peggy headed hand-in-hand towards the
house, Stuart and Mallory strolled back to his car. 'I hope
this place isn't getting too much for them,' Mallory said as
she kicked at the dirt. 'If they had someone in to trim the
lawns and hedges it would free them up for their business,
but Peg insists on getting on that mower herself apparently.'

'I think they're fine,' Stuart said. 'Every time I've met
with them, they've been on the ball with what they want.
There is a lot of land here that's not being used I must
admit, but then that's the appeal of the countryside.'

He draped Mallory's coat over her shoulders.

'I wouldn't want to live off the land, or run a farm,'
Stuart said then added with a smirk, 'I've picked up quite a
few city habits; like finding tucked-away whiskey bars down
alleyways and enjoying the occasional gallery exhibition.
But places like this are always within reach to visit so it's the
best of both worlds.

'And there's your work,' Mallory added, not quite ready
to leave.

Stuart nodded. 'These rural jobs are dream jobs. I
breathe deeper after visiting Mum and store all that fresh
air to take home to the suburbs.'

'I should have asked. How's Nellie?'

'The same. I'm going to see her tomorrow. Do you want to grab a coffee first then come with me, if it's not too strange going without your father being there?'

Mallory's heart skipped a beat. 'Sure, but let's make it coffee at the bakery rather than the nursery, just to be on the safe side.'

When she didn't elaborate on her comment, Stuart let it go and stepped towards her. His hand was firm on her upper arm, his lips warm as they pecked her cheek. Had he held her for a few seconds longer than necessary, or had she imagined it? Either way, her heart warmed at his touch.

Chapter Eighteen

WHEN MALLORY HEARD Stuart's car pull into her driveway, she locked the cottage and skipped down the stairs. For some reason, it seemed less formal than him collecting her at the front door.

'Good morning,' he said with a wide grin. 'Ready for coffee?'

'Absolutely,' she replied happily.

As Stuart hung their coats on a nearby hook, Mallory rubbed her hands together and glanced around for a spare table. 'Everything smells divine.'

Stuart gave her a mock salute. 'I'll be quick then.'

The hustle of customers ordering golden pies, inspecting sourdough loaves, and eyeing off the cabinet of delectable cakes was somehow homely. Snippets of conversation wafted around her – who had paid what for which local property, whether the new seafood restaurant in nearby Minnette Cove was worth the high prices being charged, the need to book for someone called Zoe's latest ivy wreath-making course. It sounded somewhat superficial, but she knew there were deeper layers to her town that were more authentic to how she remembered her childhood.

She had snared the last remaining table by the window and Mallory was gazing out at the rain-drenched street when Stuart returned with two fresh rhubarb Danish pastries.

'Coffees are on the way. I hope you like rhubarb. What are you thinking about?'

'That the nursery café has a lot of competition in this bakery.' Mallory stifled a giggle. 'Actually, I was feeling a little on show sitting in the window here and wondered what Heather would think if she walked past and saw us. Surprise that we're having coffee together or annoyance that we're not at her business?'

Stuart laughed as he tore open a sugar sachet. 'What did you mean when you said you need to clear your thoughts? Or don't I want to know?'

Mallory held her pastry and cut it in half, Stuart following her finger as she licked the stickiness from it. The arrival of steaming cups of coffee broke the moment, but Mallory had noticed his attention, and had felt a welcome twinge in her belly. With a shake of her head she decided she was tired of charades and would run a few thoughts past him; lying awake at night hadn't answered them for her.

The coffee was strong, warming her from the inside. 'I saw Heather at the market, and she was very brusque, and told me they didn't need my help. Not that I'd offered anything except to patronise the café and buy some flowers.'

'And ...?' Stuart rolled his hand, obviously knowing there was more on her mind.

'Well, it was the strangest thing. A stream of strange

things. Firstly, Dad had apple slices in his room and I saw Heather in the home's car park ...'

Stuart lowered his coffee cup slightly, his lips tweaked in a slight what's-your-point grin but his eyes urged her to continue.

'... then there was that comment at the market. And she and Olivia were at Dad's funeral.' She shrugged. 'I only saw them as I was leaving.'

'I can't imagine old HP charming anyone, but maybe he did just that in his old age. Maybe he used to frequent the café; after all they've known each other their whole lives and he knew Heather's parents.'

'To the degree that mother and daughter had completely decked out the funeral home with beautiful floral arrangements? I'm sure it was them. But the flowers would have cost a lot of money, plus there was a sweet little card.' Mallory clicked her fingers, her eyes wide. 'Oh, unless Dad paid for the flowers before he passed, to give them a large job. Or something. And the card tucked under the lavender was a final thank you from them to their customer. Mind you, the flowers weren't Dad's style – if anything, he'd be more likely to have jugs of apple branches. But, I just can't see any other connection.' She nodded as if ticking one mystery off her list.

'I don't know. I mean it would be a bit presumptuous to put a note on a customer's coffin, wouldn't it?' Stuart said. He shrugged before changing the subject. 'You must be enjoying catching up with old friends again. How long do you think you'll stay?'

'I'm not sure. Now there's Dad's estate to sort out and that will probably take a few months to go through the channels. I haven't been involved in this type of thing before. Mum just left everything to Dad when she passed.

In the meantime, the will is being read next Friday which Vivien is returning for. She's worried Dad left Pepper Farm solely to Patrick.'

Stuart winced. 'That will be interesting, but hopefully HP did the right thing by all his kids. Pepper Farm is a beautiful property so it will be tricky to work out and keep everybody happy, no matter what the will might say. Would you buy the others out, do you think?'

Without thinking, Mallory replied, 'I can certainly afford to. Oh ...'

'Sorry, it's none of my business. I just remember how you used to love racing around the orchard, but it would be a fair amount of upkeep. No doubt your brother pays someone to do it out of HP's account. And it depends on where you want to live too.' He lifted the cup and then realised it was empty. 'Shall we have another one and wait for the rain to ease?'

Mallory nodded. Stuart's reference to their childhood had thrown her, flashes of them together in the orchard surfacing. They would sneak under the low branches with a blanket and spend many happy hours talking, kissing, and hoping HP didn't find them. Often her school dress would be damp with the twilight dew when she snuck back inside. In spring, when the bees buzzed above them between clusters of blossoms the two of them would whisper to each other about their dreams, of leaving Appletree Hill to see the world together. Then they had sealed their devotion with the first hint of summer.

As if he felt her gazing at his back, Stuart glanced over his shoulder and sent her a warm smile. Like a wisp of smoke, it curled across the other patrons and landed on her skin, the sensation lingering as he turned back to give their order. Mallory laughed as he squeezed between the tables on his return, sucking in his stomach to ease through.

'I probably shouldn't have had that danish,' he said, gripping his waistline.

His light-heartedness encouraged Mallory to feel relaxed, even cheeky. 'Oh, I think you look pretty good for an old fellow.'

'As do you, Mallory. It's good to see you again,' he softly replied. 'I can't believe I'm this age with grown-up children. Most of the time I feel twenty again. Well, maybe thirty.'

Mallory laughed. 'I don't think I'll ever feel twenty again, and I don't know that I want to.'

Stuart gave a brief nod. 'I'm glad I grew up in the country though, aren't you? There was a certain freedom, a connection to nature.'

'Your parents were a lot more liberal than mine – you could pretty well do what you liked,' Mallory replied. 'But yes, it was an interesting time without city pressures. But then, I guess the flipside is that when the opportunity came, I was more than ready to leave, to travel with a girlfriend, go to college.'

The time flew by over their second round of coffees, the conversation easy as they dissected old times – the good, the bad, the funny, the disappointing.

'Each season has a reason they say,' Mallory said.

'And on that profound point, we should brave a visit to Nellie who is definitely in her final season,' he said, the hitch in his voice not going unnoticed.

'IT IS strange being here without seeing Dad,' Mallory said

as she leaned back into the car seat and looked at Hillview's entrance.

'Why don't I drop you home and I'll come back,' Stuart suggested. He reached across, wrapping his fingers around Mallory's hands gripped in her lap. 'It was insensitive of me to suggest you come.'

'Not at all. Let's go and brighten Nellie's day.'

Although Mallory had only met Harold's close carers once, they recognised her and extended further condolences. The manager emerged as well, giving Mallory the chance to enquire if all the paperwork was complete and if any outstanding expenses needed to be paid. Her heart gave a kick when they passed Harold's old room, another nameplate already in place.

'There's a waiting list so no room is left empty for long,' Stuart said kindly, noting her surprise. As they continued down the wide, deserted corridor, an occasional raspy cough could be heard, plus the faint sounds of a guitar.

'That music sounds like it's coming from Mum's room. She must have the radio or TV on,' Stuart said.

Mallory tilted her head, listening to the tune closely. With a start, just as Stuart entered Nellie's room, she remembered where she'd heard it before. Perhaps Keith was practising his composition by playing for the elderly.

'Guy ...'

The music stopped abruptly. 'Dad!'

With Stuart blocking the doorway, Mallory stood in the corridor, confused by what she was hearing. A room alarm lit up further down the hallway – Mallory's subconscious hoped the occupant was alright.

'What are you doing here?' she heard Stuart ask as he finally moved forward.

Mallory eased inside the doorway, unsure if she was

imposing on a private moment. She was still confused by the name Stuart had called her neighbour. Nellie dozed in her wheelchair.

Keith had stopped playing, turning to place his guitar against the wall. When he turned back, his eyes flicked from Stuart to Mallory and back again. 'Mallory?'

'Hello, Keith,' Mallory said.

Stuart spun towards Mallory. 'Do you two know each other? Why are you calling him Keith?' Surprise and questions mingled behind his eyes.

'Because that's what I told her my name was.'

Mallory found her voice but was still unsure if she should be part of the scene at all. 'What is your name then – Guy?'

He nodded, looking somewhat embarrassed. 'I said Keith, after Keith Richard. You know, the guitarist with The Rolling Stones.'

Mallory nodded. 'I know who Keith Richard, Richards is. But why ...'

Stuart leant to say hello to his mother who had stirred at the sound of voices.

Guy stared at his father. 'This is awkward.'

Stuart crossed his arms. 'How do you know each other? Mallory, if you knew he was my son, why didn't you say something?'

As Guy stood and faced his father, Mallory shook her head, waving her hands in front of her in a gesture of not having known a thing. She opened her mouth to reply, but Guy stepped in first.

'Don't jump to conclusions. Again. Mallory has no idea who I am or why I'm here,' Guy insisted.

Their attention was diverted to Nellie as she started to shuffle in her seat.

'She's been perfectly fine whilst I've been playing to her for the past half hour,' Guy said defensively as he gently wrapped her fingers in his hand 'It's okay, Gran.'

Of course, Nellie would be his grandmother. 'Why don't I take Nellie for a bit of a stroll down to the lounge and back?' Mallory offered.

'Thanks. Good idea.' Stuart said as he released the brake and wheeled his mother to the door for her to take over. For a brief moment, their hands touched, although she doubted Stuart noticed.

Mallory sent Guy a sympathetic smile, caught by Stuart as she turned. She pushed away the slight tickle of guilt.

It was very tempting to dawdle, to try to catch their words but Stuart eased the door shut after her. A carer walked past and nodded, so Mallory kept walking. Her head spun with what she'd just witnessed. So, the musician squatter next door was Stuart's troublesome son, Guy – this visit back to Appletree Hill was becoming more complicated by the minute. She hoped he was explaining to his father that she had no idea of their relationship; even more, she hoped neither man presumed she had been trading their comments about each other as she was unwittingly caught in the middle.

As Nellie's breathing settled into the rhythmic puffs of an elderly's sleep, Mallory slumped onto a couch alongside the wheelchair in the plush corner lounge. She needed to take a moment, but the first thought that came to mind was how she hadn't realised Keith, or rather Guy, was Stuart's son. She could see they shared the same cheeky wit, the same laconic way of walking, and very similar facial features now that she'd seen them together. Why on earth had he lied about his name to a stranger – had it been before or after she'd commented that she had grown up in the town, or that he wasn't meant to be living in the house? What an amazing coincidence to visit Stuart's mother just when Guy was also here, but as Bridie would say, 'sliding doors.'

Mallory checked her watch, conscious of Nellie's routine, presuming it must be close to the residents' early lunch hour. Stuart met her half way. Frowning, he wheeled his mother into her room, to leave her with the waiting carer.

Stuart rubbed the back of his neck. 'Guy says I owe you an apology.'

On a whim, Mallory looped her hand through his arm as they walked towards the exit. 'Not at all, although I'm still at a bit of a loss as to all the secrecy. Has Guy left already? We could have all come back to Fruit Flan for a long walk, a drink, or something.'

The short laugh from Stuart was steeped more in frustration than humour. 'I doubt having a drink with his old man would have been on Guy's agenda.' Mallory was sure she also caught a tinge of regret in his words.

As Stuart walked with his head down, obviously deep in thought, she let the silence linger between them. Guy couldn't have filled his father in on many details in the limited amount of time she had been gone. On the short drive home, she contemplated just how far she should go with her opinion or observations, but decided to wait for Stuart to take the lead.

'I do apologise for my hasty comments,' he said as they parked at the front of the B&B.

'You're welcome to come in anyway,' Mallory ventured as Stuart opened her car door. An old-fashioned but rather lovely gesture in her opinion.

'I'd best be heading back to the hotel,' he said. 'Um, I need to go over the girls' plans again.'

Mallory doubted that very much. 'Okay. It was nice to see Nellie, if only for a moment,' she added, offering the opportunity for Stuart to open any conversation but he just muttered 'thanks for coming'. As her key met the front door lock, she turned to see him sitting in his car, the engine still idling.

Through the windscreen spun a silent 'come on then, let's chat' from Mallory, a sigh in agreement from Stuart. He turned the car off, strode up the stairs, and followed her inside.

'Is it too early to open that bottle of wine?' he asked.

'Sounds like a great idea; it will help dilute all that caffeine,' she replied, nodding towards a bottle of red sitting on the kitchen bench.

'And surprises at the nursing home. Who would have thought,' Stuart said as he undid the screw top, picked two glasses off the shelf, and wandered back to the front veranda.

Well, at least he is mellowing, Mallory thought. I might be able to broach the subject after all. By the time she had tidied herself up, grabbed a wool rug each, and joined him, he had poured the wine and was staring across the fence towards the not-so-abandoned house next door.

'So, he told you that he is my noisy squatter?' Mallory paused as she passed him a rug. 'Oh, I don't suppose you actually own that house, do you?'

Stuart shook his head, extending his glass to hers in cheers. 'No such luck, in fact I'm not sure who does. But the fact that my adult son is squatting and told you a fake name! I just don't get it.'

Mallory decided to go all in. 'Even though he's

squatting, he's doing work around the place, tidying it up. He's planted a vegetable garden too. He's a great fellow Stuart, from the little I know.'

'What exactly do you know?' Stuart didn't turn to her, his stare lingering on the bushes dividing him from his son. A slight edge had crept into his words, but Mallory was no longer someone to be intimidated. Her teaching career had taught her how to placate many confused or upset students, as well as their parents.

But she had to tread carefully. 'Well, he said he comes here to see someone in town, so Nellie confirms that. I heard him playing the same song he was playing to her today. It's his composition and I rather like it, don't you?'

'Why didn't he just tell me this was where he was living, and what's wrong with a hotel?' was Stuart's reply.

He obviously wasn't going to be swayed by Mallory's attempts to compliment his son. 'I can't answer the first question, but perhaps the answer to the second question is because of Rooster,' she suggested.

'Who the hell is Rooster?' Stuart threw his arms in the air as if this was the final straw to trying to work out his son's life and motivations.

Mallory made her eyes wide as if to say, 'don't you know?' 'His dog. A staffy who is rather gorgeous I might add, even though he made me incredibly muddy one stormy night. Oh, it's his girlfriend's dog, isn't it?'

'I have no idea,' Stuart muttered. 'And why you'd be getting muddy because of my son's dog makes me think you know him more than you're saying.'

'For heaven's sake, Stuart. Don't be ridiculous. He said you disliked dogs anyway.'

Mallory was tempted to walk next door and summon Guy herself, to drag him back to the cottage and leave the two men to sort themselves out. Without her. When she glanced across at him, Stuart was shaking his head.

'I don't dislike dogs. You might recall I was attacked by one when I was young, so I guess I'm wary of them but that got misinterpreted. Why is communicating with kids so complicated?'

Mallory glanced at the old scar on his chin. She used to run her finger along it, tenderly calling it his touch of Indiana Jones.

'It's a while since eating that pastry so I'll get some nibbles to go with the wine,' Mallory offered. As she gathered cheese, biscuits, olives and grapes onto a platter, she tried to fathom how the father and son could have strayed so far from each other. Stuart had mentioned Guy wasn't happy about the divorce, but also that his ex-wife sided with Guy over his musical career aspirations. It wasn't any of her business, but she liked her neighbour and had to face that she also liked Stuart. But any more revelations of the Forbes family story would have to come from this man.

Stuart was leaning on the balustrade above the garden, his wine glass gripped between his hands. Mallory placed the platter on the table between their chairs. Weak autumn sunlight found its way through the remainder of the day's cloud and sent a milky apricot filter across the pastures. An eerie cow's call echoed somewhere in the distance, and closer to them the bushes rustled with an animal making its way home.

'So beautiful,' Stuart said. 'Look, you can see some kangaroos across the road there. That's the downside of driving at twilight – they can jump out in front of you so quickly, either roll under your car or bounce across the bonnet and windscreen.'

'Bridie and I were saying how weird it felt to be sitting

on Fruit Flan's veranda, imagining Vern and Doris welcoming us, and not being someone who had just rented it on Air B&B.' Mallory smiled. 'Despite all the family dramas, I'm enjoying being back.'

'Not that it's any of my business, but if you can afford to buy Pepper Farm, as you said, then why not buy this place? It played such an important part of your early life and it's clear you're still attached to it.'

She turned to face him, unsure whether enough water had gone under that bloody bridge that needed crossing. 'I'll need to see what pans out with Dad's estate and the farm first, but I must admit I'd never even thought of doing that. Um, I have a few final things to sort out with John too.'

She paused. 'I actually won some money in the lottery a while back which will make things interesting as he's still trying to get his hands on some of it. Not that he can apparently.' She laughed. 'I'm rambling, I'm sorry. I just get nervous when talking about money.'

'Well, we'll change the subject then,' Stuart said, a slight frown interrupting his friendly suggestion. 'Should I go and see Guy? I can't ignore how much I appreciate him visiting Mum, and I just know that deep inside Nellie loves him being there. She always had a soft spot for him and she did seem to like his music. I got distracted by the bizarre reference to Keith Richards, but I guess I should have thanked him today.'

Mallory shuffled closer as she turned her back against the balustrade, her shoulder resting gently against his arm. She turned her face up towards his, needing to see his eyes. 'Yes, I do think you should visit him and soon. He's your son,' she replied softly.

Stuart's hand was warm as it gently cupped behind her neck then brought her face to his. His lips tasted of red wine. As her eyes closed, she could feel his body turn towards her, their lips not breaking as he reached for her waist and drew her against him. Mallory balanced her wine glass on the railing, her arms reaching around his back, her palms resting against his leather jacket. Stuart's other arm looped around her shoulders as he held his glass carefully in the air.

A lifetime seemed to speed past as she relived his kiss. Gentle at first, then more urgent as her lips parted and they sought each other as they had as teenagers. Stuart's touch was tender as his hand moved across her back, underneath her jumper, pulling her even firmer against his chest. When the kiss broke, he pecked her smile before running his cheek against her forehead. It felt bristly and comforting as Mallory fought the fine pinprick of her unwanted tears.

Stuart eased away, bringing his arm and glass back to the safety of his side, but the familiarity of his hand remained on the small of her back. He searched her eyes, a worried expression relaying silent words.

Embarrassed, Mallory gave a short laugh and flicked at the one tear that had managed to roll down her cheek. 'Must be the night air,' she joked. Reluctantly, she eased her arms from Stuart's body and picked up her glass, took a sip.

'Mm, that brought back sweet memories,' Stuart murmured. 'Or did it just add to your Appletree dramas?'

'Certainly not the latter,' Mallory replied, not quite sure if she believed her words. She just knew it felt so good to be wanted, as if she was being cushioned from the world. She quickly rose on tiptoe and kissed him quickly on his parted lips. Her breath was on the verge of panting, her heart rate well over where it normally sat.

Stuart brushed her hair away from her face, a cheeky grin spreading across his own, uncertainty lingering behind it. 'I'd better leave you here, with the ghosts of Vern and Doris. Until another time. Thank you for your advice, the wine, the cheese we didn't eat, and that delectable kiss.'

Mallory let out a deep breath as she watched him stroll to his car. He sat watching her before flicking his fingers in goodbye with a cheeky smile to follow. She would have loved to be able to read his thoughts at that moment. As he drove away, she quietly called to watch out for kangaroos on the road, wishing he would come back.

Chapter Nineteen

HER THOUGHTS KEPT TUMBLING BACK to Stuart's lips, to their shared kiss. *And where do you think that will lead, Mallory Campbell?*

Little sparks of – was it joy or arousal, or perhaps both – flicked throughout her body. Stuart's hands on her, the strength in his embrace, the kindness in those searching eyes as they had gazed down into hers were happily replayed in her mind over and over. She had given up hope of sharing intimacy again with someone special, more specifically of having mind-blowing sex. Could that be possible? She couldn't deny that she yearned for companionship, but only with the right person. She would never settle for someone just to have company, not after the last year of working hard on enjoying her own again.

And trust – would she allow herself to trust again? Her intentions were authentic, but who was to say she wouldn't pull away at the last minute. Particularly with someone from her past. That had been the attraction of potentially 'letting loose in Italy', as Zarni had hoped she would. She could have casual sex with handsome Italians and no one would ever know – but that choice just wasn't in her DNA.

As Stuart was now back in Sydney for a couple of days, Mallory decided to drive into Melbourne for the day and spoil herself with a shopping spree. After parking at the Arts Centre, she wandered across the bridge spanning the murky Yarra River and along the windy city streets. As the department store escalator sailed past the travel department, she smiled, recalling the cornflower blue suitcases she'd purchased on a whim. Her life had been blown apart only hours later – despite the lingering sludge of betrayal, it seemed so long ago now. She stepped off and strode into the lingerie department and did some serious damage to her credit card on La Perla.

Bridie had recommended coffee and cake at the popular Tea Rooms, so after enjoying a stroll through side streets and arcades, Mallory waited in the café's short queue for a table. Lingerie and the incredible cakes on offer didn't complement each other, but she happily nestled into her seat with a pot of tea and a slice of fruit-adorned red velvet cake and reflected on where to head next. Department store clothes were the same everywhere she found, but she needed to upgrade from her usual jeans and shirt ensemble. Between sips of Earl Grey, she googled where to find a selection of locally made independent labels. The nearby laneways appeared to be full of different designers, so off she went.

An hour later, feeling like Julia Roberts in *Pretty Woman* with large glossy shopping bags hanging from each hand, Mallory made her way back to her car. It hadn't escaped her that her sudden need for new clothes had popped up since Stuart's lingering attention.

When her cell buzzed in her bag, she didn't have a

spare hand so let it go to voicemail. Once at her car, she checked it – seeing a missed call from Stuart, she quickly called him back.

'Stuart, sorry I missed you. I'm in Melbourne and well, couldn't get to the phone quickly enough.'

'Are you at an exhibition? I heard there's a good Banksy one due to start.'

'No, to be honest I should have checked the galleries' programs but I got waylaid shopping instead which has been enormous fun. It's ages since I visited Melbourne, although it's a bit quiet in the CBD; not as I remember it.'

'There's still a hangover from offices closing during Covid unfortunately, but it's slowly returning.' There was a slight pause as if he wondered if she needed to play around that line of small talk. He continued when she kept silent. 'I'll be heading back to Appletree and thought we might have dinner Thursday night. If you're free that is.'

A small smile tweaked Mallory's lip. 'I'd love to.'

'Great. I'll book at the French place in the square and pick you up at seven?'

'Sounds good. See you then.'

Mallory turned on the ignition. *I knew these new clothes would come in handy.*

THE NURSERY CAFÉ had been closed whenever Mallory had passed it over the past few days with a sign of apology propped at the door the only indication it may re-open soon. Rooster was the beneficiary of her extra time.

The stocky little dog hit her like a cannonball as Mallory walked around the side of the neighbouring house.

Little tail wagging at a million miles an hour, Rooster rubbed against her legs making her feel welcome. Until Guy appeared at the door.

'Hi, Guy. Feel like a walk with Rooster?'

'Why?'

'Why not?' Mallory couldn't keep the sigh out of her voice – why the drama more to the point? 'Oh come on, Guy. I wasn't aware you were Stuart's son, or he was your father, or whatever. I got as big a shock as he did when I saw you in Nellie's room.'

'It just seemed a bit cosy when you both appeared to visit Gran,' he said, remaining inside the screen door. 'I suppose he told you how I'm throwing my life away by pursuing music, that I don't have any financial security.'

'I'm not your parent, Guy, but I did a lot of the talking, saying I liked your music, that you were fixing up the garden here ...'

'I can fight my own battles.'

Mallory ventured to a cane chair and took a seat, sensing she would need to spend a little time around the subject with her neighbour. Rooster dropped at her feet as she scratched his ears. They both looked at Guy and waited. Reluctantly he emerged and plopped onto the other chair.

A small spider was busily spinning a web, its total focus set between the gutter and veranda post. Mallory watched its escapades for a moment then took a deep breath and began. 'I knew your dad when I was in school. In fact, he was my first boyfriend.' She sensed Guy shifting uncomfortably.

'He was the sports jock and well, I guess I was the nerd. We broke up towards the end of the year and went our separate ways. We both married. I live in Brisbane but came back to Appletree Hill to stay for a while to see my dad who, as you know, has just passed.'

'Your dad was at Hillview too,' Guy stated. 'I was waiting in reception and overheard a conversation about his funeral; hence the flowers I left for you. Is seeing your Dad in such a facility why you think nursing homes are okay?'

She nodded. 'He was in a different home to start with, but I liked Hillview better. I thought they'd take better care of him,' Mallory replied. 'I remember Nellie so well. She was such a gracious, attractive lady, much loved by everyone and I would only wish the best for her in her old age. She seemed to like your music.'

Guy sniffed. 'At least someone does.'

'Oh, that's not true. I like it and I've said as much. Hopefully, you've got more than one song in your repertoire though,' Mallory teased. When Guy laughed, his shoulders relaxed and at last Rooster stretched out and started to snore.

'Yes, I've got quite a few tunes.' He looked sideways at her. 'I'm thinking of performing at the open mic session at the restaurant in Minnette Cove next week.'

Mallory clapped her hands. 'Fabulous. Can I come? Can we come?'

Guy's expression clouded. 'I'm not sure about Dad, but you're welcome.'

Tiny steps, Mallory, tiny steps. She gave Rooster a final pat and then stood to leave, resisting passing on advice that perhaps he could invite Stuart himself.

'Thanks, Mallory. I didn't mean to be rude,' Guy muttered, scratching the back of his neck like his father.

'No problem. Oh, and Guy? What if you wrote a song about a little boy, or a girl called Daisy, who set out to have grand adventures with a pet emu?'

A frown creased across his brow as he squinted into the middle distance. 'I don't know why I would. That's not my bag at all, but I seem to remember ... Hey, do you know those books?'

The warmth of acknowledgement spread through Mallory's body. She nodded. 'I wrote them, so understand the importance of a creative outlet. See you at the gig.'

As she wandered back to Fruit Flan, she rang Bridie to divulge Stuart had contacted her with a dinner invitation. 'He's in Sydney at the moment but suggested the French restaurant in the square.'

She laughed at her friend's response. 'Oh, wonderful. The girls will be pleased too – not that we were talking about you. You and Stuart I mean. Well, we were but it was all positive.'

'I have to be at the lawyers in Freestone first thing Friday morning for the reading of Dad's will, so it will be a good distraction.' She smiled inwardly, recalling how her heart had tripped with pleasure when Stuart had called with the invitation.

'That will be pretty straightforward, won't it?' Bridie asked.

'I imagine so,' Mallory replied. She suspected she was lying to herself though as a chill inexplicably coursed through her body.

WHEN HAD she become so unsure of something as simple as what to wear to dinner? The short mirror behind her bedroom door didn't help, as she moved back and forth trying to see her full length. One hand held a simple, long-sleeved knitted dress, but the black felt too formal and it would mean stockings – did anyone wear stockings these days? From the other hand hung a new dusty pink and grey silk blouse teamed with her new light wool dove grey trousers; together with a pair of sterling hoops and bracelets it would have to do. At the last minute, she swapped flats for heels and undid another button on her blouse, adjusting to the warm haze of anticipation that had settled around her.

When Stuart's car's headlights approached, she opened the front door, instantly hit by a cold wind that had found its way from the distant bay and across the paddocks. Quickly she ran to grab a wrap. Stuart was stepping inside as she returned – so much for a confident, relaxed welcome.

'Ready?' he asked with a wide grin.

Mallory's heart gave a little lurch as she wrapped the shawl around her shoulders and returned his smile. He leant in, one hand on her arm, and gently kissed her cheek. 'You look, ooh, and smell, fabulous.'

'Thank you, but I think I've underestimated the chill. I'll be fine once inside.' She kicked herself for sounding like a fussy old woman, so shot Stuart a dazzling smile. 'Thank you.'

The ten-minute drive passed with Stuart sharing reviews he'd checked for the restaurant and Mallory assuring him it sounded perfect. She would have loved to know how he was feeling; if he was excited, nervous, calm. It probably didn't matter if you forgot about 'the kiss', after all, they were just two old friends having dinner together. But the kiss had changed everything. In Mallory's mind anyway.

As Stuart spoke with the restaurant's front of house, Mallory ran her eye over his charcoal-toned trousers, patterned shirt and tailored jacket. His hair was slicked back on the sides. *Very nice Mr Forbes*. The French Table's rustic atmosphere was very welcoming, with delicious aromas from the kitchen mingling with the warmth of a corner open fire. The country-style décor of crockery-laden sideboards, damask tablecloths and serviettes drew on Mallory's distant memories of lazy days she had spent in little French villages.

'Champagne?' Stuart asked.

'Absolutely. This place is gorgeous isn't it, so cosy. I must say I'm rather hungry too,' Mallory replied as she opened the menu. She squinted slightly, trying to disguise the fact she'd forgotten to bring her glasses. 'Although snails are not going to happen.'

Stuart laughed. 'I'd offer you my glasses, but they're for distance so wouldn't be much good. But back to the menu, apparently their duck is a specialty, so I will try that. We could share the terrine de foie gras; unless you'd like one all to yourself?'

Mallory flicked to the desserts. 'If we share an entree, then I can lash out with ... ooh passionfruit Crème Brûlée. The fish with lemon butter sauce might be my pick.'

As Stuart gave their entrée and main dish orders and their champagne was poured, Mallory glanced over her shoulder and around the restaurant. Only a few small tables remained empty. Her eyes settled back on Stuart. She liked how he'd aged; faint laugh lines around his eyes that creased into deeper grooves when he laughed, the way he still dipped his head and looked under his brows when unsure. His athletic youth had paid off, probably with untended injuries but outwardly a body that had remained solid and fit. She could spy part of it between his shirt's open lapels.

'Cheers,' Stuart said, watching her over the rim of his

flute. The flicker of candlelight caught in his eyes like midnight fireflies.

Mallory watched his lips touch the glass, a slight buzz rolling within her stomach as she remembered how soft they'd been on her own mouth. 'This is nice. Thank you for suggesting it, Stuart.'

He nodded, hesitating. 'Should we get the subject of Guy out of the way first?'

'The subject of Guy?' Mallory tilted her head as she repeated his phrase, although she was well aware of where he was heading. 'He's your son, Stuart. I don't want to interfere.'

'Are you going to tell me you haven't been in to see him since being with Nellie?' His tone was friendly, more teasing than accusing.

Her surprise at his accurate presumption was outweighed by amusement. She gave a cheeky gasp. 'Maybe, maybe not. Why is it important? Have you a chest full of dastardly family secrets you want to keep hidden?'

Stuart laughed. 'No, not at all.'

The terrine was placed in front of them. Stuart waited while Mallory slid some onto her plate, added a small gherkin and a few crisp slices of baguette then helped himself. 'You know what, it's not important and I don't think I want to go there at the moment. Sorry.' he sighed. 'Tell me what you've been up to – are you okay since HP's funeral?'

'Oh golly, I'm not sure I want to go there! The meeting with the lawyer is tomorrow morning so ask me after that.'

'Okay.' He gazed at her over the edge of his glass, his lips paused on its rim. Slowly he took a sip and then stated, 'So, you're divorced, living in Brisbane when you're not in Appletree. And an unemployed woman of means.'

Mallory laughed, tilting her glass towards him. If the comment had come from anyone else, she would have glossed over it, but Stuart's cheeky grin betrayed his knowledge.

'Ah yes, Harold's well-known opinion of women not earning their keep. I always thought it was rather odd, considering the era that Mum and Dad were brought up in. He always wanted Mum to be home in front of the stove and raise us kids yet made references to not knowing what she did all day. And of course, the subject of money always brought a chill to the Pepper Farm air; any possibility of her returning to work to have her own income would have been disastrous. Mind you, Mum was happy with her life.' Mallory frowned. 'I presume. We never really had those kinds of conversations.'

The waitress presented their main meals and topped up their wine. 'Thank you,' Mallory said. 'He used to say 'woman of unknown means' too as a dig from when I earned money from my books – he never understood how something as, to quote "so simple to do", could be an income, yet it was proof I was earning my keep. John had the same attitude.'

Stuart leant in. 'Well, it's certainly not an opinion I would share.' He smiled. 'My folks were always pretty liberal too. Remember Mum had that job at the local accountant's office for years to help pay for my sports gear and trips. You know, I still remember HP taking me aside when we were dating and saying, "Stuart, you've got to plan your life early and work hard". I really had no idea what he was on about at that age.'

He took a bite of the duck. 'This is delicious. What's wrong? Did you need another salad, more pommes frites?'

Mallory shook her head and picked up her cutlery then

paused. 'There it is again. That phrase that Olivia told me – I couldn't place it but then Vivien repeated it at the funeral, and you've just referred to it. Dad used to say it.' She shrugged. 'No matter.'

A gentle buzz from fellow diners and a faint rendition of La Vie en Rose accompanied them savouring their meals. Mallory's body felt soft, relaxed, with any worries of what the next day's meeting would bring well and truly suppressed.

'Did you continue to play football, you know for district teams?' Mallory asked.

'I did for a while, but the old body gave way after a few years. Too many injuries.' He rolled his shoulders as if backing up his statement. 'I was thinking about both Harold and Nellie being in the same nursing home at the same time. Mum wouldn't have been aware of him, but I wonder if your dad recognised her and spoke with her,' Stuart said.

Mallory paused, thinking about Stuart's comment. 'I doubt it. He wasn't happy to be there and stayed in his room most of the time, I think. Apparently, Patrick hadn't visited and presumably Vivien hadn't made contact, which is sad.'

'It's a real shame,' Stuart agreed. 'I'd like to think my kids will visit me when I'm old, remember me when I'm gone.'

'I'm sure they will.' Mallory placed her serviette on her lap and took a sip of her wine. 'Well, that was amazing. We might have to wait a while before dessert though' She stood to go to the bathroom. 'I'll be back in a minute.'

It had been a delightful evening, with them sharing many laughs and memories as they avoided any further mention of Guy or the elephant in the room. Their kiss. Was she playing it too cool, too much of a friend – she didn't know, nor did she feel confident in questioning it further.

Yes, there had been a small amount of flirting from them both but probably the kiss had been a heart-fluttering one-off. With a sigh of disappointment, she reapplied her lipstick and then headed back to the table, prepared to let things run their natural course. Despite her body yearning for more.

When she saw Stuart's unwavering gaze, she followed his line of sight across the room to pinpoint a table obscured behind her chair. As the waitress moved to the side, Mallory gasped. Vivien and John sat with their heads close together over the little votive candle, eyes locked. John was rubbing his finger along Vivien's hand as she giggled. Panic rose through Mallory's body as she hustled to her seat, eager to turn her back on the couple.

Stuart leant forward. 'Oh, Mallory. I thought I recognised Vivien and by the look on your face, I presume it is her. And John?'

Mallory nodded, taking a drink of water. 'Did they see me?' she whispered, not daring to peek back over her shoulder.

Stuart shook his head. 'They've looked around the room, but she can't have recognised me. Have I aged that much?'

Mallory coughed into her water at his attempt to lighten the situation. 'No, you're still very handsome,' she stuttered without thinking.

John glanced across as she continued to cough, but the restaurant was dimly lit and Mallory's back was to him so his attention refocused on Vivien.

Mallory gave her body a slight shake, taking back some of her composure. 'He's here for the reading tomorrow. But it's beneficiaries only so he won't be in the room.' Mallory paused. 'Shit. How dare she bring him, how dare he come to support her.' Tears pricked her eyes as she cleared her throat. 'Sorry Stuart.' The last thing she wanted was for the couple to spoil their evening together.

Stuart reached for her hand and held it tightly. 'Don't you dare apologise. I agree, it's totally tasteless of them. But you have me, Mallory, don't forget that. You know, the handsome, aging bloke?'

She sent him a weak smile, although warmed at the cheeky twinkle in his eye.

'Now, what are our options? Sit and have another wine, regain our appetite for dessert, or march out of here as though we own the place?' Stuart asked.

Mallory placed her other hand over his, like the hand-stack game from their youth, and thought for a moment. When she opted for the last suggestion, Stuart gave a firm nod and signed off on the bill. With false bravado, Mallory stood, picked up her shawl, and walked towards the exit. She paused ever so slightly as Stuart held open the door for her, sending Vivien a look she wasn't quite sure of, but it certainly wasn't sisterly. Out of the corner of her eye, she was surprised to see John snatch his hand away from Vivien's. Mallory and Stuart left The French Table as though they owned it and headed to the car.

'So, that's John,' Stuart said slowly as if he'd spent the last decades conjuring an image of Mallory's husband. Mallory knew that wasn't the case.

'Yep.'

Stuart kept his thoughts to himself on the drive home, allowing Mallory to process hers. He parked at Fruit Flan and strode around the bonnet to open Mallory's car door before wrapping his arm around her shoulder and hustling them both through the crisp air.

Her heart leaping like a frog around her chest, she

rummaged in her purse for the key. Turning, Mallory leant against the door and looked up into Stuart's face, holding his gaze with her own. 'I can think of more exciting things to do than think about my ex-husband and my sister, can't you?' she murmured against his lips.

Chapter Twenty

STUART EASED her into the warmth of the cottage, kicking the door closed behind them. His lips lingered at the corners of her mouth as he lowered her shawl and then flicked it to the side. Mallory's body tingled with anticipation as his arms wrapped around her, tugging her against his chest. His hands moved swiftly, earnestly, in circles across her back as their lips parted against each other's.

Mallory's fingers interlaced through Stuart's curls as their kiss deepened. Stuart shrugged off his jacket, Mallory flinching at the absence of his touch. Inch by inch they shuffled towards her bedroom, buttons being undone with every step. The bedroom glowed a warm yellow from a bedside light Mallory had left on, unaware of the important role it would play later that evening.

No words had been spoken but, to Mallory, nothing felt more real, more needed than this intimacy.

The bed creaked as he sat on its edge and brought Mallory to stand between his legs. She tugged his shirt from his trousers and rolled it back over shoulders that had obviously seen many years of labouring. As she suspected, he was still in great shape, muscled and tanned. Mallory ran a fingernail down his chest, remembering the first time she had done that same gesture whilst snuggling between sand dunes – she had been just as nervous then as she was now but for different reasons. Stuart let her blouse join his crumpled shirt on the floor; deftly unclipped her bra and eased it away from her body.

Surely he could hear her heart as it buzzed within her, as if caught in a field of electricity. She waited, hesitant to gauge his reaction as his eyes devoured her body. Warm hands cupped her breasts as he leant forward, gently kissing each nipple before running his tongue around its edges. As his hands moved to her buttocks to pull her even closer he looked up at her – was it possible for those green eyes to now be an intense black, could desire do that? Mallory hoped so as she offered a smile to the boy who had been her first lover.

'You're beautiful,' Stuart whispered. 'I hope you know that.'

'Thank you,' she whispered, taking the compliment. She silently thanked La Perla's pearl and lace range as he undid her belt and eased her trousers over her hips to puddle at her feet. She stepped out of her heels and, placing her hands on Stuart's shoulders eased him back onto the covers and undressed him down to his boxers.

'Let's get comfortable.' His voice was husky, sexy.

As light escaped through the lampshade and danced across the ceiling, Mallory settled amongst the cool, oversized pillows. Stuart slowly lowered his body over her. A gentle breeze whistled around the windows, as if blowing wishes their way as Stuart kissed her passionately. Mallory pulled his whole body onto her, his hardness now pressed against her stomach. His face was warm as she held it between her palms, their eyes locked. As she smoothed her hands down his arms and between their bodies, feeling his length, a small gasp escaped his parted lips. Mallory smiled with his response, with his pleasure and what was to come.

'Shall we dance?' he murmured into her ear, making her give a small laugh of recognition. It had been their sign to each other as teenagers, when they had yearned to escape friends or family, to have time alone.

'Oh, yes,' she sighed, her breathing shallow, her hips tilted.

His boxers and Mallory's panties hit the floor and Stuart eased her legs apart. She reached for him, running her hand along his shaft, directing him into her. He didn't need any help entering, nor continuing a long, easy rhythm as Mallory's hips rose further to meet him.

A LAZY MIX of post-sex pleasure and amused surprise lit Mallory's reflection in the bathroom mirror after she had quietly slipped out of bed. *I'm like a Cheshire cat preening after some naughty act of rebellion.* She fluffed her hair and ran her eyes over her naked body. Yes, there were lumps and bumps but she couldn't deny how liberated she felt. Her lips were red from Stuart's kisses, her cheeks the same from his rough cheeks; her legs deliciously heavy while her whole body yearned for more. But what happened now?

Shivering, she tiptoed back to the bed and slipped between the warm sheets. Stuart stirred, opening his eyes slightly, murmured 'Okay?' then drifted back to sleep. Mallory lay on her side listening to his easy breathing, watching the flutter of his long eyelashes as he dreamed, she hoped sweet dreams. Perhaps he was reliving, as she was, their earnest lovemaking, their tender strokes of each other's bodies until the cool night air had forced them under the covers.

Now, the silence was heavy around her forming a comforting cocoon as she nestled a little lower. Not even a possum scurried across the roof. It was as though the countryside was allowing her space to enjoy this post-coital moment, to revel in its unexpected joy and possible meaning.

Had it merely been a needy reaction to seeing Vivien and John earlier in the evening? After all, it was the first time she'd witnessed them together. No, deep down she knew that Stuart had been playing at the fringes of her memory and thoughts on and off for years. And hadn't he shown with every piercing gaze, with every caress and sigh that she had possibly been on his mind too?

Things happened in threes, didn't they? Did it apply to life's surprises as well, when one course suddenly veers away in another direction? Because if it did, she had got the trifecta. One, winning the lottery. Two, John and Vivien's affair. Three, having sex with her old boyfriend.

'What are you thinking about, or shouldn't I ask?'

Stuart's sleepy voice murmured to her across the pillow as his heavy eyelids eased open. He reached out from under the sheets and ran a finger across her creased forehead. Mallory smiled and shuffled closer, relaxing against his chest. His arm rested over her hip, his palm against her bare buttocks pressing her closer.

'I was enjoying how quiet it is, and contemplating ghosts. Perhaps Doris and Vern still walk the halls and witnessed us making love.'

Stuart let out a bark of laughter. 'You're kidding me!'

'I didn't expect this, Stuart. Did you?' Mallory wasn't

sure why she was whispering, but she relished the closeness that still lingered, her words were for him alone even though there was no one else to hear.

'No. But I do have to say that when I saw you again at the nursing home, my heart raced so much that I thought I'd be the one needing care.'

'Well, you hid that very nicely, Mr. Nonchalant.'

'Are you going to tell me there wasn't even a little spark of happiness to see me?' He gently kissed the end of her nose and lingered on her deliciously bruised lips. 'Mmm?'

'I won't deny it,' she teased. 'I just wish my life wasn't so complicated; I just don't know if there's room for any more decision-making. I've got this meeting in a few hours and must face Vivien again and ...'

'Well, how about we just live in the moment? This moment.' Stuart eased her knee onto his hip, his hand then sliding between her legs. 'I could distract you from any dire decisions if you like?'

His touch moistened her in a moment. Mallory gasped and smiled at his innocent expression as he gently massaged her. She closed her eyes with pleasure, obviously having made that difficult decision. As the foggy morning light filtered between the curtains and a rooster crowed somewhere in the distance, their bodies clung together, moving as one until they climaxed.

Chapter Twenty-One

THE LOVERS HAD SAT QUIETLY over coffee and toasted muffins the following morning. At one point Stuart had reached across and taken Mallory's hand and, rubbing his thumb across its back, held her attention in those deep green eyes. His hair was still wet and slicked back from the shower, one grey curl escaping to drop onto his forehead. Mallory thought she had never seen him look so sexy. Well, except when he was stretched above her the previous night. She yearned for him to press his palm to her cheek so she could lean in against his warmth – and he did just that.

His lips tweaked at the corners. 'I know your mind is probably on what the day will bring, but my mine just keeps revisiting last night.'

She smiled. 'It was good wasn't it.' So she wasn't the only one going over and through a range of emotions.

'More than. And I just want you to know that I hope there can be many more, that it wasn't just a one-off.'

'And I want you to know that it wasn't a knee-jerk reaction on my part after seeing John. Our beautiful date would have unfolded just the same.'

As one, they started to laugh. 'Well, that was very Oprah of us,' she said.

Mallory was grateful to have someone calming to talk to apart from her girlfriends, to be able to melt into Stuart's strong embrace. She would have carried on regardless of whether he was around or not, but his presence was a huge comfort just the same; as if her foundations had somehow been strengthened. Once again, she marvelled at how the previous evening had unfurled – one moment she had been eating terrine with a friend, the next they had been sharing a night of romantic passion.

'I probably should be giving you a pep talk, but I know you'll have no trouble handling yourself this morning. Remember that you're all on an equal footing, even though Patrick will be puffed up with importance, no doubt. I've rearranged meetings so I can stay for at least another few days.' He asked her to call him when she was available, then left her with a supportive bear hug and prolonged kiss.

NOW, as she stepped out of the elevator into her father's solicitor's office she summoned Stuart's words of encouragement and took a deep breath to dampen her stomach's butterflies. Patrick was standing, legs astride and hands on hips, regaling the receptionist with some story.

'Ah, here's one of them now,' he announced, his tone light and confident. As he leant in for an air kiss, Mallory smiled across the desk.

'I'm Mallory.'

'And I'm Vivien,' came a voice behind her.

Patrick darted across and repeated his over-zealous

greeting, unaware of Mallory's backstep away from their sister.

The receptionist caught her eye, noting her hesitation. 'Let me show you through to the meeting room and Mr Stephens will join you shortly,' she offered.

As Patrick and Vivien headed for one side of the long conference table, Mallory eased to the other side. A pitcher of water and glasses had been placed down its centre. A small stack of papers sat in front of the end chair. Here we go, she thought as the solicitor came through the door, leaving it ajar. After shaking everyone's hand, he sat with fingers interlaced on the pile.

'Help yourselves to water. We'll just wait a moment,' he directed.

Patrick frowned. 'What for? We're all here.'

'We have one more party to arrive, Mr Pepper.'

'Would anyone like a coffee?' asked the receptionist from the doorway.

'Who? What do you mean? I thought only beneficiaries attended,' Vivien stuttered, ignoring the offer.

Mallory held her gaze on Vivien. Obviously, her sister wasn't as calm as she was pretending to be; perhaps she was wishing John was by her side to give her assurances, a hug. She glanced across at Patrick in time to see his eyes narrow, more with malice than curiosity.

'My thoughts exactly. Who are we waiting on?'

'No coffees thank you, Helen.' The solicitor was keen to downplay their swift reactions. He began to open his folder, to unclip several papers, being careful to keep them out of sight.

Silence curled its way around the group, tripping over the tension surrounding Patrick and Vivien. Mallory was unsure what to think about this unexpected turn of events.

Perhaps Harold had left some money or an item to a local charity. His watch? He had always loved his gold and leather watch, which had been given to him on his 21st birthday by his parents apparently. But it wouldn't be worth anything surely, and Mallory hadn't sited it anywhere. But then she hadn't looked. She smiled to herself realising she had flicked her eyes to Patrick's wrists; he was in the clear as they were bare.

Patrick drummed his fingers on the tabletop. 'I don't ...'

'Aah, here they are,' the solicitor announced as the faint murmur of voices filtered through to those already assembled.

Collectively, Patrick, Vivien and Mallory swivelled sharply towards the open doorway, waiting.

Hettie McMunn shuffled through the door, closely followed by Olivia. Perhaps they knew who would be there, perhaps they didn't but they stopped abruptly like deer caught in headlights.

Patrick and Vivien jumped to their feet, their heads pivoting between the newcomers and Mr Stephens, who was dashing to the women's side. He quickly ushered them beside Mallory, keeping a seat vacant between them, no doubt as a buffer.

Although Mallory was as surprised as her siblings to see who had walked in, she felt remarkably calm. She couldn't put her finger on it, but something was trying to work its way to the surface of her mind – a comment, something she'd seen, a premonition? Mother and daughter flicked their eyes towards her, then quickly away as the solicitor firmly directed Patrick and Vivien to sit down.

'If everyone is settled, I will read Harold Pepper's last will and testament and then I'll be open to any questions.'

His voice was a background drone as he shared the

preliminary details, as Mallory took hold of a suspicion and gave it a shake. Had she already suspected there was more to her father's relationship with the café than being a customer happy with his apple slices? An image of all the beautiful flowers at his funeral was so powerful that she almost smelt their fragrance. Then there was Olivia sharing her mother's saying which was repeated by Vivien as being from Harold, together with other fragments ...

... 'You were friends weren't you', 'your parents were friends', 'Harold drove us to footy with Barbara', red hair ...

Out of the corner of her eye, Mallory saw Hettie's hands clutched tightly around her jiggling knee, Olivia's body glued to her seat as still as could be. Mallory half turned to offer a smile but they didn't glance her way.

'Now, we reach the particulars of Harold's wishes for his property after any relevant debts are cleared.'

Mallory turned back to Heather, this time her eyes being met by a piercing stare; it wasn't malicious, more fearful. A little silver cross around her neck caught the morning light, and suddenly everything became crystal clear.

You're his daughter aren't you, Heather McMunn. Good lord, you're my half-sister. A whisper of surprise escaped her lips.

The realisation must have been painted all over Mallory's face – Hettie jumped to her feet.

'I just need to go to the bathroom,' she blurted before rushing to the door.

Her daughter started to follow but Mallory was quicker. 'It's okay, Olivia. I'll go.' Mallory followed on Hettie's heels, leaving the others behind to wait, no doubt with a great degree of impatience. She imagined a totally confused Patrick would be huffing and puffing and trying to pump the solicitor for more information in their absence.

Hettie paced the small ladies' room. 'You knew didn't you!'

Mallory gave her head a small shake as she lay a hand on the woman's trembling arm. 'Not until just now. But I gather you have known all along who you are?'

Hettie nodded, stepping away from Mallory's touch as though it was scorching hot.

'And Olivia?'

Again, she just nodded. There was no defiance in the action. Perhaps she was relieved to have the secret out in the open, Mallory thought. Time will tell.

Mallory sucked in a breath and then let it out slowly, the sound echoing around the tiled walls. Her head spun with questions, possibilities, and doubts. 'Well, I'm stunned I'll admit.' She paused and then unwittingly spoke her jumbled thoughts aloud. 'I'm not sure where that places my mother, except firmly on the outside of ... of what happened. And Barbara!'

'Don't judge my mother, Mallory,' Hettie retorted, colour rising in her cheeks. 'She loved your father, our father.' Her voice was a forced whisper as though she feared the walls were listening to her words, but once she'd started it seemed Hettie needed to keep going. 'You'd remember as well as I do how Alfred used to spend his whole time at the pub, would only come home when he'd run out of drinking money. He never did anything for Mum. He only stayed for those card nights because he was suspicious of Harold but never twigged I wasn't his own daughter. *I* didn't know until ...'

She faltered. 'Anyway, do you know what it was like walking into that room just now with all of you sitting there all high and mighty? I warned Olivia, told her to keep her chin up, but it was like flailing into a spider's web with all of you waiting to pounce.'

'Oh for heaven's sake, we didn't know anything about this. We expected it would just be the three of us here this morning, so don't blame us for being surprised. As well as being rather horrified that our father was a philanderer. Ugh, what a stupid word. That he knowingly had a child we knew nothing about. It's a hell of a lot to take in.'

Mallory chewed her bottom lip to cut off any further comments, fighting back tears. Helen poked her head around the bathroom door, quickly appraising the two women. 'If you can, could you both return to the meeting please?'

'We'll be right there,' Mallory said, wiping her eyes with a tissue. Her head ached, spinning with more and more questions. Heather brushed past her, obviously steeling herself for the next battle.

As she re-entered the room Hettie extended a reassuring nod to an obviously nervous Olivia. But it was the look of don't-underestimate-me determination that she shot Patrick and Vivien that surprised Mallory. Maybe some of HP's stubbornness had filtered through to this daughter. Mallory studied her siblings for a sign they had realised Heather's true relationship with their father.

With instructions for them all to remain silent, Mr Stephens cleared his throat and began. 'Upon trust for Patrick Pepper, Mallory Campbell and Vivien Holding, as tenants in common in equal shares between them absolutely, I leave the property at 27 Blueberry Lane, Appletree Hill in its entirety.'

'Blueberry Lane?' Patrick frowned, obviously trying to place the address which certainly wasn't where he lived at

Pepper Farm overlooking the golf course and sparkling waters of the bay. He frowned across to Vivien who shrugged, then to Mallory.

'But Blueberry Lane is where The Getaway is, rather where Fruit Flan was. But that's number 29. Number 27 must be ...' Mallory floundered, trying to order her thoughts, then without really knowing why she burst out laughing.

'What the hell is at Blueberry Lane?' Patrick asked. 'Why are you laughing?'

Recovering, Mallory straightened her shoulders, rather chuffed she knew something the others didn't. And now we know whose property Guy is squatting in, she mused. 'It's an old house on a few acres of land. It's run-down but rather charming actually.'

'Good. I still don't see the humour, but we'll sell it and split the proceeds. Between the three of us,' Patrick said pointedly as he glanced across the table at Hettie and Olivia. 'Now, on to Pepper Farm.' He rolled his hand impatiently for the reading to continue.

Mallory felt a shiver of apprehension spread through her body, the light relief about Blueberry Lane now gone. She held her breath, already aware of what words would be read to them.

'To my daughter, Heather ...'

Loud gasps erupted from Patrick and Vivien. 'What the fuck?' Patrick shouted, whilst Vivien covered her mouth with her hand, eyes wide, looking as though she may vomit.

'Please calm down Mr Pepper while I continue,' the solicitor instructed. 'To my daughter, Heather I ...'

'Daughter, my foot!' Patrick again interrupted with a certain amount of smugness. 'Prove it.'

The solicitor closed his folder and folded his hands on the top, exhibiting the control that only a career facing disgruntled families would bring. 'There is no requirement to prove anything. Heather and Olivia McMunn are beneficiaries in their own right.'

'What's the date of this will?' Patrick demanded. His voice had started to shake, Mallory not sure if in fear or fury but obviously the instructions being read out weren't the same as the will of Harold's that Patrick had seen.

'You will all receive copies of course, but the date is April just passed,' Mr Stephens replied.

'When he was in that nursing home you moved him to,' Patrick hissed at Mallory. 'Clearly, he wasn't of sound mind.'

Vivien shot to her feet, jabbing her finger across the table at Mallory. 'You knew about this, didn't you!' Her eyes darted between her sister and Hettie who was gazing silently somewhere over Vivien's shoulder. 'You knew and you're just trying to get back at me out of spite. It's fine for you, you don't need the money ...'

'What are you talking about?' Patrick demanded, side tracked for a moment.

'No, Vivien. It seems that affairs and infidelity must run in some families.' Mallory bit her lip, wishing she could snatch back the comment. She didn't want to buy into trading nasty comments around the conference table and there were Hettie and Olivia to consider. She couldn't imagine how they must be feeling now that their secret was out.

She took a deep breath and then added. 'This is all news to me as well.'

The door eased open, and Helen began to enquire if anything was required, but a sharp glance from her boss suggested she not interrupt. Mallory gripped her hands in her lap and tried to focus on what was being said in the room. Her siblings sat dumbfounded.

'Mr Pepper was of sound mind I can assure you. I met with him myself,' Mr Stephens said firmly. 'Now, I can only continue if you all settle down and respect the deceased's wishes. Please.' He waited a moment then continued. 'To my daughter Heather McMunn and granddaughter Olivia McMunn, as tenants in common in equal shares between them absolutely, I leave Pepper Farm at number 2 Old Clifftop Drive. There is a personal note Mr Pepper requested be read out here and that is, "The one condition is that no subdivision of the property take place and the apple orchard remains, as I know would be the wish of the beneficiaries also."'

'But ...'

Heather's one word was the only sound in the room. Its softness bounced around the walls, without meaning or impact. Olivia turned to her mother, a look of joy spreading across her face with obviously no idea of the ramifications that would soon be let loose. When a single tear rolled down Hettie's cheek, Mallory realised that she too had no idea of what Harold's last will would disclose.

'Is that it?' Vivien asked, her eyes searching the desk for further pages.

The solicitor nodded. 'The bank funds as part of the estate as mentioned earlier will be distributed in addition to an amount allocated to Pepper Farm upkeep. We now wait for probate and the estate to be cleared.'

Patrick pushed back his chair and stood, towering over the table. 'Well, it's not the last you'll hear from me.'

'Nor me. Although I still don't fully understand what has just happened here.' Vivien shook her head as she followed her brother out of the room.

'Wow,' was all Mallory could utter as she remained seated. She saw Hettie reach across and clutch her daughter's hand, give it a squeeze then reach for her glass of water. She took a sip.

'I guess I should say we're sorry. In a way.' Hettie said, her tone a little clipped to be entirely sincere. 'After all, it was your family home.'

'I'm not too sure how to feel, to be honest,' Mallory said sadly. 'What was he thinking to exclude the children who lived there, with our mother? I for one loved that orchard.'

'If there are no more questions, I have another meeting,' Mr Stephens said. 'But you can stay here if you'd like to, have a coffee, and digest what has been read.'

'No, we'll be going, but thank you.' Hettie started to rise, pausing as Mallory turned to Olivia. 'Would you mind asking Helen for coffee? I think I'd like to stay for a few minutes and chat with your mum.'

Neither woman spoke while they waited, each deep within their own thoughts. Heather angled her chair away from Mallory, her attention directed out the window. Mallory sat in her shadow and took in the woman who suddenly became part of her family – was she family? Hettie's stiff back told of her defensiveness, but it also reflected Harold. Mallory could recall her father straightening back his shoulders and holding himself in such a pose when there was a 'serious discussion' to be had, or he had tried to contain his anger. Had he just been nervous, like his daughter was now and Mallory had misread him all those years? No, she refused to believe it. This was just a similar habit they both had. She ran her eye over Hettie, looking for other signs, other traits.

Mallory jolted, guilty, as Helen breezed through the door and Hettie quickly swivelled her chair. The half-sisters sat sipping hot black coffees, ignoring the cream biscuits on offer. Olivia had taken Mallory's hint to leave them alone and was no doubt waiting in reception.

'What do you want, Mallory?'

'What do I want? To be honest, I don't know what I want.' Mallory gave an unexpected hiccup of emotion. 'It's funny how life turns out, isn't it? I mean it gives generously with one hand and just as suddenly it takes away with the other, and somewhere in-between there's a giant question mark. I think the important thing is to work out which is the more important. Up until recently, I would have said that memories and childhood experiences are what you should hold onto no matter what because they're something you can trust, but that's, well, it's not true.'

Hettie toyed with her coffee cup, not making eye contact. 'I know you won't believe it, but it's been tough on me too. Tough on Olivia not being able to share the identity of our father and grandfather. When I saw you were back in town, I went to pieces. I didn't know if you'd found out, were here to interfere or make trouble. Plus I didn't want Patrick coming around harassing Olivia. I always worry whenever he comes into the café, which isn't often thank heavens.'

She paused. 'Harold's funeral was especially difficult, having to keep to the back of the room. Not being included. Maybe I should have just got up and given a little heartfelt speech of my own.' Her lips drew into a tight line of bitterness.

Mallory didn't miss the challenge in her words but couldn't deny that Harold's death and funeral would have been especially difficult for daughter and granddaughter. She frowned. There was a piece missing.

'Why did you keep quiet for all those years when you

lived in the same town? Both your apparent parents had passed, so there would be no finger-pointing at Barbara, and Dad could certainly stand up for himself. He would have just ignored everyone.' Mallory smoothed her hand across the tabletop as if calming waters but looked directly at Heather. 'You still haven't told me how long you've known.'

Hettie shrugged, her knee setting up its jiggle again. 'When I was a teenager, I overheard Mum and Harold arguing one afternoon – she was crying, saying she wanted to leave Appletree and to be with him; for the world to know they shared a child, being me. She didn't care what people thought, and suggested we leave Appletree. But Harold wouldn't leave Stella, his family, or his precious orchard.'

Mallory rubbed at a coffee stain on the table. She heard the edge of sarcasm spike her comment. 'And all the while we carried on with our lives not having a clue. Poor Mum. I presume your brother was kept in the dark as well.'

Hettie nodded.

Images of Harold and Barbara, Vivien and John floated through Mallory's blurred vision. They were like little Lego people, all holding hands and smiling.

'What a huge secret to keep from those close to you. How I wished I'd known at some point. Or does everyone just live a life of denial, not caring about the hurt their actions cause?' she murmured.

'We weren't like your family, Mallory. Our household had to work hard for everything; nothing came easily for us although I don't expect you to remember that. But I always liked Harold and Olivia was able to get to know him too when she got a bit older. It's good for her to see he didn't forget us, even after death and I'm grateful for that.' A look of tenderness softened her frown. 'He was always kind to us, but this time it was his choice.'

'What do you mean?'

Hettie jumped to her feet and gathered their coats and handbags. 'We've got to go. Have a think about all this Mallory and I hope you are happy with what your own father decided and will accept his wishes before you go back to your life. Just believe me when I say I didn't know about the outcome of Pepper Farm. But I welcome it and we will look after it.'

Chapter Twenty-Two

MALLORY STRODE DOWN THE BEACH, her body fighting a headwind, her mind fighting what had just been revealed. Her hands dug deep inside her cardigan pockets as her hair became windswept and sandy. Tears tugged across her cheeks and into the cold air. The reading of the will had spun her world on its axis – how was she supposed to digest all this new information about her father, about her and her life as she thought she'd known it? She needed help.

'Hi, did everything ...? Mallory, are you crying?'

'Are you free, Stuart? I need someone.'

'Of course. I'm just leaving Guy's place. It sounds like you're in a wind tunnel somewhere.'

Her voice was small, unsure, as she tried to shield the mouthpiece from the buffeting wind. 'I'm at the beach, below the golf course cliffs. You know?'

'Sure. I'll be right there.' Frowning, he said a hurried goodbye to Guy and dashed to his car. Perhaps, whatever had happened at that meeting, hadn't been as straightforward as Mallory had presumed.

FROM THE CLIFFTOP, Stuart scanned the stretch of foreshore in both directions. The tide had turned, leaving patchy platforms of exposed rocks. Wave foam, picked up by the onshore gale, flicked into the air and across the shallows. A few hundred metres beyond the access staircase was a lone figure standing as still as a sentry at the shoreline, gazing at the horizon. Clutching two of his coats from his car, Stuart hustled towards her as fast as he could.

Mallory turned when she saw him. She walked straight into his open arms. The coat he firmly wrapped around her shoulders was comforting in its weight as well as providing protection against the world and all its secrets. As he hugged her close her sobs echoed through his chest, her thanks for his swift arrival muffled within. Finally, gasping for a deep breath she eased away and allowed Stuart to feed her arms into the coat's warm sleeves.

'You must be freezing,' he said gently. 'Do you want to walk?'

Mallory shook her head. 'No, I've been pacing enough for one morning. We can sit near the cliff wall over there if you don't mind a hard rock. It looks sheltered.'

They nestled next to each other and gazed out across the bay as small hawks swooped on the hunt for anything that might run from the grasses above. Stuart let Mallory take her time with whatever she had to share.

With a deep, shuddering breath, she began. 'The other night, you asked me what I was thinking, and I was wondering if surprises came in threes. In which case I reasoned I'd had a trifecta. One, I won the lottery. Two, my husband had an affair with my sister. Three, I'd just had sex with my old boyfriend. Well ...'

Stuart held up his hand. 'Hold on for a second. There are so many parts of that that I need to come back to later; firstly you winning the lottery when only 'some' money was mentioned previously? I hope the third surprise was an amazingly pleasant one and miles better than point two. Anyway, sorry I interrupted.'

'Yes, it was amazingly pleasant.' Mallory regarded Stuart's handsome face. To anyone else, they would probably only see a nonchalant smile, but she wasn't oblivious to the concern that pooled below the surface. He was beginning to suspect she had something deeply personal to disclose.

'But it seems that surprises come in fours.' She waited a beat. 'Because I've just learned that my father had an affair with Barbara McMunn and Heather is my half-sister which makes Olivia my ... um ... I can't think really.' She flicked the question towards the waves, hoping the seagulls would carry them away like a lukewarm chip.

When Stuart found his words, they were stammered in a tone of disbelief. 'Are you kidding! Harold and Barbara? Heather McMunn? How do you know?'

'Because Dad left Pepper Farm to his daughter Heather and granddaughter Olivia.'

There, she had said it aloud. She shuddered. When her hands were safely clutched inside Stuart's strong fingers, Mallory recounted what had happened at the solicitor's office. With every new revelation he squeezed her hands, with every recounted outburst from Patrick and Vivien he uttered a tsk of disapproval.

Finally, Mallory dropped her head onto Stuart's firm shoulder as they both let it all sink in. She could almost hear the questions of *when? how? could it be true?* ping-ponging silently between both their minds.

'There you have it,' Mallory whispered. 'My family in a fucked-up nutshell.'

'But, I just keep coming back to the fact that none of us knew, that they actually had a child together. If nothing else, it explains why they both came to footy practice.' He cringed. 'Gawd, the things you remember at such times.'

'It all dawned on me just before it became clear from the will. Then Heather rushed to the bathroom, clearly upset, so I followed. She confessed that she and Olivia knew of their relationship to HP but I didn't get any deeper than that before we had to rejoin the others.'

'How do you feel about it?' Stuart asked gently.

Waves rushed up the sand, paused as if listening to their conversation then quickly receded, none the wiser. 'Well, there are so many parts, aren't there. I mean, firstly that Harold deceived Stella, that he had a child growing up in the same town as his own family. Then there's the fact that I'm related to Hettie. Who would have thought any of this could have happened.'

'Poor Stella. Now that you know this, does it make anything from the past somehow make sense when they didn't before?'

Mallory shrugged. 'I'm exhausted thinking about it.'

'Well, that's understandable. It's so fresh and raw.'

'Surely Patrick will contest it,' Stuart said, scratching the back of his head. 'Can't say I've ever warmed to him. Sorry Mallory, but you'd have to agree he was always opportunistic and self-centred.'

Mallory sighed. 'I know.'

'Did you say you were at Guy's when I rang? I need to think of something else for a while – how did it go?'

'I took your advice and went to see him, to thank him for visiting Mum. To be honest, I also needed to fill in time until I heard how you had gone, but once we sat down together, we covered a fair bit of ground. It was good. You know, I have no recollection of that property he's living in, from our younger days I mean. The house seems well constructed, just very neglected. I did notice Guy's squatter status seems to include putting in some effort with the gardens though.'

Mallory could sense he was doing his best to do as she'd requested, to distract her from her own somersaulting emotions. She blew her nose, determined to clear her head with better thoughts. 'You don't remember it because we spent most of our time in the apple orchard ...'

'You taught me about the constellations as we lay under those trees ...'

'And you took me to the beach and taught me to surf.' Mallory nodded towards the rough waves as they pounded a rocky point. 'Amongst other things. Ah, the freedom and simplicity of youth.'

Stuart squinted towards the horizon. 'You know, I guess some things have a positive side. I don't regret those decades away from here, just the way I left. My marriage didn't last but I have two amazing sons as a result.'

'I agree. I did tell Guy that we had 'history' at high school.' She hooked her fingers and then quickly returned them to Stuart's grasp. 'Were you okay with Rooster?'

Stuart shook his head with mock exasperation. 'Why does everyone think I don't like dogs? I love dogs but after being bitten I probably went overboard with the warnings when the boys were growing up. Guy said he and Sasha have broken up so Rooster will be around for a while.'

'Oh, I didn't know. Is he upset?'

Stuart shook his head, an amused glint appearing in his eye. 'To quote my newly dedicated son, "I'm not sweating that she's gone, Dad. If she doesn't want to hang around for my success, then so be it. Anyway, it frees me up to be wherever I need to be.'"

Mallory laughed. "Well, who says he's "newly" dedicated anyway, but I'm glad his heart is still in one piece. And I rather like having Rooster around.'

'I offered to return him if he wanted to stay in Appletree and keep seeing Nellie,' Stuart said.

'Really?'

'That was Guy's reaction too. Hey, I even got an invite to his gig at the marina.' He sighed. 'I guess I should be happy he's pursuing what he loves rather than settling for less. Less is the wrong word.'

'Heavens, this country air is working its way into your soul and finding the goodness.' Mallory flicked a teasing smile across at him. 'But I know what you mean.'

'Had Guy told you he'd stayed at that house when visiting his Gran in the past? And to learn HP was the owner all along – such a coincidence. There must be money in apples.'

Instantly, Mallory was transported back to the solicitor's office, and the announcement that Harold had owned the property next to Fruit Flan.

She nodded. 'You should have seen Patrick and Vivien's faces when the properties' addresses didn't line up. Patrick must never venture around the town because he has no idea where Blueberry Lane is. One thing's for sure though, he and Vivien will be checking it out sooner rather than later, probably with a For Sale board in the car boot. Oh!'

As one, they realised what that would mean. 'Call him, quickly, Stuart,' Mallory urged, jumping to her feet.

They scurried back along the beach, Stuart redialling as he went but there was no answer from Guy. As they arrived at their cars, Stuart took Mallory into his arms. 'Whatever comes from all this, you know I'm here to help, as are all your friends, I'm sure.'

'Thank you.' She stood on tiptoes and kissed him.

'Never in doubt,' he replied softly.

The sincerity of his words, reflected in his concerned eyes, warmed her whole body.

Stuart held Mallory's door as she jumped in. 'I'm sure everything is fine, but we need to tell him he needs to move out now. Shall I meet you there?'

She nodded. 'He and Rooster can stay with me.'

'Oh, but that would cramp our style,' Stuart replied, flashing her a broad grin.

'MAYBE WE PANICKED FOR NO REASON,' Stuart said as he held up hands on either side of his face and squinted through the kitchen window. 'His gear is still here, and there's no sign of visitors.'

Mallory peered around to the rear of the house where Guy parked his car out of sight. 'The old car he rented isn't here though. Maybe he took Rooster to the beach. Is that him now?'

A car engine cut off, doors slammed, and voices drifted from the driveway. A loud knocking on the front door was followed by the sound of approaching footsteps along the veranda. They were slow, and measured, their thumps interrupted by the possible rapping of knuckles against a wall. As the voices approached, Mallory shook her head, visualising Patrick pretending to check out the house's structure as though he knew what he was doing. She moved to Stuart's side and waited.

They watched Patrick lean in to peer through the windows and then run his hand across the top of the doorframe as if he would discover a spare key. 'Bloody hell. Someone's living here,' he muttered.

Vivien and John were the first to see Stuart and Mallory. What possible explanation had Vivien spun to their brother about John being by her side? Mallory wondered. One thing was obvious – they were a tight little group.

Patrick came up short. 'I saw the cars out front. You didn't waste any time checking the place out, did you.'

Vivien and John hadn't dragged their eyes away from Mallory and Stuart. Mallory saw John's eyes flick to their joined hands. Her lips tweaked in a smile as Stuart gave hers a squeeze.

'You're the guy at the restaurant the other night,' John said, flicking his head back as if that had been a crime.

'You remember Stuart Forbes, don't you?' Mallory said to no one in particular.

'I thought it was you,' Vivien said. 'As John just said, you don't waste much time do you Mallory, checking out the house and an old flame.'

Stuart's grip tightened around Mallory's fingers. She was unsure if the gesture was to reassure her or keep his own reaction under control.

Patrick turned his attention to the couple, running his eyes up and down Stuart. 'I remember the name, but what are you doing here? This is family business.'

No one pointed out the obvious that John was standing amongst them as Patrick droned on. 'That meeting this morning didn't quite go to plan but all is not lost. Vivien and I intend to contest the will's outcome re Pepper Farm and it's up to you whether you side with us, Mallory.'

Mallory's reply was firm. 'No. It's sad and disappointing in so many ways, but if that's what Dad wanted then Heather and Olivia should inherit the property. I can't say I won't miss it though.'

'All very well for you to say, Mallory. You don't need it.' Vivien's words were sharp and pointed.

Mallory ignored her sister's inference. 'I was just as surprised as you were about Barbara and Dad's affair. It will take a while for it to sink in; how none of us had any idea for all that time. But what's done is well and truly done and we should respect his wishes, which includes him providing for Heather and Olivia. At least he took some responsibility for them in the end. Isn't that what we should be focusing on?'

Stuart gave a small start but when Mallory glanced across at him, he was staring towards the garden deep in thought.

Patrick patted the air, palms down as if he alone could placate the group. 'I'm quite sure that, despite those allocated funds, when Hettie McMunn sees the cost of running Pepper Farm not to mention the taxes on the property, she'll be ringing to offload it. And I'll be waiting. But that's if it lands in her hands in the first place.'

Mallory heard Stuart mutter under his breath. 'Condescending tosser.'

Patrick wasn't to be put off, however. 'I'll get the agent to come and look at this place, toss out whoever is bunking down here, and give us a valuation. Once the estate is cleared, it goes on the market.'

'To be divided equally between three siblings I believe,' Stuart said, staring at John. Obviously, the previous distraction had passed and he was back in the conversation.

'We'll see about that too,' John chipped in as he looked at Mallory. He may have come across to the others as taking a stand, but Mallory heard a certain softness beneath his words. What was that about?

How has it come to this, Mallory thought sadly; everyone trying to impress or second-guess the others. The trio turned as one and stalked off to their cars. Raised voices hovered in the air for a few moments before the sound of engines could be heard receding into the late afternoon. As one, Mallory and Stuart let out deep sighs, then started to chuckle.

'Thank heavens Guy didn't choose to return just then,' Mallory said.

'Gawd,' Stuart puffed as he dropped onto a chair. 'And I thought my family had problems.' He reached across as Mallory sunk lower into the other chair and rubbed her eyes. 'You must be exhausted.'

'It's been a big day, that's for sure. Thank you for being there,' Mallory added.

He nodded silently.

'I wonder what Patrick thought about John being here. Maybe he's so pre-occupied by the outcome of Dad's will that he doesn't even care.'

Stuart shrugged. 'It was weird.'

Mallory gazed across to the vegetable patch, to the empty stakes and a few new carrot tops. 'I'm not sure how many salads Guy hoped to make out of that lot. Are you okay, Stuart?'

Quickly he turned to her, a warm smile once more on his lips. Mallory leant across and brushed them with her own.

'I'll wait here for Guy and fill him in if you like,' he said. 'Why don't you head home, have a nice long bath with a glass of wine, and curl up on the couch.'

'Will you come across later?' she said, stifling a yawn. 'I

have a choice of casseroles we could heat up for dinner. Bring Guy.'

Her heart ached at the loving look Stuart sent her, even though she feared she'd soon be asleep despite the early hour.

'Those clowns won't be back so there's no great hurry for Guy to move out today. I'll come and rescue one of those casseroles but stay here for dinner with Guy then head back to the motel. Is that okay?'

If Mallory was surprised, she didn't show it. Her head ached and she certainly had a lot to think about, but she also suspected that Stuart had something on his mind too.

Chapter Twenty-Three

THE NEXT MORNING, Mallory was on her second cup of coffee and wondering if she should call Stuart when Guy and Rooster appeared at her door.

'Just returning this,' he said, holding up the washed dish. 'The curry was delicious, thanks.'

'Come in, come in,' she beckoned.

Guy tied Rooster to the veranda post, took off his shoes, and walked into Fruit Flan. 'This is, um, different,' he said, scanning the pristine décor.

Mallory laughed. 'I'm with you. I like a bit more character in my home, but it's easy to keep clean. Coffee?'

'Got a green tea? I try and cut down on the caffeine when I'm writing.'

'Ooh, that sounds promising, although aren't musos supposed to be primed on caffeine and whiskey? Is this new material for your gig?'

He nodded. 'Yeah, but anyway Dad told me about your day yesterday. I hope you don't mind. It's none of my business really, except that I'll have to move. He said you'd offered for us to bunk here but I understand if you'd rather we go somewhere else. My girlfriend, ex-girlfriend has taken off interstate so can't take Rooster back yet and I don't think the motel allows dogs ...'

Mallory smiled as she passed him a mug of tea, green as requested. His deep frown and rambling words showed this disruption to his routine and space didn't come easily – the opposite of the way his father would have reacted. As a teenager, Stuart had been up for anything; the more thrills and last-minute changes the better.

'Of course, both of you can stay here so move your gear across whenever you're ready.' She held up her hand and smiled. 'No music at midnight though, okay?'

'Deal. Thanks, Mallory. I wouldn't want to be around if the estate agent called in next door.'

A moment's silence fell between them. Guy leaned back against the kitchen bench; his hands wrapped around the mug as he watched the steam rise. Mallory tried to appear busy by wiping down the clean benchtop. She liked this gentle fellow and his determination to lead a fulfilling life, and she wanted to keep their easy conversations going.

'It's good you had a chance to chat with your dad. Family's important,' she said, a hitch in her voice to be saying such words.

Guy nodded. 'We nutted out a few things and I think he's a bit more open to where I'm heading. I've just got to make sure there's a future for me in music.' He paused, tapping the side of his mug. 'It sounds like you've got yourself some new family too – it might be nice to reconnect with them as well, yeah?'

In all the upheaval and disclosures, Mallory hadn't dwelled on the fact that, yes, she did have new members of her somewhat fragmented family. It was looking as though Hettie and Olivia could be the only family she could be in the same room with, without wanting to murder someone. Did they feel the same way? Hettie's upbringing certainly explained her anger toward Mallory, but would that continue now everything was out in the open? Maybe it was time she found out a little more about the past.

'DAMN IT.' A handwritten Closed sign greeted Mallory as she approached the nursery. Realising she had no idea where the mother and daughter lived (and why would she?), she was about to turn away when a flash of orange raffia being flung into the air caught her attention. Quickly she knocked on the door and motioned Olivia to let her in.

'I'm sorry, the café's closed, Mallory. We have a large flower order to get ready for a luncheon today.'

Mallory couldn't help but notice the change in Olivia's conversation. Her earlier confident tone had been replaced with a timid, apologetic voice as she looked everywhere but into Mallory's eyes.

Her heart sank, but she eased the door open anyway. At the same time, Hettie burst through the back door another large bouquet of native flowers raised high and dripping water.

'Olivia ... Oh, Mallory.'

'I know you're busy but please, can I just sit in a corner and wait or do something to help? I need to speak with you both.'

Mother and daughter glanced at each other as the heady scents of lavender, lilies, and herbs circled their hesitation. Cut rosemary, mint, and delicate filler flowers were scattered across the counter, ready to be made into small posies. Mallory was sure her visit was the last thing they needed or wanted. Just as she was about to back away, Hettie thrust the bouquet against her chest, the stems quickly soaking her jacket.

'Get these dry then go to the back room and get another couple of skeins of raffia.'

'Yes, Ma'am,' Mallory quipped with a smile as she flung her damp jacket onto a chair. A hiccup of laughter came from Olivia. For the next hour they worked together, Hettie ordering Mallory around and Olivia stepping in to quietly help when Mallory floundered. Which was often. It went without saying that there would be no chatter of any kind before the job was finished.

Finally, the client's knock came on the door and the flowers were dispatched to the event. 'Coffee time?' Mallory asked in a hopeful tone but was told sternly that would only happen after they'd cleaned up the mess of foliage remnants.

When Mallory returned from yet another trip to the compost, it was obvious the two had been whispering. Hettie cleared her throat and propped her broom against the counter as Olivia put the final touches to three coffees. She's nervous, Mallory noted as Olivia messed up their trademark leaf design of latte art. As Olivia grimaced and glanced up, Mallory sent her a reassuring smile. The Closed sign stayed firmly on the door as Hettie cleared a small round table and dusted off metal chairs before pulling them to the table. No one spoke.

'It's good to see you're busy,' Mallory finally ventured, flicking away an imaginary petal.

'Like I said, we don't need your help,' Hettie said, rattling her cup onto the saucer.

'Mum ...'

Mallory offered her a warm smile and then tried to extend it to her mother, but Hettie's posture was stiff and unwelcoming. A peek across to Mallory from under lowered eyes showed uncertainty more than hostility so Mallory decided to focus on why she'd come.

'Neither of you have anything to worry about with me. Truly. I'd just like to have a chat. Yes, I have some questions which I hope you'll answer because this has all come as an incredible shock.' She paused, hoping she didn't sound patronising. 'The other thing is, um, I'm here on my own. Nothing that is said will be passed on to Patrick or Vivien. Let's just say we're not on the best of terms.'

'Why not? Because we inherited Pepper Farm?' Olivia whispered.

'Things weren't great before that,' Mallory said realising that if she expected HP's daughter and granddaughter to be open with her, then the same should be offered to them. 'I've never had a great relationship with Patrick, you know the overbearing older brother scenario ...'

Hettie muttered, 'That's an understatement.'

Mallory continued. 'I came back to check on Dad and to see that everything was in order with his estate and Pepper Farm. I'm afraid that since Mum died, I haven't exactly trusted Patrick's motives and I needed to check Dad wasn't being taken advantage of.' It was on the tip of her tongue to disclose it had been her decision to move Harold to Hillview and to pay for his care, but let it go. What did it matter?

'And Vivien? Well, I haven't spoken with her for some

time.' She took a sip of her coffee. 'Not since she ran off with my husband.' There, it was out in the open.

Both women sat upright, their gasps ricocheting off bottlebrush and potted cumquat trees. 'Bloody hell,' Hettie blurted. 'So, that's what you meant in the lawyer's office.'

'But that's awful!' Olivia added.

Hettie recovered quickly. 'Are the three of you going to contest Harold's will?'

Mallory shook her head. 'Patrick says they have plans to, but I understand they don't stand a chance of winning. I won't be.'

The relief on the faces staring at her tugged at Mallory's heart, but she also knew that Hettie could shut down any conversation at a moment's notice so pushed ahead.

'Can I ask you a few questions?' When Hettie flicked a frown toward Olivia, Mallory kicked herself. 'Or should we make it another time?'

'No, no,' Hettie replied. 'Olivia knows all about her family so now is fine.' She crossed her arms and waited.

'Can I just say something?' Olivia said, her hand raised as though in a classroom. She flicked her eyes to her mother who returned with a minute nod. 'I feel guilty, Mallory for pretending I didn't know about, um things. I mean, I didn't know who you were at first but then Mum explained, and I kept on as though ...'

'Oh, Olivia, thank you. It's all so complicated, isn't it! Let's just try to move on, okay? Hettie, I don't understand why you were so nice to Harold for all those years when you knew he was your father. When you knew about his affair with your mother? They kept you a secret and ... oh wait. You said that he'd always been nice to you both – what did you mean by that?'

'Why ...?' Hettie's voice suddenly shook with emotion, her eyes narrow with suspicion.

'Mum, give her a chance.' Olivia put her hand over her mother's and turned to Mallory. 'Harold promised Grandma that he would provide for Mum in every way so that Grandma wouldn't leave Appletree like she wanted to. She loved him so much and her own marriage wasn't happy apparently. Harold bought this land where the nursery was for Mum, for her to build a house when she got older. But then Mum left town. When she returned with me, she was determined to make a future for us, and the property was in her name, so she kept it as a garden nursery. Harold paid for all the setup and legal stuff, for us but more for Grandma.'

'Where do you both live then?' Mallory asked.

'In Barbara and Alfred's old house on the outskirts of town.'

'You'd remember it from the card nights,' Hettie muttered.

The card nights. All together in each other's houses, with such a huge secret fizzing between them. Hadn't Stella realised? But then maybe she had, and Harold had denied it, so her mother chose to ignore what she didn't want to confront. Mallory had always presumed that both mothers were friends, but either it was all for show like a murky agreement between them, or Stella was in the dark.

'I just find it incredible that no-one realised. This was such a close-knit community,' Mallory said hoping that it formed more of a question.

Hettie shrugged, obviously used to the long-term lie. 'Mum kept to herself a lot because her husband was so anti-social and drank too much. She always told me that suited her just fine, that we didn't need any locals around, except for the Peppers. Of course, when I overheard the conversation about who my real father was, I ranted and raved and called her some pretty awful names, but deep down I knew she loved her kids so much. And who would start wondering when you and I were so close in age, Mallory?'

Mallory toyed her coffee spoon across some spilt sugar. She had been at the older end of the year level in terms of age, and Heather had been at the younger age limit. How long before Barbara became pregnant had the affair been burning? Before she could ask more, Olivia jumped in, seemingly eager to add to the conversation.

'He was proud of us, I think.'

Proud of you? Bitter tears pricked behind Mallory's eyes. 'That's good,' she whispered.

'Did you know I'd left Appletree to have a baby?' Hettie asked.

'Bridie mentioned it,' Mallory replied. She glanced across at Olivia, and ran her eyes over the girl's red hair. Fleetingly, she wondered if Bridie had been right about Banjo being her father. So many questions still to be answered but that one didn't make any difference.

'Do you know why I think he left us the farm?' Hettie didn't wait for a reply. 'I think it was because for all those years he felt guilty that he couldn't, wouldn't, publicly acknowledge us. He refused to take us away from here, but he wouldn't own up either. It hurt Mum so much, I know that. After I'd settled down at the news and accepted she hadn't had affairs with every man in town ...'

'Mum!' Olivia said.

Her mother shrugged. 'Well, it's true. It was so out of character for her so I started to doubt everything. But then I'd study how they were when together and how her eyes would light up. Anyway, we grew a lot closer, Mum and I.

I'd come home and say things like "He winked at me in the butchers today", or Mum would do a twirl in the kitchen in a new dress that had been delivered for her.'

Mallory was stunned, trying to visualise her father in the role of a lover with two children so close together, as someone who bought dresses and winked.

'And what was his excuse for the way he treated Vivien and me?' Her fingers snapped the twig her hands had been toying with. She tossed it aside. 'He never said he was proud of us, never bothered coming to any of our events. Even just before he died, he wouldn't acknowledge me, my life, how I was trying to help him.' Her voice started to break, from anger and sadness.

Hettie made no move to physically comfort her, but when she spoke her words were sincere. 'Perhaps his gruffness came from compassion, that over the years he hadn't done more for Stella, you and your sister. He was caught in a way.' The option was left hanging.

'I know he was old and sick, but, well, he could have tried and make up for it in his final days,' Mallory said finally. 'As for the farm, he obviously knew you wouldn't subdivide it, that you loved it and would keep it as is.'

Hettie nodded, a soft smile finally creasing her face. 'We often spoke about it, over an apple slice or two but I presumed it was just small-talk and we'd never be able to go there after he passed.'

Mallory didn't ask how often Hettie had been to Pepper Farm, or when.

'Thank you for coming, Mallory. It's weird, that we're sort of family,' Olivia said, echoing Guy's words. She glanced across to her mother but when no similar sentiment came, she fell silent.

Mallory stood to leave, her hand paused on the handle

as she turned back. 'The flowers at Dad's funeral were beautiful. Thank you.'

FEELING the need to be alone, Mallory strolled to the rotunda. What was she to do now? She was telling the truth about not contesting Harold's will. The realisation that she would no longer be a part of Pepper Farm was more complex. It wasn't as though she had spent a lot of time there during her adult life; the fact remained that in the back of her mind, she always knew the property was there. Waiting. Whether Patrick was 'in residence' or not, she was entitled to sit in the orchard, walk its gardens, plop onto the window seat and gaze at the view. It would soon belong to Heather and Olivia McMunn – who in their wildest dreams would ever have believed that. Maybe she could visit now and then when she was back in town. She sincerely hoped so.

The scattering of Harold's ashes was yet to be organised, but it would be soon. It would be her final visit to the orchard for a while.

A young family meandered along the path through the park, the parents bent over as they balanced a child each as they wobbled on small scooters. A couple in business suits talked earnestly as they passed the rotunda, folders in hand – real estate agents, Mallory presumed. They were the only people to suit up in small towns. Perhaps they were on their way, under Patrick's instructions, to 27 Blueberry Lane. What was she to do about the house left to her and her siblings, and what a sly old fox Harold had been for never mentioning he owned other properties. So many secrets.

An image of Patrick, red-faced and blustery popped up.

She could only imagine how incensed he would be. No doubt he'd further explained the ramifications of the will to Vivien, and that they'd be eager to finalise the settlement of Blueberry Lane as soon as legally possible. If they did intend to contest the will concerning Pepper Farm, she had been left out of the pow-wow.

Another thought had started to wiggle its way into her mind – was it because she didn't need the proceeds that she was prepared to accept Harold's wishes and relinquish Pepper Farm so easily? Perhaps winning the lottery had softened the blow of needing the inheritance, even though it had been her childhood home. She felt guilty for even contemplating that money could outweigh sentiment. If it had all panned out as they had presumed, how could the three siblings have shared ownership amicably anyway?

Warm sunshine washed across the rotunda, urging her to stretch her face towards the sun, close her eyes, and breathe deeply. She could smell damp leaves and hear the drone of a distant mower.

'Are you sending a prayer to the heavens, or conjuring a hideous spell to be cast on some poor unsuspecting relative?'

Mallory's heart jumped at the sound of Stuart's voice. He was standing at the foot of the rotunda steps, hands in pockets and a broad grin across his handsome face. How wonderful it was to see him, to presume he'd sought her out.

'Guy said you'd come into town, and I had a feeling I'd find you here.'

Mallory patted the seat beside her. 'Come on then. Sit down and keep me and my racing thoughts company.' As he approached, she could sense a hesitancy, and see concern in his eyes. 'Guy is moving across to Fruit Flan if that's what you're worried about.'

With a nod, Stuart lowered himself onto the bench. 'Who said I'm worried about anything, although you do seem to be able to read me. Is that a good thing? How about a coffee?'

'No, I've just had one thanks. With Hettie and Olivia. It was good, despite me pushing my way into their space. We cleared the air about a few things. I told them I wouldn't contest the will and that Patrick's efforts would most likely be in vain. It sounds beyond weird, but I think we might be friends at some point in the future.'

'Oh? Are you planning on staying?'

Mallory would have been happy to chat about her various options, but something was amiss. She frowned across at him as he took a sudden interest in a nearby magpie. Maybe this was where he said goodbye, that he didn't appreciate her becoming so involved with Guy, that he was heading back to the city for good.

'Have you got something you need to say, Stuart?' she murmured before chewing her bottom lip.

He grasped her hand in his and sent her one of his happy faces. Somewhat relieved she squeezed back and waited.

'There's been something dancing around the corners of my memory, Mallory. I haven't been able to understand it but I've connected the dots, and now I realise how some things actually panned out all those years ago. I'm just not sure how important it is or that you're going to like it, and I don't want to add ...'

'Stuart, you're worrying me.'

'No, it's nothing to worry about. It's a little thing, but if it's a big thing to you, then I think you'll be hurt. And hand on my heart, I don't want that. But you made it clear the other night that you needed to get things straight in your head, to understand more about your family, what happened, and why.'

He sighed before continuing, aware that Mallory now wanted to hear what he was on about more than ever. 'It's so long ago, ridiculous really that we're even referring to it, but now I realise that when Harold saw Heather and me together at the dance he was angry because he thought I was taking advantage of ...'

Several heartbeats thrummed around the rotunda before Mallory murmured, 'His daughter. When he said to keep away from his daughter, he was referring to Heather, not me.' She shook her head, taking a moment for that realisation to sink in. 'And all this time I hung on to that one reaction when I thought he was being a protective father to me. How stupid was I.'

A small stone of regret and resentment lodged in Mallory's stomach. 'I'm glad you said something – it seems that what happened so long ago actually bears relevance today. But it's not only about me; he got his friends together to make life in Appletree very unpleasant for you. All the while, he knew you were my boyfriend but that didn't matter a jot. You tried to explain to everyone that you were only trying to include Heather in the night. You didn't deserve that.'

As Stuart gathered her to him, she thought back at how her young heart had been broken. She'd sobbed on her bed day after day, how her mother had tried to cheer her up with promises of more fish in the sea. She hadn't wanted Stuart to leave but he hadn't any choice after her father had gone into action.

'I don't care about that,' Stuart said.

'Heather could have backed up your version, but she didn't.' She paused. 'It was a way to get back at me for being

Harold's legitimate daughter; out of jealousy I guess.' For a moment she contemplated returning to the nursery but shelved the idea.

Stuart tilted her face to his own and kissed her gently. 'I hope it was the right thing to drag it all back up again, and I'm sorry if it wasn't. Like I said, I don't care about any of it. It's the future I'm more interested in.'

Chapter Twenty-Four

'ROOSTER, ROOSTER. COME HERE,' Guy called. 'What's the matter with him? There must be a rabbit or something in there.' Guy had moved into Fruit Flan, but it seemed Rooster preferred the smells and critters next door.

Mallory and Stuart headed over to where Guy was peering into the bush towards the fence line that joined the two properties. He called for Rooster again with no response.

'I can hear voices,' Stuart muttered.

'You don't have to whisper, Dad.' Guy laughed. 'But they do seem to be coming from next door. Do you think it's the estate agent rocking up for the appraisal?' He rubbed his hands together. 'Let's go make a scene if Rooster hasn't already.'

Stuart cuffed his son on the arm. 'No, but I think you should wander in Mallory because I reckon there are a few voices in there which means Patrick is probably in the wings. I know you can handle him, but shall I come with you?'

Mallory glanced at her watch. 'Do you have time before heading to the airport?'

'Dad isn't one of those people who arrives for a flight with hours to spare. You could both go in Dad's car then he can leave straight away and you can just come back here,' Guy suggested.

Mallory and Stuart glanced at each other, hiding smiles. 'Or, we could just rock up and see what happens,' Stuart said. 'Come on.'

Patrick's car and one other were parked in the driveway. There was no sign of Rooster, but loud rustling gave away his location deep in the scrub. As they approached the front door, the murmurs from within the house grew louder and a moment later the door flung open. Vivien and Patrick jumped back in surprise to see Mallory and Stuart standing on the other side.

'My invite must have got lost in the mail,' Mallory remarked to her siblings. John wasn't with them.

The agent eased forward and reached out his hand. 'Mitch Ricards. You must be Mallory. Sorry, I understood from Patrick you couldn't make this appointment. Can I take you through now?'

'No, I've seen the property,' Mallory replied, taking delight at the others' surprised expressions. 'Several times actually.'

'Right, I was just saying that although the property is pretty run down, market value around these parts is high. Patrick here is well aware of that.'

'I presume Harold Pepper's solicitor engaged you, not Patrick?' Stuart confirmed, ignoring Patrick's frown.

The agent nodded in reply. 'We've just been discussing a preliminary value but the solicitor will confirm an estate value to you all. Did you have any other questions?' He turned and locked the front door.

Mallory looked to Patrick and Vivien who were obviously still working out when she had been through the house. They certainly didn't seem prepared to comment on their opinions about the property or its condition. Probably taking the silence as meaning all was well, the agent handed his card to Mallory and left.

A flock of galahs flew soundlessly overhead. The overcast, drizzly morning had developed into a clear afternoon, the rain leaving the countryside cleansed and glistening. A faint rainbow arced in the distance, fading as sunshine splayed across it. Mallory took a step towards the edge of the veranda and gazed out across the pastures. She could hear Rooster barking across the fence and wondered if Guy was crouched in the bushes, unable to contain his curiosity. She ran her hand up and down one of the worn pillars that stood like a sentry at the top of the stairs and felt her world vibrate with possibilities.

'We'll be going too,' Vivien said behind her but made no move to try and pass.

Mallory smiled and, without turning, said, 'I'll buy you both out.'

'What?' Vivien exclaimed. 'What did you just say?'

'You don't even know the amount yet, Mallory,' Patrick added patronisingly, his eyes narrowing.

'I'll buy you both out,' she repeated, turning to face them. She felt calm, excited.

'Well, aren't you the lucky one to splash around your money,' Vivien hissed before turning to Patrick. 'I told you she'd won some money in the lottery but it's a big mystery how much it was. John will be furious if we don't get top dollar.'

Vivien faltered as if his name added weight to the deceit their relationship was based on. She waved loosely in Patrick's direction, but her remark was directed at her sister: 'I explained to Patrick about your marriage breaking down and John finding a future with me.'

Mallory spluttered and Stuart shook his head in response to Vivien's version – no words like 'affair', 'lover', or 'betraying bastards' came with her explanation. The way Vivien shuffled her feet and tossed her head was testament to her discomfort, and Mallory wasn't interested in providing any clarity for her brother's sake.

'How convenient for you,' Mallory remarked.

Anyway, Patrick's focus was still on the money. 'So that's how you afforded the fancy nursing home? Maybe we should get a bonus on the payout of this place then,' Patrick quipped. 'After all, you'll probably subdivide and make even more money.'

Mallory sensed Stuart edge forward.

'It's none of your business what plans I have for it, Patrick.'

A broad smile spread across Stuart's face as she stood her ground.

'I've lost everything ...' Patrick started.

Mallory laughed. 'Hardly. Anyway, it was never yours to begin with.'

'We'll have to discuss it,' Patrick said then glanced across to Vivien, her cue to follow. Mallory moved to the side as they scuttled past her, down the stairs to their car.

Stuart let out a whoop of laughter. 'Ah ha, good for you, Mallory.'

She appreciated that he didn't refer to the cost she had just committed to, whatever it was, but vowed to come clean to him in the future. Because deep in her heart she hoped he would be hanging around. She moved into his outstretched arms and kissed him passionately, relief and a yearning for more flowing through her like warm honey. Her hands looped behind his neck, gently touching his curls. She felt him harden.

Mallory gently rubbed against him. 'Mmm, did Guy give up his key to this prestigious abode?'

'Yes, silly fellow,' Stuart groaned. 'We could always break in.'

'How'd it go?' Guy and Rooster were walking up the driveway toward them. 'You'd better head to the airport, Dad.'

Stuart looked at Mallory, mischief in his eyes. 'Raincheck?'

She nodded, sorry to see him go for more than one reason. 'Hurry back. See you for Guy's gig on Friday night.'

MALLORY'S NOVEL lay discarded on the little table along with a cold cup of tea, her focus firmly on what lay on the other side of the ramshackle fence. If someone asked her when she had decided to buy the property next to Fruit Flan, Mallory wouldn't be able to answer. But she couldn't ignore the sense of satisfaction, the contentment that had settled within her as the words escaped her mouth. They had taken flight around the flaking walls and overgrown gardens of her potential new home, and nothing felt more right. Plans and ideas on how she could make the house her own spun around in her mind like a roulette wheel – if she could just get those balls to fall in place, the house would be where she could settle and call home. A permanent home of her own.

Her sense of excitement evaporated as her phone rang. John's number lit the screen as though accompanied by sirens and whistles. Unwilling to pick it up, she stared at it and waited for message bank to kick in. Whatever he had to say he could leave in a message; but none was left.

The sound of tyres scrunching on the driveway drifted to the veranda, interrupting her to-and-froing about returning the call. A little white van pulled up to the steps. Mallory slowly rose to her feet as Hettie McMunn opened the car door and stood facing her.

'You busy?' Hettie beckoned to the passenger side.

Any conversation with John could wait. There had been no repeat call, so she decided it must have been a pocket dial. Thank heavens she hadn't picked up. As there seemed no alternative but to join her visitor, Mallory closed the front door, walked down the stairs, and eased her way into the overflowing van. The fragrance of hundreds of flowers bombarded her from the rear.

'Where are we off to?' Mallory asked although she had a pretty good idea. After a silent, but not tense, ride along the backstreets, they turned off onto the coast road and followed the edge of the golf course around the clifftop. The van pulled into the siding where Mallory had parked all those weeks before. The women sat and watched a group of golfers finish their putts.

'Do you play?' Mallory ventured.

Hettie let out a low chuckle 'No. Haven't the patience for it.'

'Me neither,' Mallory replied. She waited for her to let loose with what was on her mind – it didn't take long.

'I think we have quite a few things in common, apart from the bleeding obvious. I also think that when we were young, there were many times we both probably felt ignored by our father. He was that kind of man. But I never felt rejected and that says a lot about him, despite everything.'

Her words came thick and fast, making Mallory wonder, not unkindly, if she had been rehearsing them.

Even if Mallory knew how to reply, Hettie took only a quick breath before continuing. 'He spoke highly of you, Mallory, he really did. I want you to know that.' She paused, squinting through the windscreen. 'I was very jealous of your life.'

A flutter of sadness came and went as Mallory considered the words of her half-sister.

'And yet, here we are looking at the most prized possession he had, and he left it to you.' Mallory didn't mean for her words to sound bitter, but they did and she wished she could take them back.

Hettie seemed unfazed. 'I think it's more for Olivia. He adored her. I know none of you had kids so maybe things might have been different ...'

'I doubt that,' Mallory interrupted. She wound down the window, suddenly feeling claustrophobic, a pain deep in her chest warning of her rising anxiety.

'The Lord's Prayer and church service were for you, weren't they,' Mallory stated, nodding curtly at the silver cross necklace around Hettie's neck. Was she hoping for some form of divine intervention?

Instantly, HP's daughter rubbed it between her fingers. 'I guess. I tried to get him to worship more often, but he kicked up a fuss. He never criticised me for my choice though.'

Mallory swiped at flakes of bark and dried leaves that had settled across the worn dashboard like snow. They floated to join the layer at her feet.

'He never wrote to me. He didn't even leave me a letter

in his will. It would have been nice if he'd written something down or at least been a bit more welcoming when I visited the nursing home. But there was nothing. He just left everything to be sorted out after he was no longer in the middle of it all.'

A cool onshore breeze made its way into the van, but it wasn't enough. Mallory opened the door and jumped out, moved toward the moonah trees that lined the cliff, and gulped in the clean sea air. She heard the car door gently open and close, turned, and walked towards it. The two women leant side by side on the car's bonnet. Mallory let out a weary sigh, her earlier plans for her new property having evaporated like raindrops in a flame. She rubbed her eyes and then squinted across at Pepper Farm.

'I was thinking about our conversation the other day and how I admitted to liking seeing Harold around town,' Hettie said. 'Um, I hope it didn't seem like Mum and I thought it was all a game, you know the new dress remark and everything. It wasn't.'

Mallory waited, now sure Hettie had spent many hours preparing for this conversation. *Whereas you, Mallory, have been tied up with emotions wrapped around Stuart and buying houses.* A worm of guilt wriggled through her body.

'Okay,' she whispered.

'Ask me anything,' Hettie prompted.

'How long did their affair last?' Her question had come quickly as though it had been simmering, eager for an escape from all her others. It was an echo of her conversation with Vivien – why was it such an important one?

Hettie frowned. 'Depends on what you mean by affair, I guess. The bottom line is, I don't know for sure. I did ask Mum once and she just said it had finished long ago, which

246 • JULIE HOLLAND

I took to mean the sex. Obviously, he kept in touch with us.'

'What did you two talk about as he got older?' Mallory asked, her shoulders relaxing.

Heather shrugged. 'Apples, the seasons, farming. Even when he was younger, that was the conversation. He didn't care about much else. Did you know he could tell when a frost was due by the smell of the wind, that he had his own secret way of pruning apple trees that would produce twice as much fruit as other orchards?'

Hearing the warmth of memories in Hettie's tone, Mallory glanced across to see unshed tears glistening in Harold Pepper's daughter's eyes. 'No, I didn't,' she murmured.

'My apple and quince jelly, made with his apples, always won First Prize at the produce fair, but Harold never liked it. Said it tasted like baby food.'

They both chuckled.

Mallory took a step towards the distant house and heard others close behind as Hettie joined her. Together the women gazed across the golf course. 'Well, at least you'll care for the trees which is more than Patrick has done. He's also diluted a lot of the house's character but it's yours now to either bring it back or make it your own. Are you planning to renovate?'

'Olivia and I will make it our own but it's important to keep memories of Harold alive too. We've stayed up late a lot, tossing around how lucky we are to even think about living there.'

'You shared a special connection with him,' Mallory said, the edge of her bitterness now softening to acceptance.

'I hope you can visit when you're in town,' Hettie offered.

Mallory laughed, keeping her surprise at the invitation in check. 'Be careful what you wish for but thank you.' She paused, glancing sideways. 'I've offered to buy out Vivien and Patrick for Blueberry Lane. I think I might like to stay in Appletree.'

Her bark of laughter cut through the wind. 'Well, well. And does Stuart Forbes play a part in that decision?'

Mallory shrugged, not willing to reveal too much. Some things were still private, for her to hug close for the time being, but she was pleased to have shared a little with Heather McMunn. 'I'm not sure yet. His work on Peggy and Martha's new barn will have started by the time the estate settles so who knows.'

The women circled back to the car. Mallory glanced over the bonnet as Hettie opened her door, the ghost of a smile on her lips. 'So, Banjo Carruthers?'

'Tsk. Yep. The jerk shot through at the first sign of me being pregnant, but Olivia and I don't need anyone else.'

Both women shook their heads and smiled in mutual understanding.

Chapter Twenty-Five

WEAK RAYS of sun tried to push through thick clouds as Mallory wandered through the cemetery grounds. Her fingers clutched a delicate bunch of flowers gathered with a rubber band, bought at a roadside stand on her way from Appletree Hill – it didn't seem right to purchase her offering from the nursery café. Considering.

The district's crematorium and cemetery were only twenty minutes down the hill, but it was a different landscape entirely. Mallory could recall the flat surrounds suffering under hot and windswept days during summer as the grass dried to a pale golden colour – so different from the rolling hills of Appletree. The single-story rectangular building had always seemed incredibly bland, even back when she had attended the occasional funeral of family friends with her parents. Its red brick exterior and sloping grey colorbond roof had been well maintained but still lacked any other adornments that could have been added to make visitors' experiences more welcoming. A stretch of thick native bushes softened the appearance of the silver aluminium windows, an attempt to grow a colourful flower border below them failing. The front door was firmly shut but dim light shone around the edges, so presumably someone was inside. There had been only one other car in the car park when Mallory arrived, giving the entire place a sense of abandonment as though the ghosts of the past wanted to be left in peace.

Mallory hoped her father was at peace. When she had heard Patrick and Stacey would be out of town for a few days, she had hastily collected Harold's ashes from the crematorium then fuelled by their recent connection, she had contacted Hettie. As the sun rose the following morning, the hour that HP would always hustle out the back door of Pepper Farm, they opened the plain box and slid back the lid. Touring the apple orchard, the three women took it in turns to slowly scatter the ashes, finishing at Stella's final resting place.

The grass had simmered with dew, the gnarled old trees grey and still as they bore witness to the brief words each woman spoke aloud, and to themselves. Mallory had smiled, and had given a small nod towards the base of the tree, content to have done this one small thing. For herself and her parents, for Hettie and her daughter.

Now at the resting place of many others, Mallory followed the concrete path through the rear gateway. She stopped to check the grave location map. Where would she choose to be buried, or have her ashes scattered? Certainly not here nor over depths of water, nor at some unknown parkland. Mallory chuckled when she decided she'd quite like a view when it came to spending forever time. There would have to be some connection to her earth-bound life though, which was why she understood Stella's, then Harold's, decision to be scattered amongst the Pepper Farm orchard. Vivien had suggested a split of ashes between the orchard and a memorial plaque under one of the crematorium's rose bushes when discussing Stella's resting place. But Harold had been firm that there would be no 'splitting' and no external site.

Five minutes later, she stood in front of a grave marker, its pale stone curb ending at the headstone which was carved with curling ivy and flowers. Mallory read Barbara McMunn's dates and family details aloud to the breeze – "always remembered."

A well-known poem sprung to mind. It was about the dash that sat between your birth and death dates, and how it represented not the age you died, but how you spent the time between. How you spent your dash.

'I now know how you spent some of your dash Barbara, but I'm not here to judge.'

Her eyes flicked to the neighbouring site, in memory of Alfred McMunn, then back to Barbara's. The contrast was obvious – dead leaves were strewn across Alfred's resting place whereas someone had recently tended Barbara's. Mallory placed her flowers alongside the small permanent urn which held a fresh posie. She could imagine Hettie and Olivia chatting whilst visiting their loved one, arranging their gift.

A single bench seat wasn't far away so Mallory made herself comfortable and turned her attention back to whom she had come to see; so to speak. 'So, this is interesting, Barbara. Why am I here, you may ask. I for one never knew about your affair with my dad, nor would have guessed at it in a million years. Nothing against you, it's just that it's a stretch to visualise HP in such a romantic situation.' With a firmer tone, she added, 'And of course, there's my mum, Stella.'

She sighed, fatigue suddenly overtaking her. 'I can't

imagine how she wouldn't have known what was going on, so I've decided not to try – for all I know you and Stella may have come to some arrangement. It was a different time.'

A vivid flashback suddenly came to her. It was Christmas and the Pepper family were sitting in the front lounge at Pepper Farm, opening presents. But the McMunns were there too, also unwrapping presents. Why would they have been there? Mallory had witnessed Harold pass a box across to Barbara – it was a bottle of 4711 cologne; Stella had received a box of stationery from Barbara, who then passed boxes of chocolates to Patrick, Mallory and Vivien. They had been so excited to receive such treats and placed the boxes on their bedside tables. Her father and Alfred had continued joking about how quickly the kids were growing up.

And now, sitting on a cemetery bench, Mallory chuckled. She had never thought about that day, and she couldn't recall ever spending another Christmas with the family, nor what their presents to the McMunn children had been. But one thing she did remember. The sisters had always wondered what had happened to their chocolates as the boxes had mysteriously disappeared from their bedrooms by the end of Boxing Day.

Perhaps there was more than a bit of quiet spunk in all the women who belonged to this strange and unexpected group, including her own mother.

A couple on bicycles nodded at Mallory before slowly cycling on. A moment later, a young boy peddled past on his bike, trying to catch up; although his urgency seemed to come from the challenge rather than the graves that surrounded him. Mallory watched, aware of the parents' decision to allow this token of independence within a safe distance – would she have done the same thing? It had been a long time since her what-ifs had strayed to all the challenges and love that would come with being a mother. Her teaching responsibilities had brought out a definite maternal streak with both the naughty and adorable children, but you never knew how good or intolerant you'd be until knee-deep in parenting. But still, what a pity she hadn't had the opportunity to try.

Her pangs were interrupted by a magpie as it swooped onto Barbara's headstone and sat warbling at the sky. It was a beautiful, Australian sound that Mallory had always loved. Was it visiting her? The sun was clear of the sweeping clouds for a moment, sending warmth across Mallory's body and heart; the magpie flew away, perhaps on a mission to cheer up someone else.

'I've met Olivia who is so delightful, Barbara. She has a little business with a friend making cakes for the nursery café and has a definite talent for floristry. And I've made peace with Heather. I hope we can chat more but for the moment ...' Mallory paused, uncertain. 'For the moment, I will try to bide my time with all this new knowledge about Dad and my childhood.'

She stood to leave. In a way, she felt sorry for Barbara, alone with Alfred in a place so devoid of atmosphere. Barbara McMunn had fought for her daughter's future and lived out her life with a huge secret that Mallory respected. And yet, she couldn't ignore the warm afterglow she felt at the fact that her parents were together in death at Pepper Farm.

Chapter Twenty-Six

'I'LL HAVE to meet you there, Mallory. It doesn't look like my flight is going to leave any time soon.'

Damn it. She wanted the evening at the marina to go well for Guy and Stuart. She reorganised for Bridie to drive past and collect her, and hoped the airline came through in time. Rooster was safely ensconced with a long-lasting treat in the kitchen.

Plato's at the Marina was styled like a Greek taverna with long communal tables and crisp blue and white awnings. Considering the weather around the peninsula was consistently colder and windier than in Greece, the deck area was enclosed with thick plastic pull-down walls. They allowed diners to be protected by the elements but still be able to feel they were dining al fresco, overlooking the boats and harbour. Mallory and Bridie joined other chattering guests as they wandered down the steps and along the short pier to the restaurant's entrance.

'It's lucky we booked,' Rod observed. 'This place is pumping.'

'It's because there's a great musician on tonight,' came a

voice behind them. Guy stepped forward and hugged Mallory, but it was obvious he was searching for someone else.

'Your dad's coming,' Mallory said with her fingers crossed. 'His plane has been delayed.'

Guy's eyes showed a momentary flash of disappointment, but his smile didn't falter. 'No problem. I'd better go and finish setting up. Thanks for bringing your friends.' He jerked his head across to where Martha and Peggy were waving the newcomers to their table.

Mallory took a seat with a clear view of the entrance so she could hail Stuart as soon as he arrived. Presuming he did.

'Well, here's to us,' Peggy toasted. 'To old friends, new barns, and sneaky house purchases. Now, shall we order some pita and dips and maybe their keftedakia meatballs to share? Stuart will just have to catch up when he gets here.'

Buzzing conversations and the aroma of slow-cooked lamb engulfed Mallory as she kept one eye on the door, hoping Stuart would materialise at any moment. She was happy to supply all the details as her friends gently prodded her with questions about HP's final decisions, Hettie, Pepper Farm, and her decision to buy the mystery Blueberry Lane property.

Martha plucked a flier out from under the terracotta candle holder in the middle of the table. 'Oh, I didn't realise this was a charity night. This says that the restaurant will contribute some of the profits to a potential local branch of Riding for Those with Disabilities. Now that's interesting; I wonder who is behind that great cause. And they thank Guy Forbes for volunteering his entertainment free of charge. That's nice.'

Oh dear, Mallory thought. Was working for nothing a good way to put a value on your talent, to launch a career?

A tap came from the microphone as a fellow tried to grab the gathering's attention. 'Good evening, folks. Just a reminder that there is a gold coin donation bucket in the foyer if anyone would like to contribute to our fundraising efforts. The area's equine therapy centre is under great demand from those families wishing to partake in our sessions. Every month we face $50,000 worth of vet, feed, insurance, staff, and utility bills. Plus, for those attending the program, there is a big gap in disability funding. Anyway, thanks to all those involved tonight and the young fellow here for donating his time to entertain you. Over to you, Guy.'

Mallory took another sip of her red wine as the lights dimmed except for a spotlight on a single chair placed on the small, raised stage. Guy walked out and gave a brief wave to the crowd before sitting and doing a last-minute tune of his guitar. Mallory could tell he was nervous, procrastinating, but he looked amazingly handsome in layback blue denim jeans and tan open-neck shirt, the sleeves rolled up to the elbow. His hair was caught in a small man-bun, a few black tendrils escaping around his forehead.

As the first chords echoed across the room, the chatty audience stopped their conversation and listened as Guy opened his first set with a catchy crowd-pleaser. Mallory hadn't heard this style of music from him before, but it drew her in as she tapped her foot along with the beat.

'Wow, he's good,' Rod said into Mallory's ear.

She nodded in agreement and silently mouthed, Good on you Keith. Instinct shot her attention to the entrance where Stuart was standing in the doorway. His hair was ruffled, he was panting, and had clearly run from the car park. He scanned the room until his eyes locked on hers, but shrugged when he couldn't see a way through the tables without disrupting Guy's performance. With a heart that felt it would burst at the sight of him, Mallory sent him a happy smile and raised her glass.

Guy's voice was like liquid honey as he moved through several songs and a quiet ballad then kept the crowd engaged with an instrumental piece. As his fingers danced across the guitar, it was obvious this was where Guy was happiest – all he needed was Rooster sitting by his side for the quintessential musician vibe.

'I'd like to dedicate this final song to my grandma. It's called A Tune for Nellie,' he quietly announced before performing the song Stuart and Mallory had found him singing at the nursing home. It was smooth and beautiful, bringing rapturous applause when the final notes hung across the restaurant. Mallory, her eyes misted with tears, glanced across at Stuart who was transfixed where he stood, staring at his son. She was sure there would be tears in his eyes too after listening to Guy's emotional ode.

Guy couldn't have seen him standing at the back of the room, but a broad grin broke across his face as his father approached and pulled him into a hug. Mallory's heart surged as she watched the two men who had entered her life.

The group shuffled along the bench, freeing a seat next to Mallory. No words were needed as Stuart huddled close to her after a quick welcome kiss. Mallory placed her hand over Stuart's which had instantly rested on her thigh.

It was only after wine and dips had been passed along the table to sit in front of Stuart, that he turned to Mallory. His voice faltered, still clogged with emotion. 'Wasn't he great? I had no idea. Why didn't I know how talented he was?'

Mallory patted his hand. 'But now you do. He's going to join us after clearing away his gear.'

'Your boy has talent,' Peggy said pointedly to Stuart. 'And a fine soul to donate his time like that to a great cause.'

Before Stuart could answer, Guy squeezed onto the seat. Stuart poured him a glass of red wine and slid it across the table. 'Well done again.'

Guy glanced at each person with a slightly surprised expression. 'Thank you so much for coming everyone.' He raised his glass and then took a sip before a cheeky smile erupted with his news. 'They must have enjoyed my performance because you're looking at the new resident performer here at Plato's, and Theo owns two similar establishments along the coast so I'll be rotating between all the venues. Plus, I have a few phone numbers to follow up from tonight for other functions.' He turned towards Stuart. 'I'll have to put my rates up, and maybe throw in a few covers.'

Stuart laughed and gave him a wink. 'You will indeed. Just write more of your own though – they're the good ones. Wasn't it Dylan who said, "You only need three chords and the truth"?'

Guy laughed as he clinked his glass with Stuart's. 'Whoa, Dad. Where did that spring from?'

STUART HAD CAUGHT a cab to the restaurant and insisted on driving Mallory home so she could enjoy another wine with dinner. They were in the car happily discussing the evening when Mallory's phone rang.

Laughing at something Stuart had said, she rummaged in her bag and answered without looking at the caller ID.

'Mallory,' a slurred voice said down the line. 'Mallory, is that you?'

'John?' All frivolity was sucked out of her as she clutched the phone, and Stuart sent her a sideways look of concern.

She glanced across at him and shrugged.

'Well, you sound happy. So happy you hadn't bothered returning my call.'

'You didn't leave a message, John. Why would I call you back?'

She could picture her ex-husband, lounging on a couch somewhere, feet on the coffee table, legs crossed at the ankles, a beer held high as he voiced whatever was on his mind. She presumed it wasn't the first bottle for the evening.

'Ah, Mallory. Always holding back, always playing hard to get. Well, what would you say, if I thought I'd made a mistake...'

'John, you've obviously had too much to drink. I'm not going to have this conversation. Where's Vivien anyway?'

'What do you care? What do you care about anything? How I'm feeling, what it feels like to be cast aside from your inheritance when it was me who put up with your father's moods more than I cared.'

He'd raised his voice, the tone and words easily floating across to Stuart who, frowning, concentrated on the wet road but was listening. Mallory stretched her hand across to his knee, but he kept his hands clutched on the wheel.

'You can share Vivien's inheritance now, can't you,' Mallory replied bitterly. 'Or perhaps it's not our inheritance but other money you're after.'

'I miss you, Mal.'

Stuart glanced across at her, eyebrows raised. Mallory gave his leg another squeeze as they turned into Fruit Flan's driveway. Stuart cut the engine and sat for a moment. Perhaps not wanting to appear to intrude on the conversation or perhaps feeling a deeper unease, he got out of the car and made his way inside the cottage.

Mallory watched him go as John's voice droned on. Surely Stuart wasn't worried about John's sudden and suspicious return to caring for her. One thing was certain, she would end this charade now.

'John, I'm presuming the reinvention you apparently needed hasn't gone according to plan so I'm hanging up. I don't for one second believe you miss me, that you aren't motivated by greed and ego, so don't call me again.'

True to her word, Mallory ended the call and hustled inside. Stuart was in the kitchen when she entered. He dipped his head, scratched the back of his neck as she checked on Rooster, and flicked off the kettle. Slowly she eased his coat from his shoulders and kissed him long and deep as it fell to the floor.

Recovering from his obvious reaction to John's unexpected call, Stuart quick-stepped Mallory to the bedroom. They wasted no time, undressing between heated kisses and then slipping between the sheets. As Stuart slid across her, he devoured her lips as if they'd spent months apart, instead of just days. Meeting his urgency, Mallory's hips rose to welcome him inside her, moving with his rhythmic thrusts. At his throaty gasps, she closed her eyes and gripped his back as shuddering explosions of desire overtook them.

Their lovemaking had been swift and urgent, but exhaustingly satisfying. Mallory curled snugly against

Stuart's naked body beneath the blankets. Her finger gently traced imaginary circles around his chest as his hand stroked along the dip at her waist. 'I'm so glad you're here,' she whispered.

'I would have fought for you, you know,' Stuart murmured. 'Pistols at dawn or whatever it took.'

Mallory's stomach rippled with laughter against his body. He hadn't asked about how her conversation with John had ended, and Mallory liked that presumption.

Mallory sensed Stuart's lips tweak into a smile. 'Guy may have given us some privacy tonight by staying elsewhere, but you do realise our sexual exploits will now have to be confined to this bed behind a locked door; that there can be no screams of ecstasy or outrageous calls of "more Stuart, more"; which I'm yet to hear, I might add.'

Mallory giggled. 'I'm sure we'll find a way around that. There's always the beach, I guess.'

'Ah, such happy memories, but you'd do it on the beach?'

'What's a bit of sand between friends ... lovers? She gave another giggle. 'Literally.'

Stuart flung back the covers and propped on one elbow. He trailed his eyes down Mallory's body and back to her upturned face. Such a close inspection would have had Mallory cowering once, on edge at what he might see, but his gaze was so loving and sensual that she lay still as he took his time. Her mind searched for the word, the emotion that was rising within her – freedom, and perhaps something else, seemed to sit in its space.

He eased a strand of hair off her forehead and leant down to graze her lips with his own. 'Here is where I want to be.'

Chapter Twenty-Seven

THE FOLLOWING YEAR:

Mallory watched Hettie stroll through the apple orchard. She'd tug at a weed, open her face to the gentle breeze, and generally appear to be so damned content that it made Mallory's heart sing. Over the previous year they had all been caught in the upheaval of the fallout of HP's will; including the revelation that Heather and Olivia were related to the Pepper siblings. But with absolute honesty, Mallory confessed it was a joy to see her childhood home being cared for with such affection.

Hettie had handled the constant backlash from Patrick with dignity, only resorting to her red-haired temper if he dared involve or approach Olivia. Mallory had helped her draft a letter for the lawyer to adjust and forward to both Patrick and Vivien, reinforcing the wishes of Harold and that the estate was finalised. Vague rumours about the McMunn women and the nursery café circulated in the area from anonymous sources for a time and then petered out – Patrick and Stacey then moved out of Appletree Hill.

'Hi, Hettie.'

Hetttie turned, pulling off her gardening gloves and frowning across the cuttings. Spontaneous smiles rarely graced Hettie's face, but Mallory could tell by her tone that she was always welcome by the property's new owner.

'Mallory, come through. As I've said before, if you wish to visit Stella and Harold, you don't have to run it by me. You can come to the orchard till your heart's content – or stand here and swear at the wind, whatever suits.' She stretched her arm in an arc towards the trees. 'It's looking good though isn't it.'

Mallory nodded in agreement, then toward the two small but well-tended remembrance plagues nestled at the base of one of the old apple trees. An image of Barbara's resting place down the hill came and went. Mallory hadn't raised it with Hettie or Olivia, and maybe she never would; it wasn't hers to reconcile. Stuart had helped with advice that others had made decisions long ago and it wouldn't help her in any way to question or regret.

'Dad would have been proud, Hettie. I like the water tanks too.'

They both glanced back to where the tanks had stood as an eyesore in the garden. Hettie nodded. 'I remembered you once said that you and your mum established a strawberry patch there back in the day, so I thought I'd make the tanks look like that silo art you see in magazines. Angelina is a local artist and she's done a great job with painting the greenery, those curling tendrils and fat red strawberries.'

Mallory smiled in return. 'I can almost see Mum squatting there, inspecting the leaves for bugs. She would always get a good crop though so there were strawberry muffins, strawberry jam, strawberry-everything for a good while.'

'Would you like a drink of something, or do you just want to sit for a while?' Hettie asked.

'Actually, I'm here with an invitation. Better late than never, but Stuart and I are having a bit of a get-together on Saturday night at Fruit Flan. Part belated thank you for everyone's hospitality, part pre-Christmas and part ... whatever. It's all a bit last minute but we'd love you and Olivia to come.'

Both women were fully aware that this was another step forward in their relationship. Hettie in particular had been wary, not wanting to jump into becoming close – as she kept stating, 'Olivia and I do just fine on our own.' Mallory had also been kept on her toes, careful not to intrude as the newcomer back in town. But she looked forward to visiting the eclectic little nursery café in between all the activities that seemed to have built up on her return. It was always in the back of Mallory's mind that she had the financial means to put Olivia through university. She had floated the idea of Olivia studying business or hospitality, catering, or anything else the young girl may be interested in but the answer had always been a firm no. Maybe in time, but that would be Olivia's decision.

Mallory rubbed her foot through the grass, waiting for a response from Hettie, who was frowning with indecision.

'It's not a freebie,' Mallory prompted, hoping her next words would clinch an acceptance. 'You'd have to bring one or two of your apple pies, or something else if you prefer.'

'I guess.'

'Great, we'll see you around seven, then.'

Her next house call was to Martha and Peggy's. When repeated knocks went unanswered, Mallory wandered down to the barn. Stuart's design had ticked all the boxes, with the girls being thrilled with how it complemented its surroundings, but more importantly, how settled the horses were inside it. Bridie said it had good feng shui, which made Stuart laugh and insist it was due to his exemplary design. Mallory waved to Peggy who was in the far paddock with a client, the owner of a beautiful grey mare who had recently had a foal. Martha was leaning against the barn fence, her head between her arms; Rod was patting her shoulder.

'Martha, are you alright?' Mallory called, quickening her pace.

Martha looked up and gave a weak smile. 'Yes, yes. Just getting the bad news from the accountant. It appears that there's another hiccup with the therapy centre. Bloody council wants more assurances, more checks, more this, more that. Don't they realise some people need this service immediately?'

Mallory had never seen her friend so exasperated, so fragile. At the risk of being seen to interfere, Mallory had contacted the head office of the group mentioned on the night of Guy's gig, to learn more about the centre and make sure it was all above board. She had then approached the girls with a financial offer to support its setup and sponsor families. The therapy centre would operate in conjunction with the existing facility but the riding school would operate at the girls' property. All parties were over the moon but they had met red tape at every step of the process, and the months had slid by. Several extra horses who had been specifically trained were now on site, but they were spending their days chewing grass in one of the paddocks.

'Is it money?' Mallory asked Rod.

He shook his head. 'No, just the wheels of bureaucracy turning slowly. Your generous patronage is what enabled this whole thing to get off the ground in the first place.'

'Well let me know if it needs another Lotto injection,'

she replied. 'On a brighter note, I received a lovely letter from another family saying how relieved they are to have the payment gap covered. Everything is so expensive and that's one thing they don't have to worry about for their son to take part. I'll forward the email to you both.'

'Where's that handsome man of yours anyway?' Martha asked.

Stuart had been 'her handsome man' for the past year. Following her announcement to buy the property bequeathed in HP's will, she extended her lease on Fruit Flan for at least a year, and finally got around to buying a car instead of continuing with the rental. She had met the B&B owners, a young local couple who had spent every penny on purchasing it, then had been transferred interstate for work. Their decision to turn it into a B&B in their absence, and Mallory's ongoing rent, had been a godsend for them. The stars had aligned when Stuart won the contract to design and build the nearby winery restaurant and tasting rooms.

'So, will you be spending more time in Appletree than in Melbourne?' Mallory had asked him one balmy evening as they sat on the veranda, watching the sunburnt light change hue over the pastures. Rooster sprawled between them, on loan whilst Guy was interstate with back-to-back music gigs.

Stuart had leant across and clinked his wine glass against hers, a cheeky look of expectation sparkling in his eyes. 'I guess so, and of course, you can come up to the big smoke with me when I have to head into the office.'

'Then I guess we are officially living in sin,' Mallory said.

'Oh, I hope so.' Stuart had pulled her to her feet,

crushing her lips against his own before guiding her inside to bed.

A distant whinny brought her attention back to Rod and Martha. 'Hopefully, Stuart is out collecting things for our party on Saturday night. It's only casual but it is surprising what you don't have when you're not in your own home. Can I borrow some of your large platters, Martha?'

'Mm? Yes, of course. Come up to the house,' Martha said, still obviously deep in thought about her council woes.

Mallory hugged her to her side as they walked. 'Don't worry, everything will be alright in the end.'

Martha managed a laugh. 'And if it's not alright then it's not yet the end,' she quoted from her favourite movie, *The Best Exotic Marigold Hotel*.

The couples in that movie had always intrigued Mallory, particularly when she had felt so adrift after her separation. Could she undertake such a shift in her life, to take up the adventure of moving to another country? Capri, let alone a rundown hotel in Jaipur hadn't eventuated. But then those couples hadn't won the lottery. Mallory could do anything she wanted to really, and in great comfort. Her life had motored on, an unexpected yet blessed recovery eventuating via Harold, Appletree, and then Stuart. The latter was proving to be so much more than just life getting in the way – Mallory had fallen wonderfully in love with Stuart all over again and knew he felt the same way. He had told her so and she had believed every whispered word.

There had been no further communication from either John or Vivien. It was as though a wall had been built with the cheating couple on one side, and Mallory on the other, with none of them seeing or hearing the other. The odd pang of regret spiked Mallory when touchstones of their childhood were on every corner of Appletree Hill. She had, after all, lost a sister. But her friends, Stuart, and her philanthropy work were now her bedrock, her future. She was so grateful.

SATURDAY DAWNED bright and clear with the promise of perfect weather for the party. There was a distinct shift in the air, a suggestion of summer with a certain dry crispness replacing the sogginess of autumn. Although the area stayed greener than other parts of the state, no one ever underestimated an Australian summer and the unsettling threat of bushfires it brought. But that was hopefully some time away yet and there was a party to host. Mallory and Stuart headed into the village for a coffee and to chat about what was still to be done.

'So, is it an early Christmas celebration?' Olivia asked as she placed their coffees and cinnamon muffins before them. Mallory caught a hitch of uncertainty in her voice.

'Mallory needs to be drip-fed Christmas,' Stuart said. 'She's always been the same, with tinsel and present shopping escalating from the end of November. Even as a kid, I remember she couldn't wait to go to the Christmas tree farm along Marindal Road, choose the poor sacrificial tree, and load it up with gold stuff. Thank heavens I've banned any carols until mid-December.' He shot a cheeky wink across to Olivia.

'Well, we'll see about that.' Mallory laughed. 'It was only because I insisted that we had any tree at all, let alone a 'glitzy' one as Dad described it ...' She stopped, unsure about discussing her childhood around Hettie or Olivia, uncertain about sharing what they had had or not had – hopefully time would dilute that.

'It's just an excuse to have everyone over for drinks, dinner, and a dance. Do you and Alice cater for Christmas?' Mallory asked.

Olivia shook her head. 'The Appletree Twilight Christmas Market is huge. We make fruit cakes and rum balls and hampers for that. It's fun. You should come along.'

Olivia retreated inside the café. As they stood to leave, she reappeared with a large floral bouquet.

'A thank you in advance for inviting us,' she said shyly.

'They're gorgeous. Thank you.' Mallory poked her nose into the Irish green foliage which was dotted with white daisies, red rose buds, and little ruby red wired balls that burst like fireworks through the leaves, all tied with a festive gold bow.

They headed to the large produce store which sat amongst its own vast herb and vegetable gardens. Bridie had told her there was a new butcher who had joined the popular well-stocked deli, fruit, and cheese outlets, and was receiving great reviews. Mallory clutched a list in her hand, a finger tapping against it relentlessly.

'All good?' Stuart asked.

Mallory grimaced. 'This might sound silly, but I haven't thrown a party for a long time. It's an old habit for me to get nervous before an event but I just hope everyone has a good time.' She puffed out a shaky breath.

'Well, you know my life motto? It's "Habits are meant to be broken".'

'Is that a challenge, Stuart Forbes?'

With one hand still on the wheel, he reached the other across and ran it gently down her cheek. 'Of course. It will be great. All your friends will be there.'

'I know, I know. And I'm looking forward to seeing

Zarni. I just got a text to say she's arrived at the motel and will see us later.'

'There you go. I know you've got this and I'm here to give never-ending advice.' He shot her one of his sexy winks, which she loved. 'Anyway, I reckon you could just give everyone a ham sandwich and a beer, turn up the music and they'll be happy. We've got a lot to celebrate you know.'

Chapter Twenty-Eight

AND CELEBRATE IS what they did.

Zarni arrived later that afternoon. Mallory was in the kitchen and didn't hear her car arrive, but there could be no ignoring the thump of footsteps running through the house accompanied by a shrill, 'Mallory, I'm here!'

Mallory thought she would explode with excitement to have her dear friend in town with her. 'Thank you so much for making the effort to come down at such a busy time of the year. I can't wait for you to meet all the locals tonight. How was the train trip?' Mallory said as she pulled Zarni into her arms for a huge girlfriend hug.

'I enjoyed it. I felt like I was on the Orient Express.' Zarni laughed. 'I'm kidding about the Orient Express reference, but it wasn't too bad and if it meant I didn't have to board a plane but still make it here to see you at your party-best, then so be it. And look at you, you look radiant.' She leant closer and whispered, 'Is it love?'

Mallory laughed. 'Could be! We have time for a cup of coffee and regroup before I must get showered and changed, so let's not waste a minute.'

'Are you sure? I'm happy to stand at the kitchen bench and chop something.'

'Absolutely not. Alice, a friend of Olivia's will be along soon to help. She was keen to earn some extra cash. I need to sit for a while anyway,' Mallory replied as she flicked the on the coffee machine.

As they settled on the front veranda with steaming mugs and pieces of buttery shortbread, Stuart materialised from around the side of the house. As always when he suddenly appeared, Mallory's heart gave a little kick of excitement at the sight of him.

She watched as two of the people who meant the most to her embraced. They had met only once before when Mallory and Stuart had briefly returned to Brisbane to tidy up the remnants of Mallory's life there but had liked each other from the start.

'Great you could make it, Zarni. I have to dash and collect a few things, Mallory, but I'll be back in about an hour,' Stuart said.

'Really? What ...'

'I'm sure you two have a lot to catch up on and I'll see you soon,' he replied firmly.

The women watched as he leapt down the stairs and drove away. 'What a hunk,' Zarni said. 'I think I'm drooling at little.'

'He is, isn't he.' Mallory couldn't keep the warmth from her words.

She would never have imagined she would be spending her days, nights, and future with Stuart Forbes – but what a wonderful future they had promised each other as they lay between the sheets or walked along the beach, their fingers intertwined. She admired his ability to face challenges with directness and humour; his love for his sons and the health of the world. She was grateful for the constant words, and acts, of encouragement he took the time to give her. Without even realising it, she had become used to a partner who didn't share his feelings. But now, being with Stuart and his easy ways, the contrast was plain. This was a man open with his thoughts, who was strong enough to share how happy he was to have her in his life; who would shoot her a frown when she tried to divert an argument, preferring to 'discuss the issue that had upset her' to the bitter end.

'OH, I FEEL TOTALLY UNDERDRESSED,' Mallory laughed as Martha and Peggy, adorned with flashing reindeer antlers, arrived early with their specialty ginger glazed ham surrounded by a variety of bread and salad greens. As guests arrived at Fruit Flan, they were greeted by Stuart with a tray loaded with bubbly, wines and tumblers of fruity punch and directions to 'help yourself to beers in the esky in the kitchen.' Bridie offered bowls of nuts and her homemade mini turkey and cranberry quiches. Several of Stuart's local clients, as well as trainers and volunteers from the eagerly awaited therapy centre, slid easily into the casual atmosphere. Even HP's lawyer and his wife had accepted the invitation.

Mallory shuffled her charcuterie platter towards the centre of the table where Olivia's floral bouquet was the centrepiece. Everyone but Hettie and Olivia had arrived. Mallory was just considering they may have had last minute doubts about coming when mother and daughter stepped tentatively through the doorway.

'Oh, I'm so pleased you're here.' Mallory grinned before

giving them a welcoming hug. Hettie seemed glued to the spot, her eyes darting from guest to guest, obviously out of her comfort zone.

'I brought you these. I hope they're okay.' Olivia quickly offered a plate of mince pies.

'Oh, they look delicious, thank you. Come and let's get you both a drink and I'll introduce you to Guy, one of Stuart's sons.'

Laughter and chatter echoed through Fruit Flan and across the otherwise silent pastures. It was a small house, guests resorting to propping plates on their laps and balancing glasses on the veranda handrail. But the friendship and celebration were immense – a sense of belonging rippled through Mallory's heart, and her nerves settled in no time. She had always welcomed guests in the kitchen, to help take the glad wrap off a dish, empty the bottle box, or just lean on the sink and have a chat. Her eyes skipped around the spaces, smiling at the mini Christmas tree, now laden with multi-coloured baubles, that she had insisted on including. Here she was, offering hospitality to people just as Doris and Vern had offered it to her.

It seemed that life went full circle sometimes.

There was no room for dancing, but everyone called for Guy to perform a couple of songs towards the end of the evening – so long as they weren't Christmas carols, Stuart had called out before being booed. He stood behind Mallory, his arms wrapped tightly around her, his chin nuzzling her hair as they listened to Guy bring magic to what he loved. At one point, Mallory caught Hettie's eye as she watched them embrace, relieved when she received a small smile across the room.

After the last guest had been waved away, including Bridie and Rod who had tried to remain to help clean up,

Mallory refilled her wineglass and wandered through to the kitchen. She had drunk just one glass of wine the whole evening, or perhaps several half glasses that she had abandoned throughout the night, having been too busy chatting and making sure everyone had everything they needed. Olivia and Hettie had left early with only hurried goodbyes, but Mallory was grateful they had come at all and hoped they had enjoyed themselves.

She would put away anything that needed to go into the fridge and then sit on the veranda under the Milky Way. But when she was about to suggest it to Stuart, he was nowhere to be found. Perhaps he and Guy were taking out the empty bottles or rubbish?

Despite the warm day, an evening breeze had sprung up. Mallory went inside, catching her reflection in the bedroom mirror. Sparkling eyes full of joy looked back at her. She ran a hand through her hair, repining wisps that had escaped their clasps. Her fingers dropped to the necklace that hung around her neck and stroked the drop of two diamonds and sapphire that hung on a fine rose gold chain. It had been a birthday gift from Stuart.

'The diamonds are from one of Mum's rings which she gave me last year, and I thought they'd look nice with the sapphire ...'

'It's cornflower blue,' Mallory whispered, running her thumb across the pretty setting.

'I can have it remade if you prefer a darker gemstone ...'

Mallory had put her fingers against his lips and blinked away tears. 'No, no. It's perfect. To me, that beautiful colour means new beginnings and I love it. Thank you.'

Now, she collected her shawl and made her way to the front of the house. Stuart was leaning on the veranda, two glasses of bubbly in hand.

Mallory started. 'Oh, where did you get to? Has Guy headed home already? I know he likes to still squat next door and give us some privacy, but I thought it would have been more comfortable for him here tonight don't you ...'

Stuart stepped forward and covered her words with a fingertip. 'Ssh. Here's to a great party.' They clinked glasses and took a sip.

When his lips met hers, they tasted of bubbles, of gingerbread and love. 'Mm, you taste good,' Mallory whispered. 'It was a fun night, wasn't it? When that gorgeous Italian was playing earlier, I was thinking about your wish to stay in Italy and just muck around for a while. We could do that after the house is finished ...'

Once again Stuart's lips silenced her; the reflections of the party lights adding to the twinkle in his eyes. 'Maybe. But first, there's something we need to do.' Stuart took her hand and guided her down the steps to the driveway, placed his glass flute next to hers in her hand, and took her into his arms as if to dance. As he hummed a tune Mallory didn't recognise, he slowly waltzed her down the driveway, a cheeky grin spreading from ear to ear.

'Stuart, what are you doing? I don't know if I've got the energy to walk back up again *and* I'm spilling our drinks.'

Mallory started to giggle as she was slowly twirled out of the front gate, along a few metres then into the property next door. She stopped to gather her shawl around her shoulders and ease several small stones from her ballet flats, expecting to be waltzed back to Fruit Flan. She gave in as Stuart took her hand and guided her up the neighbouring driveway. The rustling of night creatures scurrying away reminded Mallory of her first few nights in the cottage, before meeting Guy and Rooster or knowing that Stuart Forbes was only a few blocks away.

The orchard was bathed in a ghostly glow from internal house lights that had found their way into the branches. It was mystical and beautiful.

Stuart hugged her in front of him, his chest warm against her back, and retrieved his glass.

Mallory frowned, unsure of what she should be seeing. 'Stuart?'

He cleared his throat. 'This is your house, right?' When Mallory gave a little nod, he continued. 'And you've assigned a clever designer and builder to carry out your every whim, right?' Another nod. 'Well, that designer decided to make some unchartered additions.'

Mallory gave a nervous laugh and tried to turn to face him, but Stuart's arm held her firmly facing the house. She took a sip of her bubbly as he slowly raised his to the stars. Instantly, strains of "Silent Night" weaved their way through the windows. The house dropped into darkness then a moment later thousands of little white bud lights erupted around the veranda. More popped on from strands wound around the columns and down both sides of the steps. Potted fir trees, swaddled in red ribbons sparkled at the base.

Mallory gasped at its magic. 'Oh, Stuart. Did you do this? Is this where you were this afternoon when you said you had to go pick up supplies? It's glorious.' "Silent Night" faded to "All I Want for Christmas is You".

Stuart shuddered. 'Well, I don't know about Mariah Carey, but the sentiment is the same. We're not finished.'

Mallory shook her head, overwhelmed by Stuart's gift and the 'little boy' excitement that bounced off his every word. She held his hand tightly as they climbed the front steps. A shadow at one window and a quick little bark told her that Guy and Rooster were in on the secret and overseeing the light show.

Stuart placed their glasses on the ground and took her in his arms. As Mallory looped her hands behind his neck, she gazed up at his happy face, then further. Sprigs of mistletoe, dusted in rusty flakes, hung from the old gutter.

Tears blurred Mallory's eyes as she tried to refocus on the handsome face that was in front of her. 'Thank you, Stuart.' Her hand gently brought his face closer, his lips to hers.

When they parted, Stuart ran his thumbs across her cheeks, catching the remaining tears. Mallory cleared her throat. 'How lucky are we. We've found each other again, plus we have Guy and Rooster, and hopefully Tim will visit, and we can start renovating our new home – our Meleto – together in January.'

'Meleto?'

She nodded. 'I thought of it today – it's Italian for apple orchard.'

As Mallory pressed her body against Stuart's firm chest, her cheek rested against his heart. She could feel the beat-beat-beat, and hear a whispered word rumble within. 'Perfect.'

--

Here-After

Sometimes to move on, you need to cleanse the past

An old terrace house. A resident ghost eager to reveal secrets. A woman hoping to move on with her life.

At last Abigail Croucher can purchase Binalong – after all, the old building in Melbourne was the dream location for her husband's restaurant. But Luca has died.

On a whim she buys the cottage next door as well. With the help of her new neighbours and attractive landscape architect Jack Mattingley, Abigail is ready to start afresh. When it appears that her husband wasn't all she had believed him to be, Abigail needs to cleanse the past before she is able to trust her heart – and her future – with anyone again.

How could a mature, self-sufficient woman have got it so wrong?

Here-After is a story about love and betrayal, about belief and possibility. It is concerned with the notion of 'after-life' – life after heartbreak, after loss and abandonment and grieving, after great change – and the possibilities not just of an 'after-world' but a happy after-life.

"Again, another wonderful book from this author. The characters are special, and I loved the story of a woman reinventing her life, and the special connection to those who have passed" – Reader Review, Melbourne

Available now: https://getbook.at/HERE-After

That Summer in Nautilus Cove

What do you pack to pursue your dream, and what do you leave behind?

Marnie Fawkner just wanted to escape the demands of adult children, job hunting and selling her house. So when Marnie's sister, Libby, asks her to mind her house and dog, Marnie jumps at the opportunity. Who would knock back a couple of easy weeks in Nautilus Cove, a popular coastal town in sunny Queensland?

She never expected a simple favour would change her life.

When Libby delays her return, Marnie reluctantly steps in to manage Libby's homewares store, Whimsy. What could possibly go wrong? Marnie finds that Nautilus Cove is offering her more than just a temporary escape – an intriguing sculptor called Harry Mitchelton for a start. It is here, whilst tackling person change, welcoming new friends, and second-chance love, and embracing the chance to start over, that Marnie confronts what she needs to pack to pursue her own dreams.

That Summer in Nautilus Cove is a heart-warming sea change story of self-discovery. It may even prompt you to research coastal real estate.

"Pitch perfect escapism. I could feel the sand between my toes and the warmth of change shining through Marnie's life. A great read" – Reader Review, Canada

Available now: https://getbook.at/NautilusCove

julie holland

that summer *in* nautilus cove

What do you pack
to pursue your dream...
and what do you leave behind?

Seasons

Because every season has a reason

SEASONS is a little book of verses to nurture inspiration,
reflection, and joy ...

May your minutes be full of trust,

your hours full of wonder,

your months full of joy,

your years full of laughter.

A lifetime of fulfilment and love.

Available now: www.heartsandmindsart

About the Author

Photography by Lisa Pearl

Julie has worked in many industries: from advertising to travel, education to public relations. She dabbles in painting and photography, writes inspirational verse as well as contemporary women's fiction, and is a prolific reader. Julie grew up in Melbourne, Australia before making a sea-change to the beautiful Sunshine Coast in Queensland where she writes and, with her partner, owns an art and homewares store (Hearts and Minds Art).

Her novels focus on mature women who are faced with life-changing choices, with emotions, family, and location all playing important roles. Her stories are warm, humorous, and inclusive.

To contact and follow Julie, please visit: facebook.com/juliehollandauthor

"Thank you to all my readers and followers both here in Australia and overseas, and to the librarians and book shops that stock my books. Thank you to Greg for your endless enthusiasm for my writing. You are all wonderful."

www.ingramcontent.com/pod-product-compliance
Lightning Source LLC
Chambersburg PA
CBHW020005140726
47904CB00018B/1828